Terror at home

People were already dying of radiation poisoning and would be joined by more. The first emergency crews on the scene were unprepared for a radioactive spill, and the bodies were still being carted away from several miles of highway in both directions.

Bolan was appalled at the Vulture's handiwork. The man was a force moving across the land—but he was just a man.

Bolan watched the death count rising in Hollywood to over two hundred. His rage was cold and deliberate. Nothing would stop him.

He was the deathbringer.

DON PENDLETON's
MACK BOLAN.

DAY OF THE VULTURE

A GOLD EAGLE BOOK FROM
WORLDWIDE.

TORONTO • NEW YORK • LONDON
AMSTERDAM • PARIS • SYDNEY • HAMBURG
STOCKHOLM • ATHENS • TOKYO • MILAN
MADRID • WARSAW • BUDAPEST • AUCKLAND

First edition February 1997

ISBN 0-373-61452-7

Special thanks and acknowledgment to
Mike McQuay for his contribution to this work.

DAY OF THE VULTURE

The terrorist and the policeman both come from the same basket.

—*The Secret Agent*
by Joseph Conrad

When good and evil clash, there must exist a common ground if good is to emerge the winner. That common ground is ruthless determination—in my case, to stop the terror and bring retribution for the slaughter of innocents.

—Mack Bolan

PROLOGUE

Upper Chaco, Paraguay
November 23, 1982

The Chaco was no-man's-land, a hell-on-earth of thorn forests and dust that turned to deadly mud in the rainy season. They called this section of Paraguay the demilitarized zone, making it a free-trade area for conveyance and sale of illegal goods. Run by the Paraguayan army, the authorities demanded a percentage off the top of any business, legal or otherwise, that took place in the Chaco. It was the only thing that held the country together fiscally. The operative saying was: "Contraband is the price of peace." And the movement of contraband tended to involve mercenaries, a whole shifting, changing, motley crew of men whose main loyalty was to themselves.

As a general rule, Mack Bolan didn't trust mercenaries. Loyalty, once for sale, was always for sale. But that wasn't the worst part. Mercs were mostly overgrown kids playing army, all customized uniforms and beer-drinking contests. Some were hard, trained fighters, the best in the world. But those kind were few and costly. The rest were legends only in their own minds—untrained, without seasoning, without the killer instinct. They were soldiers of fortune to whom only the fortune part applied. They could get you killed in a second by improper backup, lack of stealth or jungle technique or simple cowardice when the going got rough.

And somehow the going always got rough.

But Bolan sat anyway, sweating, nursing a Peruvian beer at an outdoor cantina and making small talk with the young blond soldier of fortune called Mulroy sitting across from him.

"This your first time in the Chaco?" the kid asked.

Bolan shook his head, watching the steady stream of camouflaged men across the street as they went in and out of the large shack made of scrap lumber and corrugated tin. "How about you, Willy? You get to the demilitarized zone a lot?"

"Just once before," he said, looking hot in his long-sleeved fatigues and jungle boots. Airborne patches had been ripped from the sleeves and breast pocket, leaving stitched outlines behind. "I hired on as part of a security team for an arms shipment from El Salvador to here. We were off the job once the sale was made."

"Who were you working for?" Bolan asked.

Mulroy shrugged. "Don't know who we sold to, either. It was just a job."

Bolan pointed to the patchless pocket. "You served your tour?"

The man frowned and gulped down the rest of his beer. He was big, well over six feet, but his face was still a kid's. "Got bounced early on," he said, holding up his empty beer bottle to indicate he wanted another. "I was too mean for them."

"A shame," Bolan said. "You missed out on some good training. Marine training is the best in the world."

"Hell with it," Mulroy said, and burped loudly, grabbing the next beer while the suds from the last one were still wet on his chin.

Bolan's attention was taken by a long line of Bolivian peasants carrying huge gunnysacks full of coca leaves. They were standing aside so several carriers full of Brazilian automobiles could pass by. Everything of value moved through the Chaco, occasionally making the region's small towns places of great importance for several hours before plunging them back into poverty and despair.

"I hear this operation is big," Mulroy said, "an army, a real army."

"That's what I heard, too," Bolan replied, his eyes briefly flashing to the man across the table. Mulroy had picked him out to talk to when he'd seen him in the cantina. Since then, Bolan had been using the kid for cover. "If the amount of mercs on the streets is any indication, it's a huge operation."

"As long as the money is huge, too."

Bolan had drifted into the hamlet of Piedro Blanco the night before. Hundreds of drunk mercs cruised the streets, looking for fights, shooting up the place—like a college fraternity party with guns. According to locals, it had been like this for weeks, always with new groups of guns for hire. That wasn't a good sign.

He'd come down from the Stony Man Ops Center in Virginia at Hal Brognola's suggestion to hire on after an American agent disappeared here three weeks previously. Before he'd vanished, the man had sent back tantalizing reports about the Medellín drug cartel recruiting a professional mercenary army in order to conquer the surrounding area and create a safe zone in which to conduct its ruthless business. Medellín wanted to secede from Colombia and form its own independent nation run by gangsters. An empire of death.

Bolan's plan was to see if he could conduct his own little search-and-destroy mission from the inside. Unfortunately the Executioner wasn't the lowest-visibility human on the planet. He'd recognized some of the mercs he'd seen and hoped they didn't recognize him.

A dust-covered Cadillac pulled up in front of the shack as tinny salsa music drifted from someone's radio several doors down the street. A chauffeur in full livery climbed out of the driver's door and opened the back, and two men quickly got out and hurried into the shack.

"That's them," Mulroy said, "the dudes that are doing the hiring." He stood. "Now's the time if we're gonna do it."

Bolan was up, too, and they drifted across the street together, stepping over the sunbathing black snakes that infested the entire region. Other mercs on the street stopped and watched them—new meat.

A man in a panama hat and wearing a gaudy flower-printed shirt stepped out of the shack as a small group gathered around.

"We just lookin' for people we ain't seen before," he said in heavily accented English. "If we already give you a job, just wait, you'll get instructions later today. If we already turn you down on a job, get the hell out of here."

Everybody laughed except the men who'd been turned down. They walked off slowly, probably broke, probably stuck in Piedro Blanco indefinitely or until the next chump came along.

"Who ain't been here before?" the man at the shack door called.

Bolan and Mulroy bullied their way to the front of the group, and the man in the loud shirt gave them the once-over. "You big boys, huh?" he said. "You both Americans?"

"Yeah," Mulroy said.

"You know anybody else here?" the man asked.

"I don't know," Bolan replied. "Who else is here?"

"Funny guy. You two, up here. Are you armed? We don't allow no guns inside."

Both men shook their heads, but the doorman frisked them anyway. Bolan palmed the three-inch spring-loaded knife as he was patted down, then deftly slipped it back in his jeans pocket.

The man stepped back and pushed the door open for them, Mulroy running in ahead of Bolan. The door swung closed behind them.

The room was hot and dark. With no electricity, the only light filtered through the cracks between the wallboards and one glassless window that looked out on Piedro Blanco's main and only thoroughfare. Thick dust danced in the slices of daylight cutting through the room.

A desk was set up toward the back. A dark, curly-haired man with deep acne scars pitting his face sat facing Bolan, and another man, tall and thin, leaned against the desk with his back to the room.

Flies and mosquitoes swarmed loudly in the still, hot air. Everyone sweated profusely, and Bolan's T-shirt was already drenched. Three guards casually holding assault rifles stood by the walls.

"My name is Pablo Fuentes," the curly-haired man said, "and this is our last stinking day in this stinking town."

"Hear, hear," said the tall man, his accent strangely European. Bolan couldn't quite place it.

"But we still need a few men to join us," Fuentes said.

Bolan recognized Fuentes as the Medellín cartel's fixer, their number-five man on the cartel organizational chart.

"Tell me, what are your names? Where did you hear about our little...project?" Fuentes demanded.

Mulroy stepped forward. "In the hotel bar in La Posada in Salvador," he said. "Jerry Sparkman told me. My name's Willy Mulroy. Lots of mercs hang out in—"

"I know the place well," the tall man said, not moving from his spot.

"Mike Belasko," Bolan said. "I was fighting with Libyan regulars in Chad. Marcel Bouton told me about this."

The tall man turned around. He had a long, aristocratic face and aquiline nose. His eyes shone pale blue in the semidarkness. His face seemed lacquered in cruelty. "I spoke with Marcel just last week," he said.

"Tough proposition," Bolan replied. "He's been dead for a month." Bolan should know. He'd killed the man.

"And my good friend, Mr. Khaddafi, how is he? Does he ever speak of his friend the Vulture?"

"I wouldn't know," Bolan replied. "He's too busy changing palaces and hiding out to talk to his troops."

"Mr. Garcia," the tall man said to the man in the loud shirt, "would you go down the street to the flea-breeding farm they call a hotel and ask Mr. Sandoval to join us?" He looked then at Bolan. "You'll get to have a reunion with your old comrade from Chad, eh?"

That was it, the bad break Bolan had been hoping wouldn't happen. He'd be dead thirty seconds after Sandoval came into the room and exposed Bolan as an impostor. He locked eyes with the man who'd called himself the Vulture and saw animal cunning staring back at him. A beast who loved the jungle.

"That's a legendary name you threw at me," Bolan said casually as his mind sketched the outlines of his backup plan—kill Fuentes, then escape. The operation was a wash. Garcia had gone to fetch his death sentence. "Are you the same Vulture who's linked to the train-station massacre in Rome?"

"My fame precedes me," the tall man said, bowing slightly.

"The mysterious Vulture," Fuentes said. "The elusive Vulture. Never seen. Never photographed."

"Never arrested," the tall man said.

"Are you in charge of the Medellín operation, sir?" Mulroy asked.

The man smiled. "We are going to remake the maps of the world."

Of the three guards, only one of them had his Uzi at the ready, and it hadn't been primed. That would give Bolan a couple of seconds with him and an extra second or two with the other guards, maybe three, depending on their reaction times. Fuentes was a dandy. Even here in this dusty hellhole, he wore a tailored shirt, pressed and starched. He wouldn't be carrying iron. The tall man, on the other hand, would be lethal with both hands. He had to be taken out first. Mulroy didn't count. It would be over before the kid knew what was happening.

The tall man, the Vulture, walked out from behind the desk, making a mistake by trusting his underling to have conducted a thorough body search. As soon as he got within reach, Bolan would move, making sure as he went to wax Fuentes and take the education out of the organization.

Bolan, still casual, rocked back on his heels, hooking his hands into his jeans pockets. He flicked the spring on the knife, his right fingers now lying atop the razor-sharp blade.

"You're truly a soldier, I can tell that," the Vulture said, "but there's something wrong about you. Do you ever have feelings about things, Mr....Belasko?"

"Feelings?" Bolan replied, stalling.

"Feelings about things, how they're going to turn out. You don't feel right to me, Belasko. Mercs tend to have a certain...dissipation around the eyes that I don't see in yours. I tend to act on my feelings. It's a jungle-survival skill, don't you think?"

"We're in the desert," Bolan replied.

The man narrowed his gaze and moved several steps forward, his eyes riveted to Bolan's as if he could see right into his brain. Bolan had gone up against every kind of man there was, but the Vulture's singular intelligence and street sense marked him as dangerous. Bolan had to make his move—and quickly.

There was a noise at the door, and as the tall man's gaze flicked away for just a second, Bolan jumped.

The knife was in his hand, already inscribing a wide arc aimed at the throat. But the man moved like lightning, his hand up to block the thrust. Bolan's hand was deflected but didn't stop moving, and the blade jammed into the tall man's right eye, cutting through, gashing all the way to his ear.

The Vulture screamed as he fell back. Bolan dropped the knife and reached to the man's right hip to jerk out his weapon, a nickel-plated Uzi pistol, even as the Vulture spun away toward the floor, his hands covering his face.

The Executioner hit his targets in the order he had planned, first taking out the man with the rifle at the ready with a high-percentage chest shot. Three seconds had passed since he'd pulled the knife, and Fuentes had come to his feet. Bolan turned the Uzi and snap-aimed, then pulled the trigger, splattering the man's educated brains all over the shack.

He heard two automatics prime, then swung around to loose a triburst at the two men drawing down on him. The third shot toppled one of the guards into the men who came charging through the door. Less than ten seconds had passed, and Bolan turned toward the window just in time to see Mulroy charging him.

Bolan swung the Uzi around, slamming it hard into the kid's temple. Then he vaulted over the collapsed body as men poured through the front door, and dived out the glassless window and into a barrel roll that brought him back to his feet.

Mind focused solely on movement, he charged around the shack, where the limo driver was stepping out of the Caddy. The Executioner fired head high, taking him down immediately, ripping the .357 Magnum off his belt as he fell.

He jumped into the driver's seat and slammed the door. The streets were filling with running mercs who would discover any second now that their gravy train had just been derailed. Bolan goosed the ignition and dropped the car into gear, his foot already to the floor.

The Cadillac squealed loudly as Bolan took it through a one-eighty turn, spraying dust everywhere. The gunfire was constant now, bullets punching through the limo's tinted windows as the tires caught hold and the car lurched forward.

Men were all around him. He raced ahead, running

over anybody in his path, watching as other vehicles joined the chase.

He'd planned on pursuit, though. Releasing the wheel with his right hand, he went for the watch on his left wrist, pressing the wind button until it clicked.

The explosives he'd planted the night before went off in sequence. Shacks and contraband storage garages exploded loudly all along the street, followed by a rain of wood and tin.

He checked the rearview to see nothing but smoke and fire, no vehicles emerging from the conflagration that enveloped Piedro Blanco.

Foot still heavy on the gas pedal, he sped into the desolate expanse of thorn forest surrounding the city, suspecting that he hadn't killed the Vulture, only made him mad. He'd discovered a long time ago that an enemy not killed is an enemy you'd meet again.

When next they met, one of them would die.

CHAPTER ONE

New York City
July 17, 1996

The sweltering summer heat was pervasive, inescapable. The sun fired up the concrete until it radiated, the tall buildings blocking off any chance of relief from the wind. It was the kind of weather that made young people riot and old people die.

Mack Bolan sat in the back seat of the rented van. Six burly United States marshals filled up the rest of it. Everybody was hot despite the air conditioner blasting away as they cruised the streets of Brooklyn on a mission that, for once in Bolan's life, he was looking forward to.

The Vulture had been caught.

"Hey, look at those kids," said Gene Tripp, the beefy marshal beside him.

Bolan stared out the window to see a fire hydrant spewing a jet of water fifteen feet into the air to the delight of the dozen kids splashing, running and screaming below it.

"They've got the right idea." Tripp turned to Bolan. "You got any kids, Belasko?"

Bolan shook his head. "Never found a woman who'd put up with me long enough. You?"

"Damned right. Hell, I've got grandkids, two of them."

"You must have started young, then."

"This is my last run," Tripp said, his face nearly as red as his hair. "I'm retiring the minute we get rid of the meat we're picking up. I pulled all the strings I could to get this assignment. Wanted to go out on a high note, and the Vulture's somebody I can talk to those grandbabies about. You're not Marshal service, are you?"

"No," Bolan said in a way that any cop would know to leave alone. "I'm just along to identify the guy."

"You know him?"

Everybody had turned around to look. "Our paths crossed fifteen years ago for all of five minutes," Bolan said.

"What happened, for cryin' out loud?" the driver called back to him.

"I cut his eye out," Bolan said, and turned to look out the window again.

"They say the guy wears a patch," Tripp returned

enthusiastically. "We gotta be on the beam with this one."

The details of the Vulture's capture were sketchy, but Hal Brognola had told Bolan that a deep-cover NSC agent working out of Switzerland had accidentally stumbled on the Vulture. NSC then contacted U.S. Customs, telling them the terrorist would be traveling from Zurich to Kennedy International under a passport issued in the name of Charles Dorn. By the time the Vulture was arrested without incident as he deplaned at Kennedy, the FBI, the State Department, the CIA and the Treasury Department all wanted a piece of the action. While the bureaucrats fought it out, the Vulture was dumped into a holding tank at a local precinct.

After three days of infighting, a compromise was reached, allowing the federal marshals to transport the terrorist to a federal institution in Quantico, Virginia, where everybody could get a crack at him at the same time.

Everybody wanted the big fish.

As one of the most feared and successful terrorists in recent memory, the Vulture had been connected with some of the most visible acts of brutality against innocents of the latter twentieth century. Train bombs in Italy, kidnapping in South America, airline hijacking worldwide—all had his name attached. He was a criminal mastermind with a private army who'd do anything for money. And Mack Bolan had let him get away, albeit with only one eye. The Executioner was there to make sure it didn't happen again.

They were moving west on Linden, into the maze of medical-center buildings and museums just east of Prospect Park. The homes off Linden were narrow two-story brownstones in block-long rows.

"We'll be there in a minute," said one of the men in front of Bolan. DiGuisti had been a New York cop before becoming a U.S. marshal.

"How long you got to retirement, Belasko?" Tripp asked.

"The day I retire is the day I can walk out on those streets without a gun to protect myself," Bolan responded. "Can you make it on your pension?"

"Hell, no," the man returned. "What do you think they invented the Witness Protection Program for? It's so retired marshals can make extra money arranging payouts to gangster snitches and ferrying around people to debriefings who don't know nothing to begin with."

Everybody in the van laughed. "Save us a place!" the driver called.

"Pull it up," DiGuisti said. "We're there."

They hugged the curb on a busy section of street with a jumble of row houses, department stores, and restaurants. The towers of the hospital complexes dominated everything else around. Just ahead of the van, the precinct house sat at the top of a long flight of stone stairs. The streets were full of people coming and going. Bolan didn't like it.

"Let's get this over with," he said, sliding open the side door and climbing out into overpowering heat, a furnace blast. The weather was fitting. Just like Paraguay in '82. Mack Bolan, the Executioner, was one eye away from finishing a job.

"Hey, we're on expense account," somebody called. "Let's get a bite to eat first."

"Do what you want," Bolan said. "I'm going to pick up a prisoner and take him to Quantico."

Everybody groaned. "One in every crowd," DiGuisti said, and Tripp chuckled as he climbed out into the heat beside Bolan.

A black-and-white squealed loudly in front of the van, crossing over at an angle into the yellow no-parking zone. Four uniformed cops got out and moved toward the steps. Bolan kept looking at them, his attention drawn by the way they took in the surroundings, reconnoitering. As if they were in enemy territory. Then he saw their weapons.

"DiGuisti," he said. "What's regulation-issue iron with NYPD these days?"

"Rugers, 9 mm semiautos. Why?" he replied.

"We've got two cops with Glocks, one with an Uzi pistol and one with a small machine gun strapped to his leg, that's why."

"No way," DiGuisti said, turning and looking at

the cops walking slowly up the stairs. He jerked when he saw the guns. "This doesn't make... Hey, fellas!"

Before Bolan could stop him, the man had jogged off in the direction of the cops.

It all happened in slow motion then. An old step van rumbled in from the west just as the "cops" turned and reacted to DiGuisti. Their hands went for their guns as the van screeched to a dead stop right in front of the station.

"Get cover!" Bolan barked even as the men on the stairs saw the step van and rushed into the police station. DiGuisti, looking confused, turned to watch the van's driver jump out of the truck and charge down the street.

"Get down!" Bolan shouted at him, the last word swallowed by the thump of an incredible explosion as the step van went up in a huge fireball, two thousand pounds' worth of ammonium nitrate seeking release. The wrath was mighty. The marshals' van, the black-and-white, everything was up in the air as glass shards and shrapnel rained down from above and the fronts of buildings sheared off completely and crumbled to the streets with a volcanic roar.

The force of the blast slammed Bolan into a line of garbage cans. Tumbling, he came up on his knees, shaking his head, trying to clear it. He couldn't hear much, though the deadly silence gradually faded as his hearing returned, and with it, the sounds of chaos and destruction.

The streets were completely changed, reduced to rubble. A smoking crater twenty feet wide had eaten the pavement where the step van had been. The marshals' van was upside down, the driver pinned beneath it, dead, with another marshal, his legs gone, lying atop the van. The black-and-white had fallen on its side on the stairs up to the station. DiGuisti was simply gone. Vaporized.

Bodies were strewed all over the street, the survivors staggering and screaming. Tripp was on his feet beside him, disoriented, moving aimlessly, bleeding from dozens of cuts, his sports jacket ripped to shreds.

And then things got nasty.

Five dark vans screeched around the corners and jerked to a stop at the edge of the small mountain of debris that had been the front of the precinct house. Their squealing tires were muted to Bolan's fogged hearing, like tiny fingernails scratching on a chalkboard.

He turned, jerking his Beretta 93-R from its combat harness beneath his windbreaker, and reached out to grab Gene Tripp as the vans disgorged masked figures, their hands bristling with machine guns.

"Gene!" he screamed, dragging the man down behind the hulk of the upended van. "Get it together!"

The marshal blinked, trying to focus as the machine guns opened up with chain-saw rattle, spraying the street and the remnants of the precinct. Bolan shook his head again, his hearing now almost normal.

"What...?" Tripp said from beside him. "What's...happening?"

Bolan primed the Beretta as bullets chewed sidewalk all around them and dozens of thudding impacts shook the van.

"Remember the Vulture?" he called to Tripp, and the man's eyes cleared immediately.

"Son of a bitch!" he yelled, going for his gun as two surviving marshals, bleeding, their clothes shredded, crawled up beside them through deep rubble.

"This is a military action!" Bolan yelled above the gunfire. "They're trying to break out the Vulture! Gene and I are going in. There's only four of them inside. Cover us!"

He turned to Tripp, who was checking the load on his own Ruger. "You ready?"

Tripp looked him in the eye. "Your deal, gambler."

As Bolan grabbed the man's sleeve, he noticed blood dripping down his own arm. "Just one thing," he said. "You see the man with the patch, you kill him."

"No sweat."

"Try for the black-and-white first," Bolan said. Although the demolished car was only fifteen feet away, it may as well have been a mile. "Go!"

They jumped up and were in motion as the other agents stood and fired over the mutilated body on the exposed undercarriage.

With no time to pick targets, Bolan and Tripp just

fired, driving down their assailants. They had surprise and luck with them on the first run, tumbling to safety behind the crushed black-and-white on the steps as the police within the precinct began returning fire at the masked men hunkered behind the vans.

Bolan and Tripp were several steps up with a long run to the station doors. There was no way they could make it up those stairs without a distraction.

Bolan scanned the battle zone and the five vans that shielded their assailants. "You!" he called to one of the marshals returning fire from their van. "Aim for their gas tanks!

"They're going to have to rush the place," Bolan told Tripp. "This area's going to get real popular real quick." Even as he spoke, they could hear sirens mixing with the screams on the streets.

"Let's put 'em back," Tripp said, jamming another clip into his Ruger. "You want the left?"

Bolan nodded. "Go!"

Both men stood to fire over the side of the black-and-white. Bolan lined up half a dozen easy targets, out in the open and advancing. Unable to tell if the gunners were bulletproofed, he went for head shots, leaning his shooting arm on the car's side.

The masked gunmen were advancing through smoke, firing from the hip as people up and down the street screamed and bolted for safety.

Bolan's first shot picked a large man off his feet and threw him back into his van. He swung to the second, firing, sending him spinning into his comrades who were now looking for cover as Tripp knocked one down, too.

Bolan could hear the slugs thudding into the van closest to the gunners as the marshals below them concentrated their fire. It was only a matter of time, Bolan knew, before they found their targets.

"When that van blows, we're going to take the steps," Bolan said to Tripp. "Ready?"

The marshal jammed another clip home and nodded a moment before their partners hit the jackpot. The van exploded with a *whump*. Several of the masked figures rolled on the sidewalk, trying to extinguish their flaming clothing, while the other hardmen were forced to seek cover.

Bolan and Tripp bounded up the stairs two at a time, throwing themselves into the rubble of the station as the firing intensified from without.

The inside of the precinct house looked like the end of the world. The ceiling had caved in, and those who weren't pinned by the wreckage had been carved to pieces from the flying glass of the doors. Several hurt and bleeding cops fired riot guns from behind piles of debris, the entire front of their building gone.

"Holding cells!" Bolan called to one of them. The man ignored him, and the Executioner grabbed his shoulder. "Holding cells!"

The cop's eyes weren't focusing. He was in deep shock, functioning on autopilot, still firing but on the edge like a boxer ready to go down. "Third floor," he finally mumbled, and Bolan grabbed Tripp's sleeve and hauled him farther back into the devastation.

The elevator was gone, but the back stairs still remained intact. Bolan and Tripp slammed through the stairwell door, weapons out and at the ready. There was no one there.

Bolan led the way up the stairwell, moving quietly, cautiously, as the gunfight out front was muffled when the door swung closed behind them.

The stairwell turned at every landing, so the two men covered each other at the turn. As he reached the bottom of the stairs that led to the third-floor landing, Bolan could see the door hanging open, seemingly unguarded. He didn't believe it.

Keeping close to the inner railing, they crept up the last flight of stairs, one slow step at a time. Bolan could hear firing from the third floor.

When they reached the landing, he stayed glued to the inner rail, his body crouched low. A wall defined the inner stairs, so Bolan couldn't see around to the fourth-floor stairs. He took a deep breath and launched himself across the landing.

The "cop" with the machine gun was on the stairs, guarding the door below. As Bolan slid across the landing, he could see surprise in the man's eyes and knew he had him. Beretta on target, he took him out with a shot to the neck. The man grabbed for his throat as he pitched headfirst onto the landing right beside the Executioner, blood pumping in gushes from his fatal neck wound.

Bolan motioned for Tripp to close up to him, and they walked cautiously into a third-floor hallway, stepping over the body of a cop whose hands had been filled with two cups of coffee, the brown liquid mingled now with his blood on the linoleum floor.

The hallway dead-ended in one direction and formed a tee with another hall at the other end. Hugging opposite walls, they moved forward, Bolan holstering the Beretta and taking out the Desert Eagle .44 for the close-in work. If he was going to put holes in people at this point, he wanted them to be big holes.

They made it to the tee and cautiously examined the hallway that ran at right angles. More dead cops— three of them in this hallway alone. Bolan motioned Tripp back into the stairwell hall, the only exit.

The booking station seemed to be off to the right, down a long hallway. Bolan decided to investigate to the left first, a quick run-through to let him know the killing ground was safe. He'd moved fifteen feet when the man with the Uzi pistol walked out of a room directly before him just as Bolan heard men running from the other direction.

He prioritized instantly, swinging the .44 Magnum to the assailant in front and pulling the trigger from three feet away, slamming the body hard against the wall before it hit the floor.

He swung back quickly toward the approaching footsteps to fire from a crouch. From a distance of twenty feet, he found himself face-to-face with the Vulture, the man's good eye opening in shocked surprise.

Bolan had him.

CHAPTER TWO

Bolan could feel it.

He had a half second's advantage on the Vulture and planned to knock the terrorist into his two accomplices with a well-aimed shot, thus creating enough confusion to quickly take all three out.

But Tripp, thinking he was protecting Bolan, jumped into his line of fire, and the Executioner's finger froze on the trigger.

The terrorist with the patch had no such restraint. He blasted the marshal three times at point-blank range, his burst pushing Tripp backward to stumble toward Bolan.

Still cursing Bolan, the Vulture was dragged down the stairwell hallway by his men as the Executioner grabbed the still-stumbling Tripp, going to the ground with him.

Tripp had taken three slugs in the chest, and blood pumped out of him furiously, covering Bolan. "B-Belas...ko," he whispered as the Executioner rested him gently on the cold floor. "M-my jacket p-pocket...hurry."

Bolan reached into his breast pocket, withdrawing a sealed letter-sized envelope. Tripp was fading quickly, the light dimming in his green eyes as his lifeblood pooled beneath him. "What do you want me to do?"

"Read..." the man rasped, trying to raise himself on his elbows. "Give...give...Annie."

He fell back, his head moving to the side as blood bubbled between his lips. He was still trying to talk, and Bolan bent to his lips.

The voice was barely a whisper now. "Get...that... s-son...of...a—"

He was gone, and Bolan closed the man's eyes.

Then he was up and running, jamming the envelope into his back pocket. He hit the stairwell on a dead run, and took the stairs in long strides, banging the door open to reenter the carnage of the precinct's lobby.

Masked men in black were falling back, withdrawing to the street. Bolan got one in the back of the head as he raced out.

He plowed through the debris, looking at his watch. Five minutes had passed since they'd first pulled up to the station, so the place would be crawling with firemen and cops within a minute or two.

The front of the building was now filled with nothing but dead cops. Bolan ran into the sunshine just in time to see the Vulture diving into an open side door of one of the vans, then it lurched away behind two of the other vans already under way.

He charged halfway down the stairs and shot one of the retreating attackers as the man ran across the rubbled sidewalk, going down as his van started up. His comrades fired from inside the van, killing him rather than letting him be taken.

Bolan kept running as the vans sped off, vaulting over the just-killed terrorist, charging after the van containing the Vulture as it sideswiped a Toyota just on the perimeter of the debris and careered down the street.

A woman jumped, screaming in fright, out of the Toyota. Bolan charged past, then backtracked when he heard the engine still running. He jumped into the driver's seat.

"I'm the law," he said, and hit reverse and floored the pedal. The car screeched backward, smoke curling from the tires.

The vans had scattered in all directions, but Bolan still had the Vulture's in sight as it squealed a hard right onto Flatbush Avenue.

Bolan approached the turn just as the street was rocked by another huge explosion. This time he had to look up. The top two floors in the main tower of the King's County Hospital Center were blasted to pieces. Gray smoke billowed above white glowing flames. These weren't homemade bombs. The hospital had been taken out with a military incendiary, a big one. Another explosion went up and the botanic gardens erupted in volcanic fury before him.

"Diversion," he said bitterly. "These people are maniacs."

Cars were stopped all over the street, and Bolan dropped the Toyota in gear and bounced up on the sidewalk, honking at a growing crowd of bystanders.

He bounced onto the street again a block later and spied the Vulture's van parked in the middle of Flatbush where it cut through the guts of Prospect Park, blocking traffic.

He sped to the van, stopping ten feet from it and falling out of the car door to roll into firing position behind the front fender.

Alert, he eased over the hood, looking at the van idling in the middle of the street, its side door half-open. He stood, moving cautiously toward it, the .44 ready. He moved around the front end first, looking down into the seats and peering through to the back. Nothing.

He hurried around to the side and stuck his head inside without opening the door. Empty, except for a small satchel sitting near the rear. It was rigged with fishing line to the side and back doors. Booby trap.

"Freeze!" came a voice from behind. "Police!"

Bolan turned, his hands in the air. Two cops, their black-and-white sitting next to the Toyota, were standing behind their open doors, guns drawn. "This van is rigged to explode," he said. "Keep people away from it."

"Right," a tall blond cop with a gray mustache said. "Just put the weapon on the ground and kick it over here."

Bolan did as he was told. "My prisoner is escaping," he said. "Would you kindly let me go?"

"Hands on your head," the other cop ordered, both men moving toward him, their guns still trained on Bolan.

The cop with the mustache shoved him from behind, toward the police cruiser. "I'll check the van," the other one said.

"Don't open the doors!" Bolan called over his shoulder. "It'll blow!"

"Shut up!" the cop with the mustache said, shoving him against the side of the cruiser. Bolan turned his head to see the other cop's hand on the sliding door as he leaned around it.

Bolan tensed, then dived over the open cruiser door just as the van blew, tearing both cops and bystanders to ribbons.

The satchel bomb had been packed full of nails. The cruiser and the Toyota were bristling with them.

As for the Vulture, he was gone. He'd changed cars, as all of his people probably had, and escaped on Flatbush, which turned into the Manhattan Bridge and gave him access to the rest of the country.

Bolan climbed back into the Toyota, which was battered, with all its glass broken out.

He was summing up the implications of what had just gone down. There were many ways to break a man out of jail. Not all of them involved so many people, so much destruction. The Vulture had chosen this method to signal that his army was here and he was going to conduct business as usual.

Was it possible to stop him, to bottle him up in Manhattan? It seemed unlikely. No one knew whom to look for—a man with a patch, certainly, but what then? People with guns? It wasn't likely they would openly advertise their presence.

He turned the car around and headed back toward the precinct, negotiating through police and fire-rescue teams crawling all over the area. The hospital was still blazing like a torch, with God only knew how many people trapped inside.

The woman was waiting for her Toyota, her eyes wide as she saw the nails and broken glass.

Bolan stopped beside her and climbed out of the car. "Ma'am," he said, nodding and walking away.

He pulled his headset out of his harness and put it on, juicing the battery pack as he walked to a body covered in concrete and plaster dust. He punched up Hal Brognola's number at the Justice Department, although the man spent much of his time at the Stony Man Farm in Virginia. As head of the Operations Group, Brognola was responsible for resolving America's defense problems with the help of Able Team, Phoenix Force, a full support staff, and of course, Bolan. As he waited, he started pulling debris off the man who'd been the driver of the van carrying the ammonium nitrate-fuel-oil cocktail.

"Brognola," came Hal's voice. From his tone it was clear that he already knew about the Vulture's jailbreak.

"It's me," Bolan said, starting to go through the dead driver's pockets.

"What the hell happened?" Brognola asked.

"He's gone, Hal. Gone." Bolan glanced over at the area on the other side of the debris where they'd pulled up. As he feared, there was no one alive over there. "All the guys you sent up here to get him are gone. Except for me."

"Was it a car bomb?"

"Yeah. Blew up right in front of us. What's being done?"

He found something in one of the pockets and pulled it out. It was a matchbook with Bob's Texaco, Harrisburg, Pennsylvania, printed on the flap. He stuck it in his pocket.

"I just found out thirty seconds ago," Brognola said. "It takes a minute to get things moving. Striker, get back here so we can debrief you."

"Hey!" a cop called, running up to him. "What are you doing there?"

"Just a minute, Hal." Bolan stood and reached into

his pocket. He pulled out the Vulture's photo, taken when he was booked. "Officer. Here's a picture of the man who did this. We have no idea what name he's traveling under now. There are twenty-five to thirty people with him. We have no information on them except that many of them will be Europeans. There are some dead United States marshals. I'll identify them in a minute. Oh, and this man here was the driver of the van with the bomb."

The cop moved off, looking at the photo. Bolan didn't need it. The Vulture was imprinted on his mind.

"What were you saying, Hal?"

"I said we need to debrief you."

"No can do, pal. I'm seeing this one through all the way to the end."

"Striker, listen to me. You know we can't engage officially at this end with this business, but every law-enforcement agency in America is going to be looking for these guys, if they're not out of the country already."

"They're not out of the country. They're here for a reason. It's business, Hal."

"Any idea where they're headed?" the big Fed asked.

"Nope. But I'll start by putting myself in the Vulture's place and doing what I would do in his situation. He's good, Hal. He's really good.

"First off I need you to clear Stony Man for computer access to police records and intelligence nationwide. Second, I want you to find out about the Swiss connection. If an NSC man knew the Vulture would be traveling under an assumed name on a forged passport, then he might know the guy's *real* name and where he lives. It gives us something to work with on that end."

"NSC's not easy to crack," Brognola said. "They like to think of themselves as autonomous. But give me some time and I'll get the goods. Call the Bear at Stony Man and let him know what you've got so far."

Bolan heard voices behind him but ignored them. "I'm bringing this man down, Hal, at any cost. We're wasting time."

"Good luck, buddy."

"Yeah," Bolan said, tapping off.

He managed to flag down a yellow cab driven by an Iranian and climbed into the back. "Kennedy Airport," he directed.

He tapped up Aaron "the Bear" Kurtzman's number at Stony Man Farm. The Farm's top man in the business of intelligence gathering and analysis came on almost immediately. "I hope you're ready to get to work."

"Bolan!" Kurtzman returned loudly. "You're alive!"

"Last time I looked," Bolan said, watching Brooklyn slide by as cars jammed the streets, the ghoulish or just plain curious running in the direction he'd just come from.

"What have you got?"

"Access the data base of the world's law-enforcement agencies, and look for anything on the Vulture. He's traveling with a small army. They split up, I'll bet, but will all be converging somewhere. I want to know where."

"The needle in the electronic haystack."

"I don't think so," Bolan said. "They'll give themselves away somehow—there are quite a lot of them, and many foreigners. The government's going to be methodically tracking down every potential lead. I want to go with the flow, let the instincts move me around. Start tracking down their transport. Where'd they get the vans? Rented? If so, where?"

"How about you?"

"I'm on my way to Kennedy. Get me a chopper and a pilot, stat."

"To go where?"

"Wherever the Vulture got his ordnance. If my guess is right, his whole bunch probably left New York clean as a whistle to get through roadblocks. Wherever they got the bang they used here, they're going to want some more of it. Who's close? They blew up a hospital with an incendiary, looked like phosphorous. Who's got that deep an arsenal in the area?"

"Give me a minute," the Bear said, and the rapid clicking of his keyboard was audible over the phone lines.

"And while you're at it find out who, besides government people, visited the Vulture in that holding cell.''

Bolan sat back, assessing his own battle damage, wondering where the man with the patch was right now. An underground army on the move. It was a frightening concept. He took the matchbook he'd stripped from the driver out of his pocket, studying it.

"Striker," came Kurtzman's voice, "I might have a hit for you on that arms dealer. There's a guy in Bainbridge, Pennsylvania, who is under scrutiny right now by the FBI, CIA and ATF. His name's Yosiah Masterson, but everybody calls him Sarge. He's been taped doing business with foreign nationals. He likes bombs. Missiles. He's especially fond of…incendiaries, it says on my screen.''

Bolan looked at the matchbook again. "Is Bainbridge anywhere near Harrisburg?''

"Right down the street," Kurtzman replied.

"Get me that chopper," Bolan said.

"Already working on it," the man returned. "Oh, I got something else, too. Your target was allowed a visit in his cell by a lawyer, an ambulance chaser, no big deal. They met once for thirty minutes, then the guy left and never came back.''

"A name?''

"Doesn't matter. They found him dead just a little while ago. He was shot at close range over five times.''

CHAPTER THREE

Front Royal, Virginia

Deputy Sheriff Julie Powell sat behind the wheel of the patrol car as it idled in the convenience-store parking lot and wondered how she could help her son, Jerry, bring up his English grades when school started in the fall. He'd flunked this year, mostly because his communications skills were lacking. He wasn't dumb, just lazy and TV addicted. It was part of the parents' curse, she decided, that your children would do horribly in school in the subjects you'd done well in.

Her husband, Ted, Front Royal's sheriff, was inside the convenience store, checking on a rash of shoplifting incidents and calling home to tell her sister and full-time baby-sitter, Ruth, they were on their way.

It was a general rule in law enforcement that cops shouldn't marry other cops because somebody needed to stay alive to raise the children, but that was in other places, bigger places. Front Royal was a tiny vacation town, a base camp mostly for people camping and hiking on the Blue Ridge Mountains, which towered all around them. The city's main drag was Highway 11, where Julie was parked now.

It was a good, quiet, close-knit town in which to raise kids, even if they did all up and leave once they grew up. There was very little opportunity for young people in Front Royal. This was a place that existed on pensions and feeding the tourist trade. The average age of its citizens was sixty-two.

Ted, all six foot five of him, came out of the store, smiling the country-boy smile she'd fallen in love with ten years before when they'd met as Navy SPs. He carried a cup of coffee in each hand.

He leaned in his open window and handed her a cup before climbing in.

"Let's make the rounds one more time and call it a day," he said, taking a sip. "My foot's killing me."

She raised an eyebrow. "The one you dropped the bowling ball on?"

He smiled sheepishly at her. "Yeah. I want to soak it."

She downed half her coffee in one long pull, then dumped the rest out the window. The streets were emptying as the people staying in the motels settled in for the night, leaving only cruising teenagers. "Anything from Ruthy?"

"Sarah lost that loose tooth today and she's been showing it off all over the neighborhood."

"She's just looking for a lot of tooth fairies. She—"

Their radar gun was beeping loudly. Just as they turned, a car raced past them down Highway 11, and the readout registered triple digits.

"Holy hell," Julie said, dropping the cruiser into gear and jamming the pedal to the floor. As she skidded onto the highway, she hit the display lights and siren, and all other traffic froze as they screeched after the already vanished car.

Her eyes became her brain as she swung her gaze from side to side, never actually watching the road itself, but rather all the things on the periphery.

Ted was on the horn. "Virginia Highway Patrol...this is Mobile A-1 in Front Royal. We are in pursuit of a vehicle which we clocked at...109 miles per hour in a thirty-five zone."

"Roger, A-1. Description?"

"A white Ford Mustang, late-model, GT, heading south on 11 where it intersects the Blue Ridge Parkway."

"We are deploying backup, Mobile A-1. Keep us posted."

"Out," Ted said, breaking contact.

"If they're heading into the mountains," Julie said, "they'll have to slow down." The road was already curving, weaving, gradually rising.

"Strange though," she said.

"What?" he replied, removing his .38 pistol and checking the load.

"Nobody would go through Front Royal at 110 and

into the mountains if they knew the area. You have to drive slowly and have no turnoffs. Anybody who knows the East Coast knows what the Blue Ridge Parkway is. But these guys are being stupid."

"What's your point?"

"Remember that bulletin we got—there! We've got them!"

The grade was just getting steep through the foot-hills, with many homes perched right on the sides of the mountains throughout the area. The Mustang was caught behind two semitrailers gearing down to make the long climb. Meanwhile, the last of the evening vacationers were just coming out of the mountains, making it impossible for the Mustang to pass the trucks, though he kept trying to edge to the right, to the gravel shoulder.

Julie closed the gap quickly, siren screaming. She saw four heads turn to look at them through the back window as Ted motioned for them to pull over. After half a mile they complied.

"I'll take this one," Ted said. He pulled his hat on, hooking the strap under his chin.

Julie had the handset already and was calling in the New Jersey plate on the vehicle. "Why don't you wait until we hear back on this one, hon," she said. "It just doesn't feel right to me."

"Just speeders," Ted said, winking. He popped open the door and put on his official face. "Let's stop on the way home and get some ice cream for dessert."

"You keep building that gut," Julie said, "and you won't get reelected."

He sucked it in and struck a pose. "Bronzed Adonis," he said, and climbed out of the cruiser. He used his slow walk, his John Wayne stroll, around to the driver's side of the stopped car.

"Confirmation on that license," the radio said. "Registered Joe Civit, Jersey City. Brown '93 Buick Skylark, four door."

"Wrong car," Julie said, her insides tensing as Ted reached the Mustang and leaned down into the window space. "I'm looking at a white Mustang."

"Are there any identifying markings on the vehicle?" the voice asked tightly.

"What's wrong?"

"Repeat, are there any identifying markings on the vehicle?"

"No, not really," she answered, watching Ted straighten up and scrunch up his face as he looked at a driver's license. "Mud flaps...with Bugs Bunny on them."

"Hold please—"

"Deputy Powell," an authoritative male voice broke in. "You may have part of the contingent that exploded the bomb in New York City today. These people are extremely dangerous. How many do you see?"

"Hold on," she said, opening her door and leaning out. "Sheriff Powell...we have another call. Stat."

He turned to her, an odd look on his face. Then she saw the shotgun, and life moved eerily dreamlike.

The shotgun kicked fire. Ted took the full burst in the chest and staggered back in surprise, right into the path of a semi barreling down the incline the other way.

The impact of the truck threw him straight up. Julie's eyes locked on him, unable to look away. He went high in the air even as the trucker lost control and skidded off the roadway to fall fifty feet into the Shenandoah Valley below.

Ted fell with a boom atop the hood of the cruiser, flopped like a dead fish, his body bent at impossible angles, his broken, forlorn face staring lifelessly through the windshield at her. People in the houses built into the mountainside were rushing out onto their porches to see what was happening. Somewhere in the distance a roar went up as the truck hit bottom, and a fireball shot up over the roadway to set the dry trees afire.

She fought shock only for her children's sake, dragging her gaze from Ted's broken face and concentrating on the vehicle before her.

She reached for the riot gun.

The Mustang roared to life, the driver putting it in reverse and skidding back as Julie pumped the Remington 12-gauge and fell back across the seat to aim down her body.

Wham!

The vehicle slammed into her open door, ripping it off the hinges, exposing her.

"Mobile A-1," came a tiny, forgotten voice from the floor. "Mobile A-1. Can you read?"

Screeching to a halt ten feet behind the cruiser, the Mustang's driver jammed it into gear and pulled alongside. A pale blond man with a MAC-10 gave her a parody of a smile through his window space.

She fired, the report loud, the recoil hurting her shoulder. She heard screams and return fire, and the inside of the car ripping to shreds.

She felt a dull thud in her side, then searing pain as the smoke cleared and she saw the mangled face of the man she'd just shot. The driver grabbed his SMG and aimed, while Julie tried to pump the shotgun again.

Then she heard other gunfire, from the mountains and roadway. Bullets thudded into the Mustang as the driver screeched away.

She raised herself painfully to see twenty senior citizens, armed with everything from pellet guns to assault rifles, converging on her position. The citizens of Front Royal had just driven off the killers.

"THAT'S BAINBRIDGE," the pilot said, nodding toward a small town on the eastern bank of the lazy Susquehanna River in southern Pennsylvania.

"What I heard is that the farm is ten miles south of Bainbridge, just off the river."

"You say you're speculating real estate?" the pilot asked, a local Bolan had hired in Reading when he'd had to refuel.

"Sure," Bolan said. It sounded fine. The chopper had been a good idea gone bad. His notion was to beat the Vulture here by traveling as the crow flies, but he'd been forced down with technical problems. Valuable time had been wasted waiting for another chopper. Now it was a race to see who'd get there first, if indeed this was where the Vulture was headed.

"There it is," the pilot said, and Bolan squinted into the rapidly fading light to see a farmhouse with a pickup truck in the chicken yard. A hundred yards from the house sat a hangar-sized Quonset hut of a barn.

"Set me down by the river," Bolan directed. He was wearing a black Nike warm-up outfit he'd purchased in a shop at Kennedy, the only appropriate clothes he could find there. Its chief advantage was that the loose-fitting jacket easily covered the combat harness.

"I could get you up close to the house," the pilot said, "easy."

"I want to...walk the property."

The pilot nodded. "You're the boss."

Bolan watched the grounds disappear behind a rise as the chopper set down gently on the riverbank a half mile from the house.

He started out the door, then turned back. "If there

should be any kind of trouble, I want you to crank this thing up and get the hell out of here."

"What kind of trouble?" the man asked.

"We all know trouble when we bump into it."

The pilot smiled. "I've never lost a passenger yet," he said. "I sure as hell don't intend to start now."

The Executioner climbed out of the chopper. "Just do what I say." He closed the door and jogged in the direction of the farmhouse, taking to the tall, dry Johnsongrass when the house came into view. He put the barn between himself and the farmhouse to keep from being seen.

He didn't get within ten feet of the barn. If it housed the arsenal he thought it did, there'd be safeguards atop safeguards protecting the contents. He knew men like Masterson. Their talent for mayhem tended to be quite extreme.

The Beretta came out of the harness. Bolan braced himself and charged the house from a hundred feet away, the closest he'd get to surprise in the open barnyard.

The house was white frame with a large front porch. He jumped the steps up to the porch, ran past a large dining-room window to dive and roll should he attract fire.

Nothing.

He crept to the front door, tried the handle. It was open. He shoved it to bounce against the wall, then moved quietly inside, weapon at the ready.

The house was a pit, empty beer bottles and food wrappers everywhere. A lot of people had been here. Pillows and blankets were stacked against the walls, and a television set was still on, running the weather channel.

He moved swiftly and silently through the two-story dwelling, checking the upstairs first. Beds had been slept in and more bedding rolled out on the floor, and European cigarettes were stubbed out in a bedside ashtray. This had been their base of operations and staging area. Hundreds of empty boxes of ammo were scattered around.

The search was thorough upstairs, uncovering nothing except the former presence of the Vulture's army. Bolan made his way back downstairs and found the owner of the house hog-tied on the kitchen floor.

The man appeared to be about fifty years old, his hair greasy, gray and stringy. He saw the Executioner and began trying to talk through the gag in his mouth as he bounced on the floor, arms and legs secured behind his back.

Bolan moved to him, squatted and pulled the gag out of his mouth. "You must be Sarge," he said.

"Get these damned ropes off me," the man spat, his voice rough gravel. "If you're with them other guys, they already took off."

"Where to?" Bolan asked.

"How the hell should I know?" he screeched. "Now get these goddamned ropes off me."

Bolan slid over a kitchen chair and sat, staring down as the man squinted angrily up at him. "You answer my questions quickly and honestly. Then maybe I'll cut you loose."

The man sneered at him. "Well you can just—"

Bolan's foot slashed out, the right toe of the athletic shoes he'd bought with the warm-up outfit catching the man on the left temple. Blood welled up to run down his face.

He groaned. "You're just as bad as them guys," he said.

"It's the nature of the business we're in." Bolan let the man stare at the business end of the Beretta. "Tell me why I shouldn't kill you."

"Come on, mister," Sarge said. "It's a bad enough day already. They took my goods, didn't pay me, then ran off with my wife."

Bolan smiled. "They'll be back," he said, confident now. "Who are they? How did you know them?"

"Wait a minute," the man said. "Are you some kind of cop or with the government or something? If you are, I ain't saying nothin' about nothin' until I've seen my lawyer."

"Here's the problem," Bolan said, scooting his chair closer and leaning way down, "I don't have time to play with you." He inched the Beretta closer to rest its barrel against the man's forehead. "Those men you did business with killed over a hundred people in New York City today.''

''W-what?''

''As far as you're concerned, I *am* the government. You are an accessory to murder-one, deserving the death penalty. Are you going to talk?''

Fearfully Sarge nodded, swallowing convulsively.

''I got together with them through mutual contacts in the business,'' Sarge said. ''They said they were mercs and had a job to do here and needed to lay low for a few days, too. I gave them a price for the weapons plus the board. They never argued with nothin', guess because they were never gonna pay anyhow.''

''They never talked about the job?''

''Never. Not in front of me. Seemed real well-trained, like commandos. When they left this mornin', they tied me up and took Lureen with 'em, that's my wife. Said they'd kill her if I said anything about them. You said they were coming back?''

Bolan nodded. ''They're going to want more of the same from you. Nobody packs two jobs at the same time.''

''Well, I'll be ready for 'em this time. Imagine cheatin' me like that.''

''They ever talk about where they were heading, what they were going to do?''

''A couple of them talked about headin' west,'' he replied. ''But they shut up when they saw me. Always did. Brother, I'd like to tell you a lot more, but they just didn't leave me with nothing.''

"West," Bolan said, "Everything's west of here."

The man frowned. "Why'd they have to take Lureen?"

"To make sure you didn't call anybody. They want to do business again. It's the only reason you or Lureen are alive.''

"Hell...untie me, will you? I ain't no threat to you.''

"That's the first lie you've told me today. But I'm going to untie you anyway because I want you to show me your stock.''

Bolan used a Buck knife to get the man's hands free, then Sarge flopped onto his back and worked at untying his legs. He was up in a minute, walking, stretching, rubbing circulation back into his arms.

"Come on," Bolan said. "Let's go look in the barn.''

He pulled the small man along by the arm. They moved into the yard, scattering chickens, and out to the Quonset hut, fifty feet tall. "You sell them any incendiaries?" Bolan asked.

"Sold them a couple of AR57-Ds," the man said. "Those things go for twenty-five grand apiece.''

"Phosphorous?"

The man moved to the door's intricate locking system, turning his back on Bolan to work at it. "Yeah, and gelignite, and a few other nasty things. Used 'em at night in Desert Storm to blow fifty foot up. Light up the area, plus melt the guys underneath. A bargain."

"One blew up two floors of a hospital, the other Prospect Park."

"Really?" Sarge said, as a bell went off and the latch on the door sprang. "Rough. I just sell the stuff." He slid open the door and turned on overhead lights, and Bolan walked into an emporium of death.

It was set up like a warehouse, with a straight, wide main aisle intersected by smaller branching aisles. The merchandise was piled on stacked pallets that reached all the way to the top of the huge room. A forklift was parked to the side.

There were thousands of cases of rifles and handguns, entire areas devoted just to ammunition. A whole section featured Stinger missiles and launchers. There was C-4 and timing mechanisms, grenades, antipersonnel mines. Bolan grabbed a long, zippered duffel from a stack of them on the floor. In a world of ordnance, Sarge had it all. There was even a tank with reflective armor parked in the back. Everything had price tags listing both individual and bulk prices.

Bolan went shopping, grabbing handguns and clips of ammo, a laser-sighted M-60, grenades, a bazooka with a dozen rockets to go with it. He filled his duffel until he could barely carry it, then quit. If he were going to war, he wanted to be as prepared as possible. As prepared as the Vulture would be.

"You ain't gonna pay me, either, are you?" Sarge asked as they walked out the sliding door and into the yard.

Bolan hoisted the heavy duffel onto his shoulder. "No, I'm not. Where the hell did you get all this stuff?"

The man smiled wide to show several missing bottom teeth. "Got me a buddy in Saudi who orders this crap from the U.S. government for the locals. When arms shipments show up, he always scrapes a percentage off the top and ships it back to me. We split the profits. That's free enterprise, brother."

"From where I stand, it looks like illegal arms trade and stealing."

"That's what I said—free enterprise."

Both men jerked at the sound of a truck. State Road 441, a one-laner, ran north of Masterson's property about a half mile and was connected to the farm by a long dirt driveway. They both watched the step van, lost in shadows as the day disappeared, slow down uncertainly, then turn into the dirt road leading right up to the barnyard.

"Go in the house," Bolan said. "I'll handle this."

"What about Lureen?"

"What makes you think they'd bring Lureen here?" Bolan asked. "So you could make a deal? So everybody could go on their merry way? Lureen's dead or soon will be. Go into the house."

The man walked backward, staring for a minute,

then turned and hauled ass into the farmhouse. There Bolan stood, an ordnance bag slung heavily over his shoulder, the door open to a substantial personal arsenal just behind him.

He smiled as the van pulled up, slipping one of the grenades from the zipper case to his jacket pocket. It was a diaper-service van.

Six people climbed out of the van, four men and two women. The age range appeared to be from the midtwenties to early thirties. They looked lean and hard in their casual clothes.

"And who are you?" a man with smoldering eyes and dark skin asked in a heavy Slavic accent as the others fanned out, turning circles.

"My name's Virgil," Bolan said, "Sarge's cousin."

"And where's Sarge?"

"Sarge doesn't want to do business with you," Bolan said, "after the way you treated him and all. He wants Lureen back, too."

The man smiled demonically. "Uri," he said, "go give Mulroy a ring and tell him we've arrived. Ask him for an updated list."

"Mulroy," Bolan said. "I knew a man...a long time ago, with that name. It wouldn't be Willy Mulroy, now would it?"

The man looked surprised, then nodded, and Bolan could see the wheels turning in his head as he waited for the moment to make his move.

"We need to pick up some more materials," the

man said, motioning toward the open doorway of the barn.

Bolan smiled and stepped aside to let the five people enter as the sun's last cherry rays glowed on the horizon.

"I'll handle the forklift," Bolan said. "Will you be paying in cash?"

"No," the man said. "We're charging it."

Bolan walked farther into the building with them, as they grabbed bags and carts and scattered to the merchandise. He hated to see women among the terrorists. Women would make it easier to travel; they'd be harder to catch, more normal looking.

The dark man kept looking at him, and finally Bolan asked, "What about Lureen?"

The man leaned toward Bolan and spoke low. "Lureen doesn't want to come back. She begged us to take her. She's having the time of her life...you know what I mean?"

"Nope," Bolan said, cocking his head. "Can't say that I do."

Machine-gun fire roared from the yard, where Sarge was trying to cradle a .50-caliber machine gun without a tripod, firing from the hip with a huge belt of ammo dragging on the ground behind him, every burst nearly knocking him on his behind. "Bastards!" he screamed. "I'll show you all! I'll show you!"

Bolan turned and ran from the wave of .50-caliber bullets slamming into the ordnance-filled barn. From behind him came a drawn-out howl as the dark man was scythed nearly in half.

He hustled down a side aisle, the bag full of equipment dragging him down. He stood, hoisting the bag up again. The way things were moving, he feared that if he set it down it would be gone.

There were screams from the other terrorists as Sarge made the doorway, firing indiscriminately into his own livelihood, the terrorists returning fire now.

Bolan reached the side wall as something went up, a huge explosion that set off subsidiary explosions and rocked the room, filling it with smoke. The place was on fire.

It would all go.

Bolan was blind in the smoke, feeling his way quickly along the wall until he reached the rear. The firing was centered more to the middle of the building, away from his position.

The rear of the building was reinforced with iron bars welded together in narrow, strong slats. There was no getting out there or on the sides. There was only one door.

The tank. He felt his way along the back wall until he ran into the tank, an Abrams battle wagon, then climbed up and in, closing the hatch behind him. He coughed out the smoke and hit the controls. He'd done this a time or three. It was always a new experience, but one he always figured out.

He got it cranked up, then pulled the periscope

down to eye level, watching smoke. He flipped on the radar to immediate area and watched an outline of the building and its contents come up on the screen, his tank represented by a blinking cursor. He'd do it on instruments.

He rolled forward, clanking on the concrete floor, watching the dot move along the back wall on the screen. When it hit the main aisle, he turned left, straightened and looked into hell.

The smoke was being driven away by huge blasts, filling the entire place with raging fire. Everything shook, explosion after explosion rocking the tank as chunks of building and shrapnel slammed the machine.

He cranked full out and sped through a landscape of fire that blew out all his armor and heated the inside of the turret to an ovenlike temperature. Air was hard to come by as spots swam before his eyes.

He staggered back, the world coming apart.

An explosion ripped the tank, tipping it and throwing Bolan against the side as the turret blew off to crash loudly in the fire. The tank fell back on both treads, throwing him the other way, and he was still somehow moving.

The tank broke from the inferno of the barn, the building throbbing and wheezing like a beating heart. The whole thing was going to go.

He looked up. The chopper he'd rented was hovering in the barnyard just ahead. Bolan stood, reaching, as the tank rolled beneath the chopper, then snatched a skid, the duffel still straining on his shoulder.

"Go!" he screamed at the pilot. "Go!"

The chopper rose, and in a few seconds the barn exploded. Large chunks of it were flung higher than them, and Bolan felt the heat of the leaping fire. The concussion caught them, knocking the chopper nearly sideways at a hundred feet. Bolan barely hung on as the machine was buffetted wildly by the updraft.

The explosion was righteous in its power, rising many hundreds of feet into the air, turning the night skies to daylight for twenty miles in all directions.

If Bolan looked to the east, he could see nothing but fire.

The winds rolled in, air hurrying to resupply what the mighty fire had eaten just as the pilot had precariously regained control of the bird.

The machine was buffetted again, and this time Bolan knew they were going down. They had just barely cleared the rise leading down to the riverbank, and Bolan let go to fall twenty feet as the chopper dipped quickly, then rose, then plowed sideways, embedding its main rotor deeply into the sand and tossing the pilot out his window.

The Executioner rolled down the hillside, hugging his duffel, rolling with it. He hit on the bank and jumped up, setting down the bag to run to the pilot.

The man was already sitting up, head in hands, as Bolan reached him.

"Anything broken?" the big American asked.

"I...I don't think so," the pilot returned, standing shakily.

"Then let's go!" Bolan said, grabbing his arm and hurrying toward the riverbank.

"Go where?"

"I saw a row boat. We're going downriver." He pointed to the still-bright sky above the rise. "This place will be crawling soon."

He found the boat where he'd spotted it upon landing, then grabbed the duffel to toss it inside.

"What about my chopper?"

"Get it tomorrow," Bolan said, pulling the bow right up onto the bank so the pilot could clamber in next to the ordnance. The Executioner climbed in behind and shoved off with one of the oars.

The river was wide and lazy. Bolan manuevered them into the current, then simply let them drift. The pilot rubbed his arm and grimaced.

Bolan pulled the headset out of his harness. "Hold on a minute," he said, putting the thing on. "I've got to make a quick call."

CHAPTER FOUR

Cleveland, Ohio

"I ain't never stayed at a nice hotel before," Lureen Masterson said from beside the Vulture in the Cadillac's back seat. "Sarge always said you can sleep jest as good on a ten-dollar-a-night mattress as you can on a hunnert-dollar-a-night."

"Well, Sarge just seems full of homespun wisdom," the man answered, wondering how such horribly mangled speech could come out of the mouth of such a beautiful young woman. "Noble savage that he is."

"Huh?"

The Vulture smiled and patted her on the blue-jeaned thigh. "A woman like you deserves the best of everything, my dear," he said low. "And you'll have the best. But you must remember to keep your mouth shut when we're around strangers. You do understand that?"

"Here's the hotel, boss," Mulroy said from behind

the wheel as he pulled into the circular driveway of the Framingham Hotel. Prominent on Superior Avenue in east Cleveland, the hotel was ringed by the cultural gardens, the historical society and the Cleveland Aquarium. There was even a decent view of Lake Erie a block north. A shame they'd have to leave in the morning. The Vulture made a mental note to revisit the area whenever he was in the neighborhood.

"You and Armon get us checked in," he replied. "After four days in custody, I could use a drink. We're going to retire to the bar. Meet us."

"Two rooms, boss?"

"Two rooms, Willy," the Vulture returned, the woman snuggling against him. Anyone's dog who'll hunt, he thought. She'd be amusing for a day or two.

They pulled up before the hotel, and Mulroy climbed out to wave at the doorman. "Howdy!" he called, then hurried into the large glass lobby to register while Armon popped the trunk to unload the luggage.

The fake beard that went along with the dyed hair was itchy, and the Vulture rubbed his hand against it. He'd also traded his eye patch for a pair of wraparound sunglasses.

He turned and kissed the young woman on the temple. "Would you like to go get a drink while they get the room set up?"

"Sure," she said. "I never turn down anything free."

"I'm not surprised," the Vulture replied, opening his door and climbing out of the car. Lureen was already out her side before he'd had a chance to get it for her.

He'd been hearing endlessly about her life, about how she'd been forced to marry her cousin at age fourteen and about how he'd traded her to Sarge Masterson for three machine guns at age seventeen, how Sarge had kept her a virtual prisoner ever since. The woman had enough wind to float a hot-air balloon.

Arm in arm they walked into the fancy lobby, the Vulture turning immediately toward the bar, the Orchid Room. "What should I call you?" she asked. "Nobody ever uses your name."

He smiled, reaching into the new billfold in his pocket. He got it and removed the driver's license, a picture ID of him, patch and all, smiling. It identified him as Jerry Bendorff. "Call me Jerry," he said, and they got into the bar, a dark, moody place, too small, with absolutely no orchids anywhere.

He picked the farthest table from the door, one that backed into a corner, and called to the bartender as they walked there. "Scotch straight up," he ordered, then looked at Lureen.

"Rum and Coke," she said loudly. "In a glass!"

The few patrons in the place laughed as they took their seats. "But Jerry's not your real name," she whispered, leaning across the table and kissing him quickly on the lips. "You know, the name you usually go by."

"I've got a lot of names," he said. "In my line of work, it's best that no one know anything real about you."

"Are you saying you don't have a name…no friends that call you by your real name?"

"Well…I do have a name that I bought about ten years ago, but I can't tell you that."

"Why?"

"Trust me. You don't want to be burdened by knowledge about me. Just enjoy the ride…it's free."

The bartender showed up with the drinks just as Mulroy and Armon walked in. He waved them over, then immediately ordered another Scotch from the man before he left.

The men sat. "You boys want a drink?" Lureen asked.

"They don't drink on my paycheck," the Vulture said. "We're in a war zone." He picked up his shot of Scotch and tossed it down in one drink, slamming the glass to the table, then holding it in the air.

"Hurry," he said. "Make it a double."

"I'm worried," Mulroy said. "We haven't heard from Franz yet. He was supposed to get in touch with us once they reached the farm."

"Maybe they haven't reached the farm," the Vulture said, reaching into his pocket to bring out the tiny spring knife that had been with his gear. Small, palm sized. But deadly.

"I don't know, but the minute I saw that—"

The man clammed up as the bartender returned and put a double shot of Scotch on the table. "Get another," the Vulture said.

The bartender nodded and walked off.

"That bastard from Paraguay," Mulroy continued, "I knew something was real smelly about this whole business."

"Would you look at that!" a man sitting at the bar exclaimed.

The Vulture's eyes drifted to the television over the bar. Monstrous explosions rocked the twilight sky, filling the screen with orange, streaming fire. The words "Bainbridge, Pa," were written on the screen.

"Gawd!" Lureen yelled, then immediately lowered her voice and looked abashed.

She looked him hard in the eyes. "It's the freakin' farm."

"So it is," the Vulture said, jamming the blade hard into the tabletop to quiver in the low lighting.

"I'm telling you," Mulroy said, "all this is tied up with that guy from Paraguay."

"Belasko," the Vulture whispered, knowing that, like him, the big man used many names.

The cellular phone on Mulroy's hip bleated, and he quickly answered it. "Yeah, go ahead. Uh-huh. All of them? Jeez. Hold on." He looked at the Vulture. "Delta Team is down, blown to pieces."

"That means that damned Sarge is blowed up, too," Lureen said. "Good fer him."

The Vulture held out his hand. "Give," he said, and Mulroy handed over the phone. He spoke without preamble. "Continue west, we'll find another source."

He disconnected and handed the phone back to Mulroy. "Could it be that our paths finally cross again?" he asked, downing the double Scotch and holding the glass up again. "More!"

The bartender brought the bottle, leaving it on the table and hurrying away.

Pain shot through the Vulture's eye socket, the pathetic remnants of his right eye. Air got in around the edge of his sunglasses, stinging still after all these years.

He fixed his good eye on the still-quivering blade before him. Reaching, he grabbed it and jerked it out of the maple tabletop and held it before his face, reliving the moment. He'd been tracking the man he knew as Belasko for fifteen years. The man was a professional, he knew that much, and that he seemed to be elusive and yet everywhere. He knew Belasko to be a human machine steeped in continual warfare, impossible to pin down, and wherever he appeared, death followed. The Vulture felt connected to him.

"How many people do we have left?" he asked, still staring at the blade.

"Five teams, four per team, including us," Armon said.

"More than enough. We will make our final arrangements in Kansas City tomorrow night."

"What about the big guy?" Mulroy asked.

"We'll do our job, wait until he finds us, then kill him."

He brought the blade close to his good eye, remembering. Someone had held his head down while Mulroy had strained to jerk the blade out. It had missed his brain by a sixteenth of an inch as it plunged through his skull to stick out above his right ear.

So much pain. He'd kept the blade razor sharp, used it often to keep it in shape. But it wanted to go home, and the Vulture was a good enough Samaritan to return it to its rightful owner.

Virtue was its own reward.

MACK BOLAN SAT in the parking lot of a Harrisburg, Pennsylvania, McDonald's, trying to digest a Big Mac while reading a map in the yellow light of the golden arches. He had Kurtzman on the headset.

"Take this down," he said. "I talked to the guy at Bob's Texaco, and he said a whole parade of them came through this morning filling up. He estimated twenty-five to thirty. Get that to Hal—quicker this way."

Bolan pulled the plastic top off the Coke on the dash and took a sip. "That Bainbridge farm left a rather big mess that's not so easy to hide. He might not be happy about that. But after what happened in New York, there's not much choice."

"Yeah...it's all over the TV. They found seven bodies."

"That's my count, too. And a helicopter," Bolan added.

"Sure. What else?"

"Tell him they're headed west and there are women among them. It means some can travel as husband and wife to throw off suspicion. You got anything?"

"A direct hit," Bear said. "In a place called Front Royal, Virginia. It's on the border with West Virginia."

"Hold on," Bolan said, finding his place on the map. He saw it, right at the mouth of the Blue Ridge Parkway. "What happened?"

"The cops got a make on all the cars stolen at the scene in New York, all taken within a block of abandonment. I'll give you the list in a minute."

"Never mind," Bolan said. "They'll have changed cars by the morning."

"Anyway, a Front Royal cop called in a speeder, and it was one of the target cars, except with stolen plates. They skirmished. The sheriff is dead, the deputy in the regional hospital in Front Royal, shot up. Everybody and their brother is on their way down there."

"How old is this news?"

"A couple hours."

"Too bad. That place is reeking with testosterone by now. Anything else?"

"No. Not a peep, although I've got a question for you."

"Yes?"

"Front Royal is *south* of Bainbridge, not west."

"I've noticed. I think I'm going to go in and sniff after the government dogs anyhow. It's a pretty quick shot for me down Interstate 81 from Harrisburg right to Front Royal. Once I get there, I'll probably just follow the news vans to the hospital. How many cars did they steal?"

"Seven," Bear answered. "But two were later found abandoned in the city, and you're not going to believe this—"

"They took a diaper-service van."

"How'd you know?"

"They'll find the pieces of it on Sarge's farm. Call Hal. Let me know if anything happens."

"Watch your back, buddy."

"Yeah," Bolan said, disconnecting.

He sat back, trying to force another bite of the hamburger, then rewrapped it and put it back in the bag. Five cars left. Five times four was twenty, probably all taking different routes, which would explain why the target car was in Front Royal—traveling south to separate from the others before turning west. He'd only be able to follow one trail at a time. Front Royal seemed the place to begin.

He worked the rental Cougar onto 81 and headed south, finishing the Coke, saving the ice. The back end was heavy with the ordnance bag. He'd gotten the pilot squared away, at least until hell broke loose when they traced the chopper back to him.

He was concerned about lack of sleep. The adrenaline was flowing heavily right now and he'd be okay for a day or two, but at some point he'd have to sleep to stay in fighting shape. His adversaries were probably in bed by now, tucked away for the night in motels with "clean" cars parked in front, cars they had taken not from busy streets, but from isolated farmhouses. He knew what they'd done to get those cars, too.

The anger juiced him, his mind reliving the moment as his arm arced in slow motion toward the tall man's throat, the merest glancing blow sending it upward and outward enough to save the man's grotesque life.

When he pulled into Front Royal at three in the morning, his jaw ached from keeping his teeth tightly clenched for hours. The Executioner stoked a large fire.

He found the hospital easily enough, a simple two-story building on the west end of town. There were a number of news vans parked outside, the reporters endlessly recycling the few witnesses to the shooting, asking the same questions over and over.

Bolan drove near the back of the parking lot, parking under a burned-out pole light. He rummaged through his harness until he found the badge. It was an ID card with a photo in the corner that identified him as Cliff Jones, of the Central Intelligence Agency.

Avoiding the front entry seemed to be the thing. He slipped into the ER entry, making his way quickly to the front of the building. He got through a metal-detector station with the use of his ID.

The place was swarming with cops and government people. The Vulture's entry into the U.S. and subsequent escape involved so many government and New York State agencies that they'd be fighting one another just to use the bathrooms.

He followed the main flow of investigators up to the second floor, finding a large knot of them arguing over jurisdiction in a doctor's lounge just off the nurse's station. Everybody wanted a crack at interrogating the wounded officer. Two beefy plainclothesmen, probably FBI, guarded a door farther down the hall. His destination.

An older nurse with gray-streaked hair and a puckered mouth worked in the nurse's station. Bolan approached her, speaking quietly in a hallway filled with people.

"Just checking on the officer's condition," he said with a smile at the nurse.

"I guess she's lucky," the nurse said. "One shot grazed her side, cracking three ribs and giving her a good gash. Another went clear through her left hand, right on the palm. She'll be out of here in the morning."

"Good," Bolan said, and meant it.

"Now, if we could just bring her man back."

"Rough," Bolan said. He'd heard the whole story of Julie and Ted Powell on the radio while driving to Front Royal. And he'd heard about the two children left behind, adding this to the ever growing list of payback items for when he found the Vulture. And he would find him.

He thanked the nurse and moved easily down the hallway. He reached the doorway, nodded at the two agents and tried to move past them through the door.

"Where do you think you're going?" a tall man with a gray mane asked. His ID read Darryl Johnson.

"I'm going in to ask the officer a few questions. Let me pass."

They both laughed. The other guy's name was Hobbs. He laid a menacing hand on Bolan's arm as he read his ID. "You clowns have no jurisdiction here," he said. "This is a domestic matter now, so butt out. What the hell do you think everybody's arguing about down the hall?"

"The Vulture's terrain is global," Bolan said. "I

am personally representing the President and I insist on going in that room."

"The President," Hobbs laughed. "We've had that line used three times on us tonight and we've only been here for an hour."

Bolan withdrew a card from his pocket. "There's a Department of Justice number to call. Do it, or you'll regret it later on."

Their eyes narrowed, but after glancing at each other they shrugged and watched as Bolan brought the headset out of its harness. After he punched in the number, he spoke briefly and handed the headset over. Then he watched as Johnson had a quick exchange that left him very subdued.

"Right," Johnson said, and Hobbs hurried to open the door. "Look, if I can do anything to help..."

"I'll let you know," Bolan said, and slipped quietly into the darkened room. He could hear the woman crying in bed and walked slowly to her.

Her torn and bloody uniform was wrapped in a clear plastic bundle on the night table, with her cap lying atop her folded-up belt and holster outside the bag. She turned toward him as he approached, her face wet with tears.

"I'm Special Agent Jones," he said, holding up the badge. "I'm sorry about your husband. He must have been a good man."

"What would you know about it?" she asked.

"Some," he answered.

Her left hand was bandaged heavily, and she moved gingerly under the hospital gown from the rib injury. She had small glass cuts in a dozen places, all of them cleaned and dressed. She wasn't an especially good-looking woman, but forthrightness shone out of her like a beacon.

"I thought they weren't going to debrief me until the morning," she said.

"I just want to ask a couple of questions," he said.

"How about some answers for me. I'd like some answers, too."

"This car," he said, "the white Mustang. It was heading into the mountains when you last saw it?"

"I've already told them this."

"You didn't tell me."

"The mountains, yes. What else?"

"There were four of them?"

"Yeah, four."

"All men?"

"No...I think there were either one or two women in the car."

"Describe their look."

"European...one Asian...maybe one was a Spaniard. I traveled a lot with the service and am pretty good with character types. Not an American in the bunch."

Bolan walked away from the bed. This trail was as good as any. He'd have a go at it.

"Let me ask you a question," he said, his back to

her. "The highway-patrol dragnet failed to catch these guys. Why?"

"You're asking me?"

"Yeah...why do you think the dragnet didn't scoop them in?"

"Mr. Jones," she said, and he turned around to find himself staring down the long barrel of a .38 revolver. She cocked it, her eyes burning with the fires of righteous vengeance.

"Who are you?" she asked.

CHAPTER FIVE

Bolan stared down the barrel of the .38 and could tell, even from four feet away and in half light, that no bullets filled the chambers. Hospitals had a thing about loaded guns lying around. Deputy Powell had just made her second mistake of the day—or was it?

"Easy, Officer Powell," he said, playing along. "What are you doing?"

"Who are you?" she demanded again.

He moved closer, holding out his ID tag as he did so. "I'm Special Agent—"

"Nobody told me a thing about you, that you'd be coming to see me. I consider that unusual given the circumstances."

"Well, I'm not associated with the run-of-the-mill law-enforcement agencies. My affiliations are of a highly covert nature—in other words, I can't tell."

"What do you want from me?"

"As much information as I can get as quick as I can get it about the animals who killed your husband. I'm tracking them."

"Are you going to take them down?"

"Yes."

"Good," she said. "That's what I thought. We'll track 'em together."

"I don't think so."

She looked around the room. "The first thing you've got to do is help me get out of here. There's a ledge beneath the window, isn't there?"

Bolan looked. "Yep. There's a ledge. Why would I help you?"

"Because I'll kill you if you don't."

Bolan sighed. "Look, Deputy Powell—"

"Call me Julie," she said. "How about you?"

"Mike. I really don't think you'll kill me." He moved to sit on the bed. "Please. Just answer a few questions, I'll be out of your hair and I'll get the man who killed your husband. And you, you need to get some sleep, go home, bury your dead and take care of those children of yours. They're going to be needing you in the next few weeks and months."

"After," she said, moving painfully toward the closet to retrieve an overnight bag. "Right now I want you to go into that bathroom and wait for me to get dressed. We'll try going out the window."

"In your condition?" he asked.

"Yes, in my condition," she barked.

"No," he said. "I'm not going anywhere. We're wasting valuable time."

She thought for several seconds, shrugged, then

opened the suitcase, removing a casual change of clothes, jeans and T-shirt. Still keeping the empty gun trained on him, she began pulling off the flimsy hospital gown.

"All right," Bolan said, turning his back to her. "Now, is there anything you can add that the cops don't know yet."

"There's a lot," she said. "I want first crack at those bastards."

"Would you stop it?" he said, exasperated. "You're shot, hurt. You're holding up the progress of a massive manhunt that will catch these people."

"Why don't you get out of the way of the massive manhunt?"

He could hear clothes rustling, the sharp intake of breath as she tried to pull a shirt over cracked ribs.

"I'm smarter than they are," Bolan said.

"Me, too," she answered. "Let's go."

He moved to the sealed window with her. Bolan held back, just waiting. She finally looked at him.

"I've got some information," she said, "that might possibly put you right on their trail. If you want it, you'll help me out of here, because the only way I'm giving you anything is if you help me."

He made an instant decision—to go along with the ramblings of a woman driven by shock and grief. There was something about her face, the look he saw there.

"You can put the gun away," he said. "It's not loaded."

Her eyes widened as she popped the flange to empty chambers.

Bolan reached into his jacket, into the harness, and came out with a glass cutter and suction cup. Within two minutes he was out on the hospital ledge, helping Julie Powell through the window space. The night was still all over them, but Bolan knew it would be graying toward morning very soon.

"I'll lower you as best I can," he said, "then go out the same way I came in. You sure you want to do this?"

"With or without you," she said.

"Okay." He handed her his car keys. "I'm under the burned-out pole light in the back of the lot," he said, then frowned at her. "This is going to hurt more than anything has ever hurt before in your life."

"That's already happened tonight, Mike."

"It's going to hurt as I lower you, and it's going to feel like you're dying when you let go and fall the rest of the way to the ground."

She nodded and sat on the edge of the ledge, her feet dangling toward the ground. He took her by both hands, letting her slide off the ledge until his hands were her only support, her full weight jerking her arms, pulling her rib cage. He could hear a cry straining to get out of her throat.

"Let go," he whispered, and the woman complied

immediately, crying out then swallowing it as she hit the ground and fell back.

"Are you all right?" he whispered.

She sat up, face drained of color, and nodded, waving him away.

He gave her a thumbs-up and climbed back into the hospital room. This was either the smartest or dumbest thing he'd ever done. The woman could really have something or she could be hysterical with grief. People dealt with the death of loved ones in strange ways.

He had made an emotional choice and was now going to have to live with it. Taking a breath, he walked to the door and slipped out, and the FBI men still standing guard looked at him.

"Thanks," he said. "She's weak and has gone to sleep. How about letting her get some uninterrupted time to rest?"

"Yes, sir," Hobbs said, both of them at attention.

Bolan walked down the hallway, crisp but casual as if he belonged there and nobody would even dare question his presence. That approach usually worked best. As he passed by, the bureaucrats were still arguing in the doctor's lounge. It's what they did best.

He exited through the ER, the same way he'd come in, and got through the parking lot, expecting at any minute for someone to realize the star witness was gone.

He reached the car to find Julie Powell hunched

down in the front passenger seat, shaking in pain, her face still drained. He could see blood staining the side of her T-shirt. The escape must have torn the sutures loose.

The Cougar accommodated him easily as he slid behind the wheel and started it up.

"You weren't kidding about the pain," she said quietly, scooting up on the seat as he drove out of the parking lot and headed into the darkened streets around the hospital, staying far away from the main drag.

"We haven't bought much time, Julie," he said. "If you've got something, let's go with it. But be honest with yourself. Ask yourself if you really want to work with me and not through other, more...conventional, options. Ask yourself if you can handle this physically and emotionally. Ask yourself if your kids really want to have *both* of their parents dead on the same night."

"For a man of action, you sure talk a lot," she said.

He took that as his answer. "Lady, I'm all ears," he replied, shutting down the engine on a dark stretch of narrow asphalt road fronting residential frame houses that scaled the foothills. The Shenandoah Valley lay below them, wide and fertile, not a place for violent death.

"I shot one of them," she said simply.

He jerked in the seat. "The reports didn't—"

"That's because you're the first person I'm telling." She was big for a woman, five foot ten or so, and as he looked at her she seemed larger, filling her side of the car, her eyes glowing pinpoints of fire. The searing heat from her rage seemed to roll off her in waves.

"Did you kill him?" the Executioner asked.

"He took the Remington 12-gauge right in the face," she says. "Yeah...I killed him. And I've got three more to go."

"Two men, two women?"

"Yeah. Any ideas?"

"I've got one," he said. "I've made a couple of assumptions. First that these guys don't know their way around here very well."

"Correct."

"Secondly that they must have avoided all the major and probably the secondary roads in order to elude the highway patrol."

"I've thought that, too."

He held her eyes. "You know these hills pretty well?" he asked. "Well enough to know where everything goes?"

She nodded. "I'm listening."

"We reconstruct the event, only thinking of it from the enemies' point of view. Can you drive?"

"This car?"

"No. I want you in your car. I'll follow."

"Why not go together?"

"I work alone, Julie. That's how I can concentrate

on the task at hand without worrying about the safety of others. If we get a lead here, you're on your own afterward."

"I understand," she said stoically. "The car's at my house."

"There'll be protection at your house," he said. "In case they come back to finish you. They won't, by the way. Do you have access to another vehicle?"

She smiled grimly. "The impound yard," she said, turning to look out the windshield. "Turn north at the next intersection. It's about five minutes away."

"Good," he said, starting up the Cougar and getting back on the road. "What I want you to do is put yourself in that white Mustang. You're traveling south along the Blue Ridge Parkway. You've just killed a cop and know that the HP is undoubtedly on their way. Your car's shot up and you've got a dead man lying with his head in your lap. How do you elude and, more importantly, where do you dump the body once you've eluded?"

He made the turn north and stepped on the gas, realizing that all the Front Royal cops were either dead or in the car with him. "What good will having the body do us?" she asked.

"It'll get me to the next car," he replied.

Powell stared at him but didn't say anything. "Dearborne's Crossing is the road I'd take down from the mountains if I were looking for a getaway. It's not the best way out, but it sure is the best-*looking* way out."

"We'll start there," he answered.

"Who are these people?" she asked. "Nobody's saying very much except that they killed a bunch of folks in New York. Some kind of militia or something?"

"Mercenaries," he replied. "They're working under a terrorist known only as the Vulture. They're mostly overseas people, soldiers of fortune willing to do anything for money."

"Who is this Vulture? What is he doing here? What does he want?"

"We don't know his real name or existence," Bolan patiently answered. "Got our first picture—ever—of him just two days ago. Mug shots."

"How do you fit in to all this?" she asked.

He turned and stared quickly at her. "There's a junkyard up ahead," he said.

"That's it. Kill your lights."

He did as he was told. The car rolled up through a gravel drive to stop before eight-foot chain-link gates with a locked chain holding the gates together. The sign above the gates read Pop's Salvage.

They moved up in the dark to the fence, and Powell put a finger to her lips for silence. The shadowy hulks of dead cars filled the Executioner's vision. A small mobile home, lights out, was parked fifty feet into the labyrinth. It was one of those places where only the owner knew where anything was.

Powell pointed to the mobile home. "We'll let Pop sleep," she said, and reached for the lock, giving it a quick jerk. It came off in her hand.

"It broke about five years ago," she said as she quietly slid the looping chain through the fence and dropped it. She raised the latch and pushed open one of the gates. At that second, two growling rottweilers charged through the yard toward them, baring their teeth.

Bolan's hand instinctively went to the Beretta until Powell started in with the talk. "Hello, big Bruno," she said in a gentle, confident voice as she painfully dropped to one knee. "How's the big guy? And how's my Panzie?"

The dogs became immediately docile, and the deputy hugged them as she kept talking in the same soft, soothing tones. Then she stood. "I'll be right back," she whispered, walking into the yard, the dogs trailing happily behind her.

Within a minute Bolan heard an engine start up in the distance, rumbling, powerful. A car moved slowly through the lot without lights, picking its way to the yard. It was a souped-up Camaro.

When she got through the gate, he closed it, affixing the chain and the broken lock, the dogs padding happily through the yard, wagging their stubby tails.

"Courtesy of some drug pushers," she said, patting the car on the side. "Let's go."

He moved to the still-running Cougar and climbed in. Without another word she sped off—fast. Bolan shook his head and followed.

She sped back to Highway 11, taking him down to the intersection with Skyline Drive. The area was still under investigation. Her patrol car, the hood smashed in, the door gone, was cordoned off with yellow tape as investigators worked under floodlights. One lane of the parkway was still open, and a trooper directed traffic around the investigation.

The moment she passed the place, she kicked it into gear again, speeding off, and Bolan tried his best to keep up on the winding uphill grade. Almost immediately he started seeing signs for a cutoff to Highway 211, the intersection of the Luray Caverns and the place the Virginia HP would set up roadblocks. The real cutoff would have to be before that point.

She bypassed several roads leading down off the mountain before heading down a dirt road that seemed at first to just be a scenic turnout with picnic tables. But the road continued beyond the tables, winding slowly back down Mount Marshall and heading west.

It was perfect, or seemed perfect anyway. The other roads had been too big, too exposed. Dearborne's Crossing was the kind of road Bolan would look for if he were trying to beat a dragnet.

Once down the mountain, they were suddenly into farm country. She bypassed two quarter-mile sections, then skidded to a stop at the third. He pulled up beside her.

"I think by this point, they'd realize they'd made it down," she said. "Once they'd passed two intersections in the middle of nowhere, they'd realize there were a lot more. I'd go down this road, either direction. But we'll find a body in the bar ditch."

"You go north," he said. "If either of us find something, we'll blast the horn to let the other know."

"Got you," she said, and drove off to the north.

Bolan drove slowly, his lights on high beam, looking for anything. The road was one-lane blacktop, etched heavily with a borrow ditch—more commonly called a bar ditch—on either side that was overgrown with tall weeds.

He was glad to be away from Julie Powell. If he could find the body first, he'd take off and leave her to her other duties. He couldn't help but believe that, once she thought it over, she'd realize she needed to be with her kids because of the blow the family had taken.

The sky was just beginning to lighten when he saw the flattened grass from the driver's-side window and some tire tracks leading up to the place. He stopped the car, looking around as he climbed out.

He moved to the ditch, walking the tire treads to the flattened grass, then stepping down several feet into the weed-choked gully. He walked slowly along the ditch until he bumped into something on the ground. He bent, clearing weeds, to see a man's shoe.

He leaned over and felt a leg. He pulled the legs up the incline of the ditch until the head came into view. The face was gone, blown apart by a shotgun.

Letting go of the body, Bolan climbed back out of the ditch and scanned the ever-brightening horizon. Two miles away he saw the small dot of a farmhouse atop a high hill. There was nothing else around for miles.

If he were the mercs, once the body was disposed of, he'd have to look immediately for a new car.

The distant farmhouse drew him like a lighthouse.

CHAPTER SIX

Chester Gap, Virginia
July 18

Bolan sped down the country road, then turned up the long gravel driveway. The name on the mailbox read Wortham. The house was set perhaps a thousand yards from the mailbox, up a long hill. Rolling farmland surrounded the fenced-in yard of the house, but the house seemed separate, removed. It told him whoever lived in the house was probably older, retired. People who'd spent their life working the land and then sold it off to spend their final years watching others toil as they had toiled.

The gate defining the house property was hanging open; the house, fifty feet distant, was a typical white frame farm dwelling. He drove in slowly. An old, rusted combine collecting bugs and tall weeds sat beneath an oak tree.

He saw no car parked near the house. A bad sign. Lights burned within, and the sound of a television blared even out in the yard. He parked near the concrete porch, unconcerned about finding trouble here. The Vulture's people would have put as much distance between this place and themselves as quickly as they could. If this was the place.

He pulled on a pair of tight black leather driving gloves and climbed out of the car.

He moved up the stairs to the wooden screen door. Behind it the inner door was open, a morning farm-report program blaring out of the unseen television. All he could see through the open door was a small foyer.

He knocked, lightly at first, then with increasing tenacity. He heard a dog bark mournfully, then whine, and the animal limped up to the door, dragging its left hind leg. It was bleeding.

It was an old bloodhound, its ears drooping, its tail between its legs.

"What is it, boy?" he said gently, and pushed open the door, the dog baying, low and sonorous, then turning to hurry back into the house.

Bolan followed.

He moved through the foyer and into the living room. Two old people, a man and a woman in country work clothes, sat on a worn couch. They'd been shot dozens of times, their bodies riddled, blood everywhere. They'd never known what hit them. TV trays full of cold dinner sat before them. The dog, crying softly, was up on the sofa, curled up between them.

The TV was so loud Bolan could barely think. One of them must have been hard of hearing.

Pulling the gloves up tight, he shut the set off. Anger welled within him, spilling over, at the pointless and cruel end before him.

Time was the enemy right now. He'd tracked them to this point and needed to keep going. If he was right and they'd holed up for the night, it meant they might not be that far away right now. But with daylight just beginning to suffuse the sky, they'd be on the move again and probably be looking for another car.

He went through the kitchen quickly, then the dining room. In the corner of the dining room sat a small desk with a beat-up old typewriter and a stack of mail.

Older people tended to be organized when it came to their personal record keeping. He hoped that was operational in this case as he rifled the piles of paper, looking for car-registration records.

He found them in a cubbyhole on the desktop, next to the Medicare paperwork and life-insurance forms. He grabbed up the license-tag renewal form for a 1982 brown Buick Skylark and committed the tag number to memory, though their M.O. showed the Vulture's people stealing a separate tag for every car they'd stolen.

The screen door creaked. Not much, but enough to let him know someone had entered the house. The living and dining rooms were separated by a rounded alcove. He pulled the Beretta from his webbing and bent over it, muffling the sound of its priming with his body, then put his back to the wall just on the other side of the alcove.

Floorboards creaked just a touch, and his senses tingled. He held the gun up beside his face, alert for any sound. A footfall. Closer.

When he estimated the interloper to be on the other side of the alcove wall, he swung out the Beretta in front of him just as Julie Powell approached from the other direction with her .38 at the ready.

They stood, a gun pointing to each fiercely tense face. Then they eased back their weapons.

"What have you done here?" she demanded, noticing the ransacked desk and the paper crumpled in his free hand. "What kind of maniac—"

He held out the tag application. "They're in this car," he said. "And we're wasting time."

Her face relaxed with the realization the murder wasn't Bolan's doing. She lowered the gun, holstering it. "Sorry," she said.

He looked toward the living room. "Did you know them?"

She nodded. "Tom and Rose Wortham. They were good people, real good people."

Bolan got into his harness, bringing out the headset. "The dog..."

"General Lee," she said. "That's his name. He was born on this farm and lived his whole life around those two old people. He won't get over this. Looks like he's hurt pretty bad, too."

"Want me to do it?" Bolan offered.

"No," she replied. "It needs to come from me."

"You take care of things, then," Bolan said, and walked out of the dining room and through the living room with its terrible still life on the couch. His anger felt like a physical presence or a shadow that walked him to the door.

As he made his way to the car, he punched up Stony Man, getting Kurtzman on the horn. "I'm on them," Bolan told him. "They've changed cars again. No one knows this but us."

"Give me the data," Bear said, and Bolan provided the details of the Worthams' car.

"I can't sit on this," Bear said. "It needs to go back in the net."

"Give it an hour first," Bolan said. "Now listen. Here's what I want us to do with it. I'm assuming you have no new information."

"Nothing here. They've got some identification coming in from Interpol on a few of the dead mercs in Manhattan. So far, all of these people dropped out of society several years ago and haven't been seen since."

"Figures."

"Now what?"

"I agree with you that they went to ground last night. That tells me they probably stopped as soon as they thought it was safe, somewhere within, say, one hundred miles."

"That's a big radius, Striker."

"Not if you just looked west and in another state, which is what I want you to do." He studied his map, opening it on the hood of the car, the sky just light enough to read by. "Got a map?"

"I'm looking at it now. Where are you?"

"The area is called Chester Gap. Miles and miles of farmland. Look west. Do you see a city called, Elkins, West Virginia?"

"Got it."

"Try there first. Call every hotel and motel in that city and talk about the car, not the tag number."

"Why Elkins?"

"It's west," Bolan replied, "and can be reached by secondary roads. It's eighty miles away, just about the right distance. It's big enough to have hotels, but small enough to not attract obvious attention. I'm on my way. Call me when you've got something."

"Wait…there's something coming in. Okay. Okay. Mack?"

"Yeah?"

"There's been a shooting in North Carolina, in Charlotte. Minor traffic mishap…man and woman in car get out with guns…three dead in the other car. They sped away. A witness said they were speaking in a foreign language. That's south, Mack. South."

"Ignore it," Bolan said. "Call Elkins and get back to me. Out."

As he folded up the headset and put it away, the sound of a gunshot came from inside the house, and Julie Powell exited the house within seconds, smoking gun still in her hand. She holstered it and approached him.

"Where's their car?"

Bolan scanned the yard, pointing to a small barn behind the house. "Let's check it."

They jogged to the tumbledown spare-lumber barn, the barest hint of red paint just visible when they got close. The hasp was shot off, and the lock was lying intact on the ground, the door ajar.

She started to pull open the door and clutched at her ribs with a grimace. Bolan grabbed the door. The Mustang sat within, pockmarked by bullets all over it. They walked to the passenger side, where the door was filled with pellet holes, windows smashed, blood splattered everywhere.

"I got him good," she said.

"Did you see him in the ditch?" Bolan asked, opening the door to peer within, looking for anything that would help. But the car was stripped clean of everything save a monstrous bloodstain. Professionals.

"Yeah," she said.

Bolan straightened and handed her the car information. "We split off here," he said. "Thanks for your help. I ask you to give me an hour or so before handing this over to the Feds."

"Where are you going now?" she asked, following him out of the ramshackle barn.

"I'm going after the people who killed your husband," he said. "That's all you need to know." He turned and pointed to her bloodsoaked side. "Go home. Get well. Goodbye."

He grabbed the map and climbed into the Cougar, keying it to roaring life. He slipped into reverse and turned around. In the rearview he could see her watch him drive away, her arms folded. She wore her gun high on her hip. Her eyes were staring him down from behind as he jerked it into first, hit the gas and sped away, her image disappearing in clouds of dust.

For the first time in the game, he was going to make a little time, close in just a bit on his quarry. He made it out of the farm roads, then took state roads west, moving through the Shenandoah Valley and into West Virginia in less than an hour.

About the time he crossed the state line, his headset beeped and Bolan retrieved it. "Yeah?"

"Mack, it's Kurtzman," came the man's excited voice. "We got a positive on that car."

"Where?"

"Elkins, West Virginia. A place called the Bickle Knob Inn. Two women and a man, European accents. Paid in cash. Checked in at ten-thirty last night."

"Got 'em," Bolan said, his foot instinctively pushing down harder on the gas pedal.

SPECIAL AGENT WILLIAM "Frosty" Peaks of the Drug Enforcement Administration sat in one of forty-seven coffee shops in Los Angeles International Airport, listening to his co-worker bitch while stirring his fourth spoonful of sugar into his fifth cup of coffee.

His eyes, however, were locked on to an interesting tableau just across the busy aisle, near a bank of phones.

"So, I said to him, 'Man, you've either been snortin' coke or your mustache has the worst case of dandruff I've ever seen!'" The man laughed at his own line. "Did you get it? Dandruff...cocaine..."

"Cute, Gordon," Peaks said. "Now I've got one for you. What's our friend Agent Madison doing over there by those phones?"

Gordon Dinsmore turned to casually look at the phones. Madison, in a glen plaid suit, was holding a receiver but obviously not talking to anyone. He kept eyeing a Middle Eastern-looking man on one of the other phones. The man had a large briefcase in his hand.

"Looks like he's either trying out to be the dumb-ass poster boy this year or is sniffing up that dude on the other phone."

"If they got a problem with the guy, why didn't

they nab him when he came through customs? That was Madison's job the last time I looked."

"Can't help but wonder what's in that briefcase," Dinsmore said.

"Strikes me," Frosty said, "that setting up surveillance and organizing busts is our job, not his." He pulled his cell phone off his belt.

"You really want to screw with this?" Dinsmore asked.

"Sure...why not? Who's mobile?"

"Lopez."

Peaks punched up the man's extension in the mobile unit cruising the parking lots outside. He watched Madison's surveillance. The man had all the finesse of a monster truck as he all but loomed over the foreigner with the briefcase.

Lopez picked up the page. "Listen," Peaks said. "Get your fanny down to baggage claim and look for us. And I mean look. When you see us, get over there in a hurry. We'll be tailing somebody."

"They're on the move," Dinsmore said, gulping his coffee and standing as Madison trailed after the man with the briefcase, dressed in a black suit.

Peaks clipped the phone back on his belt and threw two dollars on the table. In their casual clothes they merged with the crowd and trailed behind Dexter Madison—in their joint view the stupidest person ever to man a customs counter. He was so bad, he'd been promoted through the system to headman within five years.

The crowd flowed through the gates and drained into the escalators that fed baggage claim below. In the claims area, the Middle Eastern man waited patiently for the bags to arrive, neither pacing nor checking ground-transport boards.

A modest-sized suitcase eventually found its way to his hands, and he carried it, along with the briefcase, directly outside.

Peaks and Dinsmore hustled out at the same time, except through doors a half block down. Madison, of course, followed the man out the same door.

"Where's Lopez?" Peaks said as the quarry moved to the curb and into the passenger seat of a yellow sports car. Top down, the car was driven by a woman in sunglasses with a red-polka-dotted scarf tied around her blond hair. These two were a total study in incongruity. They didn't match.

"Here he comes," Dinsmore said. Both he and Peaks hurried to the nearly new Range Rover they'd taken from a drug suspect, just as Madison climbed into a Ford and the yellow car sped off.

"Get 'em," Peaks told Lopez from beside him in the front seat, an arm wrapped around the roll bar. "The yellow sports car."

"What'd they do?" Lopez asked, moving them into the traffic.

Peaks shrugged. "Won't know that until we get

them," he said, and pulled sunglasses out of his shirt pocket.

He put them on and laid his head back on the seat. "Meantime, I'm going to enjoy some California sunshine."

IT WAS just before 9:00 a.m. when Mack Bolan pulled his rental car into the parking lot of the Bickle Knob Inn, which had gotten its name because it sat by a small mountain called Bickle Knob. Elkins was another tourist trap, surrounded by beautiful countryside, a national forest *and* the Spruce Knob—Senecal Lakes National Recreation Area. A great place to hide. Strangers among a city of strangers.

People were up and around, campers, boaters, excited to be on vacation. But the killers Bolan was looking for were hard at work. He cruised the busy parking lot until he spotted the old Skylark, then he parked in a slot nearby that afforded him a good view of it and waited. There was no way he was going to approach or initiate a firefight amid the crowds that were checking out of the motel and loading cars and trailers.

Besides, it was the Vulture he wanted. Wherever his killers were going was where he would be. They would nest somewhere, and the Executioner would get them all at one time.

He sat for fifteen minutes, then feared he'd been too late, that they'd already taken another car and fled. Frowning, he climbed halfway out of the car, then saw them.

Two women and a man. Twenties. Dark haired. Lean and hard like knotted rope. Their clothes had a European flair. They moved with a mean aloofness, staring arrogantly at the families wandering happily past them. Bolan slid down a bit in the seat and watched them from twenty feet away, on the other side of the parking lot.

They moved to the Buick, and Bolan knew immediately they weren't going to drive away in it. They stood, chatting aimlessly as their eyes relentlessly scanned the surrounding area, trying to get a feel for what was happening around them. After ten minutes of this, one of the women, dressed all in black, pulled a screwdriver from under her loose, untucked blouse and knelt before the car next to theirs, going to work on the plate. The other two stood blocking her, making it tough to notice. Then the plate went under her blouse. At that point they stood and chatted some more, trying to pick a car.

Two men were walking through the parking lot, and Bolan strained to hear their conversation. They were deciding whose car to take out to Senecal Lake. When it was worked out, one of the men got his fishing gear out of an innocuous Pontiac and drove off with the other man in his Jeep.

The killers had their car, one that wouldn't be reported stolen for hours.

They pulled their bags from the Buick, used a slide to unlock the Pontiac, then loaded up and left. They were in, out and gone in forty-three seconds, and not a person in that area had any idea of what had just happened.

Except one.

Mack Bolan pulled out seconds behind them and established a loose tail. He'd decided to ride this train all the way out to the end of the line.

The mercs pulled onto State Highway 33 and headed west.

The Executioner's adrenaline rush was still strong enough to keep him awake and keyed up. But the next time they slept, he'd have to sleep, too.

He had a big job ahead of him.

CHAPTER SEVEN

Kansas City, Missouri

The Vulture had finished his meal and was sitting at the hotel dining-room table with Lureen beside him.

He smiled when the cocktail waitress set the eighteen-carat-gold puzzle ring on the table in front of him—eight bands intricately twisted together to form one ring. The sign.

Casually he scanned the room quickly and eliminated tables as he went, then returned to the logical choice—three slightly dark men in business suits who leaned toward one another to speak and who never seemed to smile at all. They drank coffee.

"Where're we goin', honey?" Lureen asked as they hurried across the room.

"To return a man's ring that got misplaced," he replied, nodding approval of the tight white dress he'd bought her. Lureen was definitely talented in some areas. It was a shame she was a compulsive talker.

He stood before the table, where the men were still

huddled close together. Two were older, white haired, going to paunch. The other was very young, maybe late teens, early twenties. The Vulture couldn't ascertain his purpose at the table.

"I believe someone lost this," he said, placing the ring in the center of the table. One of the older men reached out and slowly drew the ring to him. He had a small white mustache and wore thick, black-frame glasses.

"I am most grateful for its return, sir," he said. "Would you please join us? May we offer you a drink, some coffee perhaps?"

The Vulture pulled up a fifth chair for Lureen, and everyone shifted around to accommodate the extra chair. "I appreciate your hospitality," he answered, then leaned over to call to the waitress. "A couple of Scotches, please."

The other older man, who was balding, said, "We were led to believe, sir, that we would be meeting only with you. No one said anything about—"

"Ah, my associate," the Vulture interrupted. "She is my most trusted ally and greatest compatriot. Trust me when I say that by speaking before both of us, it is as if you are speaking only before me."

"That is good enough for me," the man with the glasses said.

"Do you have the money?" the Vulture asked, sitting back to get a twilight view of the Quay River just outside the hotel.

"It arrived in the country this morning," Baldy said.

"Where is it?"

"We are not prepared to tell you that yet," Glasses said. "There are—"

"I've got people in the field getting shot at," the Vulture growled, pushing his sunglasses up hard against the bridge of his nose. "How long do you think this operation can hold together while you play your little games with money?" He banged on the table. "I've already done enough for you. By God, you're going to do something for me."

"Please, sir," Glasses said, looking around the room. "We just need to speak of several things."

"What things?"

"We were...promised a large operation," Baldy said. "While devastating, the attack in New York is hardly—"

"Gentlemen!" The Vulture smiled wide. "That was just the warm-up act, the preview of coming attractions. That was my free show to you, to let you know I mean business."

"You're joking?" Glasses said. "Then that wasn't...?"

"My plans are as large as your imagination," the Vulture told them. "You said you wanted terror. All right. First I frighten them with a deadly show of power, then I elude their increasingly desperate attempts at catching me, then I hit them with the big event, something so large it will break the will of this country and make all the citizenry distrust their government. Is that good enough for you?''

"Yes, my friend," Glasses said, his tone low, sonorous. "You will be a hero in Iraq."

"I don't want to be a hero. I want my twenty million American dollars…in advance."

"Of course," Baldy said. "To that end, we have acquired a safehouse in California where the cash is being guarded. If you wish us to bring it to you—"

"No," the Vulture said, smiling. "Just give me the address and let your contact know I'm coming and will be there tomorrow night. California is perfect. More than perfect."

"I have one more request," Glasses said as the Scotch finally showed up.

Lureen turned her nose up at it, but the Vulture downed his in one shot. He looked at Glasses. "You were saying?"

"I was about to say that our…sources of funding are unwilling to trust such a vast sum to you in advance. Knowing your feelings about waiting, we worked out a compromise."

"What compromise?" the Vulture said, feeling the anger rise up his neck to flush his cheeks.

"My nephew—" he nodded to the young man "—is the son of our benefactor. If he accompanies you on this mission, we are willing to pay the cash in advance. It is a small thing."

"Civilians just get in the way," the Vulture said. "Do you want to get him killed?"

"Our family is no stranger to death," Glasses said. "That is why we wish to repay the Americans in kind for their illegal war on our people."

"So be it," the Vulture said easily, reaching a hand across the table. "Welcome to the mission."

The young man shook it vigorously. "It will give me great pleasure to kill Americans," he said.

"Good for you," the Vulture said. "But you need a name. We'll call you Arthur."

"Arthur?"

"Indeed. We should all get some sleep now. It will be a long day tomorrow."

"One more thing," Glasses said.

"You seem to have a great many one-more-things," the Vulture said, his patience nearing an end.

"Politics is complicated," Baldy said.

"Politics is politics," the Vulture replied, nervous energy building within him like a constantly tightening mainspring. "People complicate it."

"It's the thin line we must walk," Glasses said. "Our government wants credit for this…event, but wishes, for obvious reasons, to retain its deniability also."

"You came to me, sir, because of my impeccable reputation in these matters. I have invented an extremist group that will claim responsibility on behalf of your country but make it seem as if the movement sprang up spontaneously on American soil.''

"Excellent," Baldy said happily. "What exactly are you going to do?"

The Vulture looked around, then pulled off his sunglasses to stare hard at Baldy with his one good eye. The man recoiled from the torn-up eye that even fifteen years of plastic surgery hadn't been able to make presentable. "Don't ever ask me anything like that again," he rasped gutturally.

Baldy nodded silently, then looked away.

The Vulture replaced his shades, then smiled around the table. "Are we quite finished?" he asked.

Glasses had taken a notebook out of his pocket and was busily writing on it. He tore off the sheet and handed it to the Vulture. "Here is the address of the safehouse," he said. "By this time tomorrow, you'll have your money."

The Vulture took the paper and stood, committing the address to memory before tearing it up. He finished the drink that Lureen had barely touched and walked out of the club, his new charge, "Arthur," on his heels.

He was, as always, proud of his sense of calm and bearing. But inside he seethed. How dare they presume to send a watchdog to supervise him, and an idiot boy on top of that. Well, he survived in his business by following one simple rule—give in to nobody. Ever.

Lureen was prattling in his ear as they walked back to the elevators to take the ride up to the seventh floor of the aging, charmless hotel, Arthur still behind him. He wondered if the boy was armed. Probably not. But just in case, he'd be first. The woman kept intruding, like a buzzing fly, into his thoughts.

When they exited onto the seventh floor he walked out onto the tattered beige carpet, an ugly stain from water damage discoloring it in a large circle. That was it, the final indignity. He would not stay here another hour. There had to be a better hotel in town.

They moved down the hall to 714, with Lureen huddled up close to him, her hand moving slowly up and down his back. His right hand found the knife in his pocket, his thumb caressing the blade-release switch.

He keyed them into the room and immediately took care of them, one stroke each, from behind so the blood pumping from the carotid artery would squirt away from him.

714 adjoined 712. He opened his connecting door and knocked on the other. Mulroy opened it within seconds to stare down without expression at the scene on the floor.

"I think we should move on," the Vulture said. "This place is...how do you Americans say it?"

"A dump," Mulroy said.

"A dump," the Vulture repeated, wiping the blade on a handkerchief, retracting it and replacing it in his pocket. He placed the Do Not Disturb sign on the doors as they left.

THE RESTAURANT WAS called the Bricktown Brewery and was set in an old, abandoned section of Oklahoma City that had once been the industrial district and was now considered picturesque. Named for the huge brick warehouses that dominated the mile-square area, Bricktown was part of the attempt at revitalizing a long-dead downtown section. It might have worked had not the Oklahoma City bombing in '95 caused such destruction.

The restaurant was highly varnished exposed wood on the inside and contained its own microbrewery on premises. Bolan sat upstairs, on the second floor, in a gaming area full of pool tables and virtual-reality experiences. The rock music was too loud. He ate fish and drank iced tea. He had just watched his quarries multiply from three to seven and could almost feel himself getting closer to the Vulture.

He'd followed the Pontiac all day, through Knoxville and all the way to Oklahoma City. An hour before, they'd checked into the Medallion Hotel, across from the convention center, the only hotel in downtown OKC.

Under the Belasko name, the Executioner had taken his own room across the hall from the three terrorists, all of whom shared the room. He watched their room through the peephole in his door. Within fifteen minutes four men dressed as soldiers knocked on their door, which opened immediately, and the soldiers hurried inside.

They'd just hooked up with another cell in the organization. The platoons were beginning to merge for the operation, whatever it was.

He'd followed the seven of them to this restaurant, three blocks from the hotel. They'd taken separate vehicles, the impostor soldiers driving a blue sedan with DoD plates.

Now he sat eating fish and watching them play pool as the rest of the patrons cleared out slowly. It was nearly eleven. The women sat at a table near him, talking quietly together, occasionally holding hands across its top as the five men played pool and ate sandwiches. They drank no alcohol, showing signs of a tight, well-trained unit.

He'd been listening to snatches of conversation for nearly thirty minutes, trying to pick up any word, any utterance that would give him some idea of what they were planning and where they were going. They were tight and wary. He wondered if the Vulture was nearby.

He had picked up a couple of names. The women, both dark haired, were named Selena and Mischa and looked hard-bitten. The men could have all been skinheads. The one he'd followed all day was a curly blond named Yuri. All the soldiers wore full dress uniforms so they could conceal weapons beneath the jackets. Mulroy was nowhere to be seen.

He'd leave them alone for now, in fact would probably switch to following the soldiers tomorrow lest the others begin to get a notion about the same Cougar on their tail. But follow them to where?

There was one other thing. Both Yuri and one of the soldiers wore cell phones on their belts—squad leaders. He wondered how many squads there were.

It was the presence of the cell phones that finally convinced him to not try intervention at this point. Bolan was more than adept at obtaining information from unwilling subjects, but what if he grabbed one only to find he didn't know anything, that his information came in over the phone?

He was currently sitting in a most advantageous position and saw no need to relinquish it just yet.

"Well, darling, there you are," came a female voice at the table. "I've been looking all over for you."

He watched Julie Powell, in makeup and dress with heels and a matching handbag, sit down across from him. Her eyes were hard, glittering like ball bearings. Scary eyes.

"What the hell are you doing here?" he whispered harshly.

"When I got to the hotel and couldn't find you," she said loudly enough to be heard at other tables, "I had the nice man at the desk get me another key."

"Lady," he whispered low, "this isn't funny anymore. You're putting your foot in the middle of something you know nothing about."

Her stare never wavered. "I told you in Front Royal I was going to hunt down my husband's killers," she said. "And here I am and, I think, here they are. The two women by the jukebox. The blond man. Right?"

"You followed me?" he said.

"Guess us country folk ain't as dumb as y'all think we are," she said, batting her eyes maniacally. "Although I like to think that you subconsciously brought me here to exact justice."

"Get out of here," he said. "Get out now."

"You know I'm not going to, not without Ted's killers under arrest."

"Arrest?" he said.

"I'm a cop, Mike. I take my oath seriously. I want to drag them back and let the law run its course."

"They'll never let you do that," he said. "And by the way, we're in a den of them right now."

"There's more? Who?"

"If you're going to turn," he said softly, "make it natural. See our four boys in uniform?"

"So that makes seven," she said.

"And if you walk out of here right now," he said, "I'll be able to continue tracking them all the way to their source and get every stinking one of them."

She took a long breath. "At this moment in time I am unable to appreciate your dilemma. I'm sitting here while the animals who made me a widow and my children fatherless are playing and laughing and...breathing. It's *all* I can think about. Do you understand me?''

He nodded, mind churning, trying to reconcile the situation. There had to be a way to gracefully get her out of there before—

The quarries were suddenly on the move, the soldier with the cell phone pointing to his watch, giving them the lights-out speech.

Julie Powell was up in a flash, moving just before them as they flowed past and down the stairs single file with the female deputy in the lead.

Bolan jumped in at the end of the line, knowing what was about to happen but unable to stop it. He settled into the combat mode and hoped there were pieces to pick up afterward.

The bottom section of the restaurant was quieter, with a large bar and tables filling a huge dining room. It was a straight shot from the stairs to the front door, which opened onto Sheridan, Bricktown's main drag.

Powell was out the door first, hurrying around the building in the direction of the parking lot behind the place. Good cop that she was, she was avoiding confrontation in front of civilians. Bolan continued trailing a bit, figuring to make up the distance as they walked to the back lot.

He was loose and focused. The Beretta and the .44 Desert Eagle rested easily in the combat harness.

They had been primed, safeties off, since he'd checked into the hotel.

When the firefight came, and it would, he'd go for the squad leaders first. They'd be the toughest. After that it was a toss-up. He figured if push came to shove and the shooting started, Powell would concentrate on the Front Royal killers. He'd take out Yuri, then move on to the soldiers.

After everyone had exited, he waited for an endless half minute before leaving himself. No one was on the Sheridan Street side of the building. He hurried to the corner and looked down the side street, watching them moving from the semidarkness of the streets to the brightness of the parking lot a hundred feet distant.

He moved quickly, keeping to the shadows right up against the side of the three-story brick building. When he made it to the back, he drew both guns while standing in the shadows, then took a cautious look around the corner.

The soldiers were walking toward their car, ten car spaces away from the Pontiac, and Powell stood near her own Toyota, fumbling in her handbag for her keys. She'd set it up perfectly; they had to walk right past her.

As they did, the purse slipped from her grasp to reveal the .38 in her right hand. Her left held up a badge. "Police officer!" she said loudly. "You're under arrest!"

Everything happened at once.

The terrorists scattered automatically, instantaneously, as the soldiers drew guns and charged Powell.

Bolan was out from behind the building, running into the parking lot, coming up behind the soldiers. Shots rang out, one of them Powell's, and blond Yuri took a header right into the front end of a pickup truck.

Bolan assumed the stance and fired the Desert Eagle at the squad leader from behind, hitting him on the back of the neck, the man's spine shattering as he simply crumpled forward onto the hot pavement.

Bolan took out the second leader with two chest shots just as he was turning around. Blood exploded from his chest as the innominate vein blew apart under the thrust of a .44 slug.

Julie Powell and the women had taken cover behind cars and were shooting it out as the two other soldiers dived for cover in opposite directions. Bolan fired twice at one to his left, catching him in the gut and the left thigh. The man grunted hard as he flopped to ground, his MAC-10 skittering away.

Bolan swung the .44 to the right, but the other soldier was already inside a car, bringing the engine to life.

The tires squealed in reverse, burning rubber, then the man swung the big Dodge out of the parking slot. He backed it right at the Executioner, who dived and rolled to avoid the car as it bounced over the bodies of the downed terrorists.

"Julie!" he called.

"Go! Go!" she shouted amid gunfire. "I'm all right!"

He turned toward the Dodge, which skidded to a momentary stop in the side street, then jumped forward to take the corner on Sheridan on two wheels.

Bolan was in motion, charging toward the Sheridan intersection. He made it, running out into the center of the nearly deserted street. The Dodge was a hundred yards away and picking up speed.

He brought the .44 up and focused, taking a long breath, relaxing as he let his mind become the weapon. His finger squeezed ever so gently as the car approached the Santa Fe Railroad bridge that separated Bricktown from the rest of the city.

He fired one shot, letting the wind play the hand for him, his mind not consciously pushing it. There was the slight sound of the tinkle of glass on the driver's-side back window, then the car simply turned itself toward the bridge abutment, plowing dead into it at sixty miles per hour. Even at that distance, Bolan could see the driver fly through the windshield, his head turning to instant pulp upon encountering the uncompromising stone of the bridge. The car flipped onto him and burst into bright orange flame.

Bolan still heard shooting in the back lot and turned

to hurry back there. But it had stopped by the time he reached the place.

As employees tentatively stuck their heads out the back door of the restaurant, Bolan walked up to a stoic Julie Powell as she popped the spent cartridges from the .38 and speedloaded another six rounds.

"I got my three," she said without inflection. Then she looked up at him. "Should I feel bad about this?"

He shook his head. "You've done the world a favor."

"Good," she said. "'Cause I don't feel bad. I'm free now. I can bury my husband and try to make a new life with the kids. Maybe something besides law enforcement."

"Still hurts as badly, though, doesn't it?" he asked, and watched her eyes melt.

She cried then, looked human and vulnerable for the first time. She moved into his arms, and he held her while she grieved. After several minutes she pulled away, looking embarrassed.

"Sorry," she said.

"I'm not."

She nodded then and moved off. Bolan knew he'd never see her again.

He could hear sirens in the background. It was time to get out of there. He wouldn't even have time to frisk the bodies. As the sirens roared closer, he grabbed Yuri's phone from his belt on impulse and jumped into the Cougar, turning away from the main drag, slipping quietly into the dark residential neighborhoods.

He hadn't traveled three blocks when the phone tweeted. He brought it to his ear and tried to approximate the accent he'd heard Yuri using all night long. He spoke low to cover inconsistencies. "Yeah."

"Who's this?" came the response, in a voice he remembered from the past.

"Mulroy?" he said. "It's Yuri."

"You sound funny."

"I'm choked up," Bolan said. "I've been running. We've got a problem."

"Tell me."

"We were attacked...in Oklahoma City. We were with Jorge's group. It was one man, Willy."

"A big guy, tough looking?"

"Yeah. He came out of nowhere and started shooting."

"Damn it! What happened?"

"They're dead, Willy. Everyone's dead."

"The big man?"

"He went down, shot twice. I ran over him with the car."

"He's dead?"

"Dead as they get. What now?"

"You're free? You're driving?"

"Free and driving."

"Here's your orders. Don't go to bed. Proceed directly across country to Los Angeles. A room has been booked for you in the name of Erik Freund at a place called the Plantation Motel. Let me give you the address. You'll be contacted there."

Bolan listened as Mulroy gave him the address and committed it to memory. Julie Powell had just done him the favor of a lifetime. He turned south and headed toward Will Rogers Airport. He could catch a direct flight, sleep on the plane and beat anyone else who was going to be at the Plantation, giving him time to set up surveillance. On top of that, the Vulture now thought he was dead and wouldn't bother looking or waiting for him.

He'd caught the crest of the wave. Now to ride it.

CHAPTER EIGHT

The Pentagon, Washington, D.C.
July 19, Midmorning

The Pentagon was a small city of twenty-three thousand residents, forty thousand telephones and eleven thousand miles of cable. Built to run the World War II effort by Franklin Roosevelt, it slowly grew during the Cold War into a monolith of secrecy and ever-increasing government expenditure until military might became the economic stability of the United States in the 1960s. It was a cash cow.

The Pentagon had its own subway terminal, markets, barber and beauty shops, banks and shoe-shine stands. It was in the barbershop that Hal Brognola caught up with General Amos Betcher, attaché to the secretary of the Army, liaison to his boss during the meetings of the Joint Chiefs of Staff and as connected with the power structure as anyone Brognola knew.

"You know how it works, Hal," the general said as he sat statue-still, a lance corporal clipping with scissors the sides of a crew cut that looked as if it didn't need anything done to it. "NSC has a lot of leeway. It's the Chief Executive's own little Intelligence agency, so its authorization runs deep."

"From my experience," Hal replied, "it sometimes seems to run with no authorization."

"Well, the National Security Council is its own excuse for being now. Once you stock a pond with hungry fish, they're going to start eating everything in sight."

"What about this Vulture business?" Brognola asked.

"I made some calls for you. Found out all I could."

"Sounds as if you don't have much."

The general shrugged. "Depends on what you need. Here's what I know. The NSC has been interested for a long time in the ebb and flow of liquid capital in and out of this country. It seems like a good way to ferret out terrorists and drug thugs—just watch for a large cash flow not attached to legitimate business in any way."

"What's this got to do with—?"

"Let me finish, Hal," Betcher replied as the corporal buzzed his head, making it flat as a pool table. "One of the ways in which we watch this cash flow is by putting agents into Switzerland to keep tabs on electronic transfers of funds into Swiss banks from America."

"The Swiss would never allow anything like that,"

Brognola said. "They protect their banking records from any outside scrutiny."

"Which is why this is a black program."

"We're spying on the Swiss?"

"I wouldn't put it into those words," Betcher said, suddenly swiveling his chair around to look in the mirror, making the barber pause in midbuzz.

"Looks fine, son," Betcher said. "All done."

"But, sir…"

He tore off the linen covering and stood. "Thanks, son," he said, walking out the door of the small shop, Brognola on his heels.

Looking at his watch, Betcher shook his head and hurried down the long, wide hallway, which was jammed with workers going in and out of the establishments here in the commercial part of the building. He glanced over his shoulder at Brognola. "Got a meeting in D.C.," he said. "Walk me to the subway."

As they moved quickly, Betcher talked rapid-fire. "It's a black program run by the NSC Army rep but financed by NSC grant money, not Army budget. I want you to know that. It's called Operation Snowbank. Don't talk to Livingston, the Army Chair, about it, though, because he won't know anything."

"He won't?"

The man shook his head as he walked up to stand near the subway tracks where a large group of uniforms and civilians were already queued up. "He simply makes assertions on the sorts of things, generally speaking, that he wants done. That way he can retain deniability if the fit hits the shan, if you know what I mean."

"Who implements, then?"

"The Office of Covert Studies is the name of the division. Hell, you can even look it up in your government phone directory. The place is affectionately called Cove Stud and is run by a hotshot colonel named Mulligan.

"Give them a call," Betcher said, smiling broadly as the train pulled up. He started to walk off, dropping the cigar in the receptacle, then turning back around to point. "They won't tell you anything, though. Nothing. And worse…you can't make them tell you."

"Amos," Brognola called to the man. "There's a maniac loose in this country, and they can help us find him."

Betcher climbed into the train, then frowned back at Brognola. "They won't," the man called, and the doors slid closed, whisking him immediately away.

Brognola sat on one of the station benches to think. Reports of skirmishes between Americans and "European types" had grown in the past day, plus the Oklahoma City shoot-out to cap it all off.

He'd been unable to reach Bolan since the previous day, but he knew the Executioner had had something to do with what happened in Oklahoma City. Information was of the essence for all of them right now if the Vulture were to be stopped. He made two determinations on the spot. First to trust Betcher's estimation that Cove Stud would never give up information willingly, thus leaving out the direct approach. Secondly he determined he'd get the information no matter what. To the latter end, he stood, picked a quarter out of his pocket and found a pay phone on the wall beside a small bookstore.

He first called his office to get the number for Cove Stud. Betcher was right—it was there. He dialed it up directly.

"O.C.S.," answered a pleasant female voice. "This is Marilyn."

"Yeah...Marilyn," he said quickly. "Mulligan needs to get something out right away on Snowbank and we're drawing a blank on the op's name. Could you help us out...quick?"

"You mean Dennison?"

"Yeah, yeah...we know Dennison. The first name. We need the first name."

"Rennie," she said. "The colonel knows that. He's always joking about the rhyme in— Wait a minute— who is this? Who am I speaking to?"

"The name's Brognola, Marilyn. With the Justice Department. I'd like to speak with Colonel Mulligan right away on a matter of national security."

"I don't see your name appearing anywhere on the command chart. I'm sorry, Mr. Brognola, but the colonel only speaks to and through his active chain of command. It is the nature of this office."

"So...maybe I'll get my friend, the President, to set up the appointment for me, heh?"

"That name doesn't appear on the command chart, either," she replied. "Thank you for your call." She hung up immediately.

Brognola slowly set the receiver back on its cradle. He had a name. Rennie Dennison. It was a start.

RESTED AND READY, Mack Bolan stood smiling at the check-in counter of the Plantation Motel. It was set in the middle of the craziness of North Hollywood, a few blocks from Beverly Hills on La Cienega Boulevard just off the Santa Monica Freeway.

He'd flown in on a military flight Kurtzman had arranged; it was either that or arrive without his weapons, which sat in the duffel in his trunk now.

The bag under his arm contained new clothes and a jacket, and he couldn't wait to shower and change.

"How long you gonna be here?" the clerk asked him as he went over the registration form.

"I'll pay you cash for a week," Bolan said, having no idea of where any of this was leading. He pointed out the open doorway. The two-story Plantation was square with an inner-courtyard parking lot, with every room opening into the courtyard.

"I want a room on the second level, in that corner."

The clerk handed him the key to 223 after taking his cash plus an extra hundred for not mentioning him to anyone.

He drove the rented white Mustang into the courtyard and parked. The irony of his choice of rental car was not lost on the Executioner.

His room was the perfect surveillance post. He had a clear view of the entire compound from high ground, plus the wrought-iron-and-concrete stairs were right beside his room.

He climbed out of the car quickly and moved to the trunk, scanning the quiet courtyard before opening it and hoisting out the duffel. He hurried past the perfunctory five-foot-square pool and up the stairs, getting into the room as quickly as he could. The place was suitably drab, as he'd expected when hearing how cheap the rates were.

He locked the door, then spent the next ten minutes peering through a slit in the window curtain, looking for movement, looking for enemy action. If he were sent here, might the other squads be sent here also?

When nothing happened, he decided to shower and change. The waiting would begin then. He grabbed his keys and his wallet containing all his Belasko identification out of his pockets and threw them on the bed, along with a wad of cash. As he took off the warm-up jacket, he felt something in the breast pocket.

He pulled out the envelope, soaked with dried, flaky blood, that Gene Tripp had given him as he lay dying. Bolan sat heavily on the bed and tore open the envelope. A key dropped into his lap, along with a handwritten letter.

> Whoever's reading this letter is looking at the words of a dead man. A dead man who's going to ask you a favor. The key is to a safe-deposit box. In the box is forty-eight hundred bucks, all I've been able to save.
>
> Annie don't know about it. Nobody does. When I retired, I wanted to surprise her with a cruise or something. Get her the money. Please. She'll need it to bury me.

At the bottom of the letter was Tripp's address, plus the location and number of the safe-deposit box.

Bolan took a long breath. Forty-eight hundred bucks for a lifetime of service. Most crooks had suits that cost more than that.

That he would do what Tripp asked in the letter was a foregone conclusion. If the man had been looking for an easy mark, he'd found one.

Bolan grabbed a hot shower and shave, then changed into jeans and a black shirt and tennis shoes. He retrieved the headset from his harness and punched up Stony Man. Nothing going. He'd destroyed the cell phone after his talk with Mulroy, fearing any more contact would certainly give him away. It was possible the Vulture had smelled a setup at that point and moved everything.

But the man had made an arrogant mistake before. In Paraguay.

Bolan checked through the window again as he got through to his wheelchair-bound computer man. It was the middle of a hot, still afternoon, the sun bleaching the courtyard like a spotlight. The Executioner craved action.

"Talk to me, Bear."

"I assume that was you last night in Oklahoma City," Kurtzman said.

"Me and the craziest, bravest woman I've ever met," Bolan answered, unzipping the duffel to take out and slip into the black leather combat harness.

"Woman?"

He pulled the bazooka out of the bag, lining the rockets up next to it. "Never mind."

"Are you close on this thing?"

"Maybe real close," Bolan said, pulling an Uzi from the case and setting it beside the other gear. "What have you got?"

"They found the body of the wife of that arms dealer who blew up in Pennsylvania, along with some Middle Eastern guy we haven't gotten an ID on yet."

"Where?"

"Kansas City. She checked in with three men, two military-looking types, the third a heavy drinker with long, bright red hair and beard."

"His eyes, Bear, his eyes."

"Oh, yeah. He wore wraparound sunglasses day or night."

"Bingo!" Bolan said. "That's him. They're all moving in this direction."

He had unloaded the bag, filling the bed and floor around it with his weapons. He'd have it out with them here if it came to that.

"What do you need from me?" Kurtzman said.

"Keep doing what you're doing. Knowledge is power, my friend. Keep me supplied."

"By the way," the computer man replied, "the FBI put together a composite drawing of the man who walked away from the shoot-out in OKC. It's a very unflattering picture, Mack."

Bolan jerked to the sound of an engine running outside. "I've got to go," he said, and broke contact immediately, tossing the headset aside.

He grabbed the Weatherby sniper scope from the bed and moved to the window. A truck had pulled into the courtyard and was parked by the office. It was a two-and-a-half-ton, canvas-covered ten-wheeler.

The Executioner brought the scope up to his eyes, adjusting the cross hairs until the driver's-side door of the truck came into sharp focus.

The door opened. A man got out. Mack Bolan was staring into the wild-eyed, good-old-boy face of Willy Mulroy. The motherlode.

THE VULTURE, smooth-faced again, his hair back to its normal silver, sat on the elegant brocaded couch in the palatial Beverly Hills home, drinking a Kahlua and coffee and listening to the phone ring in his ear.

He had a view out through French doors onto a western exposure, an acre and a half of meticulously kept garden brightening with the late-afternoon sun. It was lovely.

"AmerAlert," came a tired-sounding female voice after fifteen rings.

"Yes, good afternoon," the Vulture said, picking up the small magazine and looking at the circled entry on page fifteen. "We're trying to coordinate a demonstration, and I'm just checking on the times."

"What shipment and where are you?"

"We're in L.A.," he said politely. "I believe the shipment originates in Eugene, Oregon."

The voice got interested. "What group are you with?"

"We're called Awaken Los Angeles. We're brand-new."

"God bless you," the woman said. "Somebody needs to get out there and let this country know the dangers that pass through its streets every day."

"What time should we expect that shipment?"

"We just heard from our Coalinga spotter who saw the truck pass his observation point at 5:00 p.m. That gives you about two hours. The truck is dark blue and totally unmarked, but it's heavy and will look heavy, reinforced lead and iron all around. It will drive slower than most vehicles. Do you know that this is the largest plutonium shipment ever put on the road? We've protested this for months."

"It is still traveling Route 5?"

"Yes. But it will switch to 405 in Los Angeles, then pick up 5 again in Laguna Hills. It will take 5 to San Diego, where it will interchange to Interstate 8 and on to the Gila Bend storage facility."

"I'm in Hollywood. Would you say we should line the roadways by six-thirty?"

"Yes. When you spot the truck, try and follow it, honk at it, call attention to it so people will know. We haven't heard anything about this. Will it be a big demonstration?"

"The biggest," the Vulture said, and hung up.

He finished his coffee, then adjusted his silk patch. His eye still tormented him, the headaches blinding his good eye, this despite Mulroy's news that the big man was dead. He didn't believe it. His eye told him differently.

He stood and walked to the living room, a large room with many sofas separated from the hotel-sized entry foyer. The house had once belonged to an old-time movie star named, he was told, Lupe Valez. He, of course, didn't recognize the name, but he smiled and acted amused anyway so that the lady of the house would be comfortable.

The woman was an enigma, more so than most

women. She had some vague connection to his contacts in Kansas City, apparently through a diamond-smuggling operation they'd been involved in with her late husband, who'd drowned in his own swimming pool. Her name was Verna Cassabian, and she enjoyed spending money, so much so that she'd run out. She was leasing the place to her husband's ex-partners for about a million dollars, a lot of money for a safe-house. It made him wary of his new compatriots.

He saw that the emissary was still gagged and bound to a straight wooden chair, his hands cuffed behind him. Verna Cassabian sat beside the man, a drink in her hand, chatting away as if he were visiting her at some kind of tea party. Verna was another inveterate talker, a habit that was almost certain to have permanent consequences attached. Too bad.

"Hi, Charlie," she said, looking good in a tight white blouse and short, little-girl skirt. Her blond hair showed no black roots. She held up her drink. "Join me."

"Later," he said, checking his watch. "I have a job to do today."

He moved to the man tied to the chair, smiled at his wide, bulging eyes. "Have you been rehearsing your speech?" he asked, and smiled when the man nodded.

"How long are you going to be staying?" Verna asked.

The Vulture smiled. He liked this one. She, at least,

had a bit of class. "Several days," he said. Which was about as long as his hostess had to live. "Do you get many visitors?" he asked.

She frowned, shaking her head. "Since my husband died, the men have come around to hit on me, but that's about it. Guess I need to get out more."

"Well, maybe you can with all that money you've just collected. Remember, it's tax free."

"You're cute, you know that?" she said, crossing her leg seductively.

"You, too," he returned, his fingers idly playing with the blade in his pocket. Mulroy needed to hurry.

He jerked the gag from the mouth of the man tied to the chair. "Let's do your speech, then. It's time."

"Why are you keeping me tied up?" the man asked, taking deep breaths, sweat running down his face. "Are we not on the same side? I brought you our end of the agreement, I—"

"Right there." The Vulture smiled, sitting beside Verna on the couch and pulling the large briefcase and the suitcase toward them, opening the latch. "You've hit on it. Your end of the agreement was to bring me twenty million American dollars in cash, correct?"

"There it is! See for yourself!"

The Vulture cocked his head and opened the suitcase to pull out a bundle of hundreds. He fanned it before his face. "Looks funny to me," he said. "Feels funny." He plucked a bill out and set it on a marble coffee table before him, then reached into his pocket.

"It's money!" the man said frantically, "I brought it to you at great personal risk." He was a little guy, a middleman of no consequence trying to save his useless life, his eyes continually darting.

"I don't know a lot about a lot," the Vulture said, bringing a hundred-dollar bill out of his pocket to set beside the middleman's. "But I have a little money test I've always done. Watch this."

He picked up an alabaster lighter from the table in one hand and his own hundred in the other. The lighter flicked to destructive life, and the Vulture set his money ablaze to the delighted squeal of Verna Cassabian.

He dropped the burning bill on the tabletop and lit the bill from the suitcase, placing them carefully side by side. "You see here," he said, "my bill is burning a sort of grayish smoke while yours is burning bright white smoke. Now, that's different. You see what I'm saying?"

"Yours is burning a gray because it's been in circulation a long time and is dirty."

"Are you saying that your money has never been used before? But it came in from out of the country and has many, many different serial numbers."

"I'm just the delivery boy."

"So, you don't know if this money is real or not?"

"I...I...please just let me go. This has nothing to do with me."

The Vulture ignored his pleas, instead taking a tiny tape recorder out of his pocket and turning it on. The handwritten piece of paper lay on the man's lap. The Vulture picked it up and held it before the man's face.

The man read, his voice just the right mixture of desperation and determination. "People of America. I am calling you today to proudly claim responsibility for the tragedy that has engulfed Los Angeles. We are the Committee for the Liberation of Iraq and are showing our power today to let you know that your imperialistic aggressions cannot enslave the world. Free my people! Free my country from your destructive sanctions! If you will not, you will feel our wrath again!"

The Vulture turned off the recorder, applauding lightly at the man's heartfelt performance.

"Excellent," he said. "One take. A real Hollywood player, eh?"

"Please let me go now," the man begged.

"What if you've given me counterfeit money?"

"I'm just the courier. If it's counterfeit, I didn't know it."

"So, you're inconsequential to the process?"

"Yes...please. Yes."

"Worth nothing to them?"

"No. I was just hired to carry the bags here."

"All right, then," the Vulture said, pulling the

three-inch hilt from his pocket and releasing the spring. The stubby blade jumped out and locked into place. The Vulture made one quick slash, and the man's eyes opened wide.

Everything was still for a moment. Then the blood rushed out of the gaping neck wound, bubbling from the man's mouth as he tried to speak.

Verna Cassabian jumped off the couch. "My carpet!" she screeched. "You're getting it all over my carpet!"

He fixed his good eye on her. "You're earning your million dollars," he said as he wiped his blade on the dying man's hair.

THROUGH THE SNIPER SCOPE Bolan watched Mulroy as he strode out of the truck and walked into the office. He checked the passenger side. Empty. The Vulture wasn't with him. The Executioner didn't like the looks of the truck. It meant they'd connected with another arms dealer and were once again loaded with instant death.

The blond man, leaner, without the baby fat he'd remembered from Paraguay, walked back out of the office and stood before the truck with his hands on his hips. He was looking around.

His eyes drifted in Bolan's direction and held for a long time, the cross hairs centered right between his eyes.

Then the man walked to the truck, reached through the open window and gave the horn two quick beeps.

Within seconds people began coming out of motel doors. Men and women, all wearing bulky jackets in the hot sun and carrying overnight bags. They didn't speak or acknowledge one another; they just moved toward the cars in the lot and stowed their bags in the trunks.

He counted eighteen, with Mulroy making nineteen.

Mulroy climbed into the truck and drove farther into the lot, working at turning it around. Bolan rushed the ordnance back in the bag and threw his own jacket over the combat harness.

The cars below started leaving the Plantation in a kind of loose convoy. Bolan ran down the stairs and into his car as soon as the last one turned north on La Cienega.

He followed, but the convoy didn't go far. They passed Olympic, then turned west on Wilshire, then wound up into Beverly Hills, where houses as big as apartment buildings gouged into the hillsides.

Two quick turns later Bolan saw the lead truck several blocks farther on, turning into a walled estate. The cars, staggered, trickled behind.

He drove slowly on, checking the neighborhood. Every house was isolated, set in spacious grounds that separated it from its neighbors. An ideal location if it came to action.

The house Mulroy had turned into had a ten-foot concrete wall with ornamental ironwork on the top, security cams, the works. The lot was deep and so heavily wooded Bolan could barely see another home in the distance. He wondered about coming in from behind.

Then he saw it. A typical DEA stakeout van, black, with the small tinted window in the side that the camera sat behind. What the hell was going on?

In the next couple of blocks he spotted several cars with plainclothesmen sitting in them. It looked as if they even had some houses covered.

How did they get here first? They didn't look like FBI. Something had gone awry. And worse, if Bolan could spot them so easily, so could the Vulture.

He ripped the headset out of the ordnance bag beside him on the seat and called Stony Man. Kurtzman, like the Executioner, didn't punch a time clock. His job ran twenty-four hours a day, seven days a week.

"What the hell's going on in L.A.?" he asked when Kurtzman came on.

"Nothing," came the reply.

"So how come me and fifty thousand cops have got the same place staked out? They've—"

He had to swerve to avoid the two blue Beverly Hills cop cars that converged at the upcoming intersection, cutting him off. He jerked the Mustang into reverse, then looked in his rearview mirror to see ten other cops running toward him.

"I've got something in Beverly Hills," Kurtzman said, "but it doesn't pertain to—"

"Tell me quick!" Bolan said as the cops swarmed the car, guns drawn.

"The Treasury Department has been tracking twenty million in counterfeit dead presidents from Iran to North Korea to Hong Kong to here. They're waiting on a warrant to go in and bust them."

"Out of the vehicle!" a cop screamed just outside Bolan's window. "Keep your hands where I can see them!"

"Tell me who's in charge here, quick!" Bolan said as faces pressed in all around him.

"A Treasury guy named Delany working with a customs agent named Madison…and for some reason the DEA is all mixed up in this."

"Here goes," Bolan said, and signed off. A dozen weapons pointed at him from outside the car.

He slowly opened the door and stepped out, rough hands grabbing him. "Take your hands off me!" he said, his voice cool and cutting. "Get Delany and Madison over here or you'll all be real sorry."

CHAPTER NINE

They eased their grip but didn't let him go. Inside the car they found the duffel, and someone opened his jacket to see the combat harness.

"Get this guy to Delany," a police captain said. His hands cuffed from behind, Bolan was led into the bushes of a large estate two blocks from the Vulture's nest.

"There's no time for this," he said. "You don't know who's inside those walls. What kind of firepower do you have?"

"What do we need, cannons?" said the sergeant leading him.

"He's got a bazooka in the bag, McAvoy," said the patrolman who had him by the other arm, the duffel weighing down his shoulder.

They walked farther into the gardens of the estate, then turned back in the direction of the Vulture's hideout, approaching the back door of the estate directly across the street.

"Those aren't street punks holed up in that house,"

Bolan told the sergeant as the man led him up thickly carpeted stairs to the second floor. "They're combat-hardened mercenaries and they're up to the eyeballs in ordnance, heavy stuff. You understand what I'm telling you? Watch your fanny out there."

The man nodded, his eyes locking hard with Bolan's. "Thanks for the warning," he said. "Who the blazes have we got?"

"The Vulture," Bolan said, and both cops stopped in the middle of the stairs to look at him. He had their attention.

"I watched him kill a hundred people in New York City two days ago."

They picked up the pace, finally stopping behind two men with binoculars at the large window of a master bedroom the size of Rhode Island. The window overlooked the walled estate across the street.

"Who's this?" asked the older of the two, turning around, revealing a wine-colored birthmark on his left temple. He scowled at Bolan.

"We stopped him at the checkpoint," Sergeant McAvoy said. "He asked for you or Agent Madison by name. He says you've got the Vulture holed up across the street."

Both Delany and Madison laughed.

"He's got enough stuff in his bag," the other cop said, "to start a small war on his own."

Delany narrowed his eyes, then moved to stare at

Bolan and the duffel weighing down the king-size bed with the black silk sheets.

"Just who are you?" he asked.

"It doesn't matter," the Executioner said. "What matters is that you've got a lot of people on the streets out there who aren't prepared for real warfare, and that's what's going to happen when you try and take that house. What are you waiting for, by the way?"

"The warrant's coming," Madison said, a real bottom feeder if Bolan had ever seen one.

"We ask the questions," Delany said. "Now, who are you."

"You think you've got counterfeiters inside that house," Bolan said, "and maybe you do. But those counterfeiters are trying to use that money to pay off the Vulture for a major act of terrorism."

"What act of terrorism?" Madison asked.

"Pull your men out now," Bolan said. "Leave them to me."

Both agents laughed again. "Your collar, huh?" Delany said. "I don't think so."

"You don't understand—"

"They're leaving," the sergeant reported, "some of them anyway."

"What?" Bolan said, charging to the window, hands still cuffed. "It's happening."

"We'll follow them," Delany directed, taking a handset off his belt and keying it on. "Units three and nine."

"Right," Bolan said. "I spotted you guys a mile away. So did they."

"Three and nine, come in, please."

"They're going to be ready for you," Bolan warned as he watched the five cars drive out of the gate, the first car pulling a small U-Haul trailer.

Units three and nine were staticking through Delany's belt speaker.

"Tell everybody to get down!" Bolan shouted as the car turned out of the driveway and the trailer uncoupled to roll into the middle of the street.

"Would you quiet—"

"Down!" Bolan yelled, diving at Delany, taking him to the floor as a huge explosion went up on the street. The bedroom wall blew out, and everything was in motion as the bed jumped, smashing itself against the wall, the dressers falling over, glass shrapnel everywhere.

Plaster dust mixed with smoke as Bolan rolled off the Treasury man, who was coughing and groaning. The room was totally exposed to the outside. Madison lay near the opening, arms flailing, his head nowhere to be seen. The sergeant was croaking down deep in his throat, the patrolman beside him skewered by a pane of glass large as a platter.

"What the...the..." Delany moaned as Bolan got to his feet.

"They'll have left someone in the house," Bolan said. "Get these cuffs off me!"

"Where?"

"McAvoy's pockets...hurry!"

McAvoy was on his knees, vomiting blood as Delany got into his pocket, pulled out the key and uncuffed Bolan. He tore into the bedroom, pulling up a huge chunk of wallboard to retrieve his duffel, and replace the Beretta and the .44 Desert Eagle into the harness. "You're going to help me get them," he said.

Delany staggered after him as they moved through the debris of a multimillion-dollar home, the stairs half-gone, small fires burning through the entire structure.

Outside was a mess. A huge, smoking crater touched the curb on either side, and surveillance cars were blown to pieces or upside down. Trees and houses burned all around them, a vision of hell. Two blocks away, at the checkpoint, dead men lay all over the street, body parts everywhere. A few still-living agents were picking themselves up off the ground, weaving drunkenly, disoriented.

Bolan ran to the dangling, twisted gate of the walled estate, Delany behind him. He squeezed through the opening left by the explosion and ran through the trees toward the house until he drew fire.

The house was his only shot. With the Vulture on the road again, the house might contain clues. He crouched behind a large redwood eighty feet from the house as a steady stream of fire kept him behind cover. The house was stone, Tudor style, all its windows blown out. A stone fountain in the curving driveway was scattered all over, the stone Cupid that had topped it lodged high in a redwood that was cracked and split right down the middle. Smoke and fire were everywhere.

Delany, his clothes shredded, fell to his knees beside Bolan, shaking his head, trying to reorient.

"You ever kill anybody?" Bolan asked him as he pulled the bazooka from the duffel, then lined the rockets up on the ground.

"A couple times...in Vietnam," the man said.

"Good enough. You're going to kill some more."

He juiced the bazooka, building the charge, then handed Delany one of its rockets. "Feed me."

The man fell into his old military training, waiting until Bolan had set the sights on the entryway of the house before shoving the rocket into the weapon's rear. He tapped Bolan on the shoulder, then ducked.

The Executioner clicked the fire control; the rocket whooshed loudly, spurting fire from the tube's back and making impact with the house a second later. The roar of the explosion was followed by billows of black smoke filling the courtyard.

"Again!" Bolan called, and fired off another one into the smoke.

"Let's go!" Jumping to his feet and using the smoke for cover, Bolan charged toward the house, not stopping until he reached the edge of the tree line on the circular driveway.

He pulled a fully loaded M-16 out of the duffel and tossed it to Delany. "If you were in Vietnam, I'm sure you know how to use this," he said.

"Too well," Delany replied, ripping off the remnants of his jacket and tie, then priming the thing as Bolan dropped the duffel and drew the pistols from the harness.

"It's the jungle," Bolan told the man. "Kill or be killed. Remember. Let's go!"

The two men charged out of the tree line and into the thick smoke. They could hear the crack of gunfire, but it was invisible in the smoke. Movement was their friend.

They reached the ruins of the entry and found two terrorists blown to hell amid the stone rubble. They hugged the wall on either side of the hole they'd blown. Bolan instinctively grabbed a grenade from his harness, pulled the pin and tossed it into the house, and another explosion sent smoke and debris back out the opening.

They charged inside. A magnificent foyer, strewed with rock debris, greeted them. Double stairs curved upward, and on the landing above, two men were manning an M-60.

"Get under them!" Bolan barked.

Delany charged toward the gunners instantly as Bolan dived and rolled, coming up with the Beretta on target just as the machine gun cut loose, its *rat-ta-tat* echoing hollowly through the house. Bolan fired twice at the gunner's hands, tearing the man's fingers off even as the breech exploded back at him.

Delany had made it beneath the high landing, angrily opening up with the M-16 and emptying the clip into the floor above him. The other terrorist jumped, taking the hits, then tumbled headfirst to the tiled foyer floor.

Movement from the left swung the Executioner to the side, the Beretta immediately spitting fire at a large man with a shotgun. The gunner collapsed in the doorway, his heart exploded, dead before he hit the floor.

Delany kicked through a door at the back of the foyer and ran through. Bolan heard gunfire from back there as he turned to the right and charged into a huge living room to dive behind one of many large sofas set up in cosy groups on the luxurious white broadloom.

Automatic fire immediately rattled the room. His sofa was torn to pieces, fluff blasting out of the upholstery to float through the room like snow.

Bolan crawled in a rapid zigzag motion, then dived for another sofa, drawing more fire. The second it stopped, he jumped to his feet with both pistols out in front of him and emptied the clips at the three terrorists who were frantically trying to reload.

It was sloppy but got the job done. The three twitched with the shock of bullet impact, the Executioner's fists spitting fire as his assailants tumbled over furniture and one another.

Guns empty, Bolan fell behind the sofa again, dropping both clips at the same time, then reloading within seconds to no return fire. Snapping a round into each chamber, he came back up over the sofa to see nothing but bodies. The whole house was suddenly quiet, the only sound that of distant sirens.

He wondered where the Vulture was.

"Hey!" came a voice from the back end of the living room, where it led into a kitchen or pantry. "Big man! It's me, Delany. I'm coming in. Don't shoot!"

"Roger!" Bolan shouted back, but kept his weapons at the ready just in case.

Delany walked in, his shirt torn off, smeared with soot. Suddenly Vietnam didn't seem so long ago. The man's M-16 was slung over his shoulder in the true dogface tradition. If the Treasury Department had more men like Delany, the country was in good hands.

He was dragging a crying blond woman by the arm. She seemed on the point of hysteria.

"Hold her here," Bolan said. "I'm going to check the rest of the house."

He hurried off, giving the place the quick once-over but finding nothing of value. When he came back downstairs, the blonde was drinking a huge glass of bourbon and sitting on a torn-up sofa. Delany had moved halfway across the room and was staring into the face of a man tied to a chair, dead, his clothes soaked through with blood, as if every drop in his body had pumped out onto him.

"Know him?" Bolan asked, walking up beside Delany.

"He's the reason we were here," Delany said. "His name's Said Jahpur. He's a go-between, a middleman connected to a great many terrorist groups. On his own he's nothing, a gofer, a messenger boy. But the interconnected chain of organizations that used him spread worldwide."

"He was transporting counterfeit money?"

Delany nodded as Bolan got down and looked at the wound. Jahpur's throat had been slashed all the way across, the same way Sarge's wife had died. From the size of the gash, the knife must have been small and squat, almost pyramid shaped, no bigger than a couple of inches long; the cut was wide but not deep. Bolan had once owned a knife like that. He began to get a sick feeling in the pit of his stomach. This had to end soon.

"The money came into his hands in Hong Kong," Delany said. "We've been watching Iran. They've been counterfeiting hundreds of millions of U.S. dollars to flood our economy and create instability. Our contacts traced twenty million, following it through many countries as it changed hands."

"So the Iranians are behind this?"

"I don't think so," Delany said. "On the last stop before Hong Kong, in Bangkok, it was exchanged for a million *real* U.S. dollars, a payment to Iran."

"Iraq, then," Bolan said.

Delany nodded. "That would explain the long and complicated travel path since those two countries hate each other so much they could never do business face-to-face, or even admit to it."

A fireplace was set on the west wall. Bolan walked over to it, giving the woman a sidelong glance as he did. "What about her?" he asked.

"Name's Verna Cassabian," he said. "She's the widow of an international thug who specialized in the import and export of contraband, including guns."

The hearth was clean as a whistle, except for what looked to be a small magazine that had been burned there. He picked the charred remnants out carefully and walked over to the woman.

"You better talk to me, lady," he said.

"Mister," she said, tears rolling down her cheeks, "I'll tell you anything you want to know, just don't...hurt me."

He sat beside her, holding the burned magazine gingerly on his lap. "Did your husband's old associates set this up?"

She nodded, squeezing out more tears. "I...I asked them for something. I was running out of money."

"Was there a man with a patch here?"

"Oh, God...yes!" she said, pointing to the corpse

tied to the chair. "He killed that man with a little knife he pulled out of his pocket. At first he had red hair and a beard and wore sunglasses. Then he changed his appearance. He was in charge. He told everybody what to do."

"Did he give you a name?"

"Just Charlie," she said. "I think he made it up on the spot so I could call him something. None of his people ever called him by that name, or any other I could hear except for 'Sir.'"

Delany had wandered up close and was squatting before the woman, listening intently. Bolan plucked the drink from her hand and gave it to Delany. Then he took her by the shoulders and turned her to face him.

"He was cruel, wasn't he? Heartless?"

"Yes."

"Then why are you still alive?"

"I found her in a closet, crying," Delany said. "Unarmed."

"In the confusion I hid," she said. "They didn't look for me."

Bolan nodded. "Listen to me very carefully," he said. "I must know why they were here. Did you hear anything...anything that might tell me that answer?"

"I know the man with the patch was in a hurry," she said. "It was like he had to be somewhere at a certain time, you know?"

"What time?"

She shook her head. "I'm a pretty good snoop. A girl has to learn to survive. But these people were closemouthed. I'll tell you one thing, though, Charlie—the guy with the patch—did something really weird. He made that poor man in the chair read a statement, like a letter, while he tape-recorded it."

"What did the man say?"

"Something about the liberation of Iraq and taking credit for the terrible things that were happening to L.A. That's not word for word, but that's what I got out of it. It scared me when I heard it. Then he killed that poor guy as soon as he was finished with the speech."

Bolan and Delany shared grim looks. It got worse every minute.

"Do you know anything about this?" the Executioner asked, holding up the charred magazine.

"I'm sorry," she said, shaking her head again. "Charlie carried it around the whole time he was here. I remember seeing once that he had circled something in it. He burned it as soon as his friends showed up, then they all left.

"What was the book called?"

"I don't know. Something about America. He kept it open and folded up in his pocket most of the time. That's all I know. Honest."

Bolan started picking at the pile of ashes in his hands, blackened pages that crumbled to dust at the touch. Somewhere in the middle of the mess he found three pages that were completely burned except for an inch-square section, charred brown, one of which contained a partial word: "AmerAl."

"AmerAl," Bolan said. "Amer Al."

"America Al," Cassabian suggested.

"Alcohol," Delany said. "A lot."

"Allot," Bolan murmured, then it hit him. "Alert. AmerAlert."

"We'll need a phone number." Delany rushed to an end-table phone and picked it up. "It's dead."

Bolan grabbed the headset from his harness and tossed it to the man.

"What's AmerAlert?" Verna Cassabian asked.

"It's an organization that tracks the movement of nuclear waste across American highways," Bolan said, "keeping their members posted as to when radioactive material will be in their area so they can go out on the highways and protest hazardous materials in their cities."

"I don't follow," the woman said.

Bolan stood. "Never mind now," he replied, walking to stand beside Delany, who had raised AmerAlert on the headset.

"Yes...yes...the Los Angeles area. Yes, we're part of the protest." He opened his eyes wide and looked at Bolan. Then he looked at his watch. "The San Fernando Valley now?"

"Ask her what it's carrying," Bolan said.

"Cargo," Delany said. "How much?.... You're kidding." He looked at his watch again. "Thanks." He hung up.

His eyes were full of fear when he looked at Bolan. "Big blue unmarked truck," he said, "heavily reinforced and in the San Fernando Valley right now. It will take I-405 through the greater Los Angeles area. It's carrying four and a half tons of highly unstable plutonium."

"Four and a half tons," Bolan repeated.

"You figure a hijack?"

The Executioner nodded. He needed a map.

"What would they do with so much nuclear material?"

"That's not tough," Bolan said with bitter resignation. "You're not from here?"

"D.C.," Delany replied.

"Los Angeles has always had a water problem. They solved it by getting their water from the central valley."

"So?"

Just then the police started moving, guns drawn, into the house. Bolan would have to get out of there quickly. "There's several hundred miles of aqueduct in which they could dump radioactive waste," Bolan told Delany.

"The water supply."

"That's a really ugly way to go," Bolan said, and held out a hand. "Get the word out."

Delany shook the proffered hand. "I will," he said, and tried to give Bolan the M-16 back.

"Keep it, and remember."

He was out the door and gone.

CHAPTER TEN

Santa Monica Mountains, Los Angeles

Bolan sped north through the Hollywood hills on I-405 after cutting onto it from Santa Monica Boulevard. Though it was evening, the winding four-lane street was jammed with traffic, but Los Angeles streets were always jammed with traffic. He was looking for trouble.

He had the map open on his lap and Kurtzman in his ear as he drove. Bathed in the setting sun, the hills rolled easily all around him.

"Who's in on it now?" he asked into the tiny wire mike set near his mouth.

"Everybody but my Aunt Matilda, Striker. You'd better back out of there. You seeing any choppers yet?"

"Yeah, plenty, I— Hold on."

Traffic had suddenly slowed to a crawl, then stopped. Bolan jumped immediately out of the Mustang and grabbed the duffel.

He jogged in the oncoming-traffic lane because there was no traffic approaching. Both sides were stopped. Fifty yards ahead he saw why.

Two men lay dead in the middle of the highway, with cars, swerving to avoid the bodies, smashing into one another. He ran to the dead men. They were all shot up and had left no vehicle behind. Car-jackings didn't happen on the highway.

"The Vulture's got the truck," he said, then turned and looked around him. The snarl would take hours to untangle, but the roadway was clear in the north-bound lane beyond the site of the killing.

He ran to the first car he came to, a convertible Mercedes, top down. A young man with extremely long hair and little square glasses gazed myopically up at him.

"Hey, dude," he said hesitantly.

Bolan opened his door, and said "Sorry, but I need this." He grabbed him by the front of his shirt and hauled him out of the car, then climbed behind the wheel. The duffel went in the passenger seat. He backed up, banging into the car behind.

"Dude," the driver said plaintively, getting up and hurrying to the car. "Oh, dude. Dude!"

Bolan slammed down the gas pedal, leaving a trail of rubber as he swung northbound again and continued the chase.

Everything had come apart for the Vulture this time. His money was counterfeit, his hideout had been staked and the whole world was closing in on him. Given that, why was he still going for the plutonium? Bolan assumed that the dead men on the road had been the drivers of the plutonium truck. Delany's fast action with the police should have suggested to the terrorist that he would never make it to the aqueduct. So why was he still doing it?

The answer came back crystal clear, perfect in its selfish simplicity—the Vulture simply wanted to use the plutonium as a diversion, a way of covering his escape.

"I think he's going to turn it loose," he said into the mike.

"That means a backup escape plan. What's your next intersection?"

"Mulholland Drive, then Ventura Boulevard."

"What are you going to do?"

"Stay on him. That's all I can do."

More choppers filled the sky, the media now joining the chase, and police cars bumped up onto the highway with Bolan, lights flashing, sirens blaring.

Then he saw the target. A big blue semitrailer with an entourage of five cars. It was a nightmare as the convoy fanned out, forcing cars on both sides of the road onto, then over, the shoulder to plunge into the valley below.

It was a claustrophobic death trap with no room to maneuver—a steep hill on one side, a drop-off on the other. One of the police choppers dipped down close to the truck, and a uniformed cop tried to call through a bullhorn. A tracer whooshed from the rear of a convertible, tracking in a second to the chopper, and it went up in a monstrous ball of flame that seemed to hang suspended for several seconds before crashing downward, right in front of him.

The Executioner jerked hard right, running up the hillside, nearly tumbling. Two police cruisers ran head-on into the blazing wreckage and exploded. All of it was behind Bolan in a second as he steered back to bump onto the roadway a hundred yards beyond the deadly parade as cars continued to smash into one another or fall off the edge of the roadway.

The warrior had felt a lot of emotions run through his scarred battlefield of a mind and body, but rarely had he been faced with a feeling of sheer frustration before. The Vulture's strength lay in his total disregard for human life, life that Bolan had vowed to protect. The Vulture was a farmer with a scythe, mowing through human fields indiscriminately. A cyclone would be easier to stop.

Automatic fire came from the entourage, and Bolan ducked as his windshield cobwebbed, then fell out. A car two lanes away flipped end over end down the highway, throwing screaming passengers out the windows.

He saw another tracer as he skidded around a burning police car. They must have a Stinger. This time a news helicopter went up, falling into the luxury homes on the hillsides. The hillsides were burning now, a long, dry summer having turned an entire state into so much kindling. And it was hell he was driving through. All the choppers were backing way off—exactly what the Vulture wanted, no one to watch his escape.

His Mercedes sped past a sign: Mulholland Drive—3 Miles.

He pulled the Desert Eagle out of the webbing and aimed it at a trailing car right through the window space, dodging debris the entire time. Managing to pull within fifty yards, he squeezed off two quick shots, taking out the back of the driver's head just as the passenger drew a bead on him with an AK-47.

The car jerked right, then flipped upside down on the hillside, dented and squashed. The road twisted the other way, and suddenly Bolan was overlooking the edge of the abyss as the hills climbed on the west side of the road. In the curve one of the Vulture's lead cars collided head-on with another truck trying to get out of the way. The result was instant rubble as the truck continued on, pushing the tangled wreck ahead of it like a snowplow, smears of blood splotching the road as they passed.

"Aaron, are you still on?"

"I'm watching you on TV. They've got cameras in those choppers."

"Do the cops know what they're dealing with here? We don't want any roadblocks, any impediments. We can follow him until he runs out of gas if he wants to play it that way."

"The police are trying to clear the roadways ahead to give it free passage, but you and I both know he's not going to play it that way."

"I think Mulholland's his street," Bolan said. "Whatever's going to happen is going to go down there."

There was no more oncoming traffic, since the cops had diverted it. All at once, the convertible with the missile drifted fully into the other lane, and the gunner turned the weapon back toward the trailing traffic.

Bolan lifted the Desert Eagle instantaneously, without conscious thought, and fired into the convertible. He hit the gunner, who jerked around as he fired, and the missile targeted his own dashboard.

The car went up with a loud *whump*. The concussion blew another trailing car, a big Buick off the road to crash down the hillside.

The convertible disintegrated, sending huge chunks and the occupants a hundred feet into the air. A tire bounced back toward Bolan, bounding over the Mercedes and through the windshield of a cruiser behind, though the driver somehow skidded safely off the roadway.

Bolan was just passing the burning wreckage when debris slammed into his hood, smashing it in before ricocheting away. Body parts fell like rain all around him, and he looked up to see the intersection with Mulholland in the distance.

THE VULTURE WAS ANGRY, angrier than he'd ever been. He'd always given dollar value. To be treated this way, with counterfeit money and a safehouse that was under surveillance, when he was on the verge of what would have been his greatest triumph, was simply intolerable. He would exact a terrible vengeance on those who had made him play the fool. The seeds of his retribution were already firmly sown, in the greed that had led to this betrayal.

"We're comin' up on Mulholland," Mulroy said from behind the wheel.

"So we are," the Vulture agreed, and removed the square metal box with the red and green buttons from his jacket pocket. He leaned forward and pushed the button on the dash that opened the sunroof. It was a Lincoln, a sturdy vehicle. He owned one himself.

They drove the outer lane right beside the truck full of nuclear waste. Such a great idea. It wouldn't have cost a cent. All down the drain because he'd had to deal with greedy amateurs. Passionate men made stupid mistakes. He'd never deal with zealots again.

He flicked a switch, and the red light on the square box came on. He pulled out a small antenna. Mulholland was a mile ahead. He turned to Armon in the back. "Do it now," he said, and the man struggled to bring the bulk of the small antiaircraft gun from the seat to rest on the back window space. He slammed the clip of ammo into place on top and braced it on its tripod. The bolt jerked back with a loud metallic clang, and the weapon was now fully operational.

In the side-view mirror the Vulture kept catching sight of the man in the convertible whom they couldn't shake. It was the big man. It had to be. His eye was throbbing like a beating heart.

"We're closing on it," Mulroy said.

The Vulture clicked another button on the box, and the green "ready" light came on. He caressed the trigger toggle with his fingers, teasing it.

He couldn't think of the big man now or of the idiots who'd betrayed him. Self-preservation was the key. He stared at the nearing exit ramp. He had to time it just right.

Eight hundred yards.

Seven hundred.

"I hope you gentlemen can still shoot straight," he said, setting aside his timer to prime the SMG between his legs.

"Ready, Willy," he said, picking up the detonator again. "Ready...."

Five hundred yards...four hundred. "Now!"

Mulroy gave a cowboy yell and tried to jam the gas pedal through the floorboard. They shot past the truck, startled faces peering at them from the cab. Mulroy waved out his window as the Vulture flicked the switch, and the C-4 he'd planted just above the truck's rear axle went off, physically lifting the back of the truck in the air. When it slammed back down, there were no wheels beneath it.

It screeched loudly, gouging the highway, then tipped over, taking the cab with it. The semitrailer skidded on its side down the highway amid a shower of sparks and banshee screeches.

It whiplashed for a hundred yards, then the cab finally slammed into the hillside, crushed flat behind the weight of the truck and its contents, everything creaking loudly, like the roar of a dying prehistoric beast.

The contents of the truck lay all over the highway.

As Mulroy took the exit ramp at a hundred miles per hour, the Vulture stood in the front seat to take aim through the sunroof at the half-dozen police cars deployed in front of them at the bottom of the exit ramp.

The Vulture watched the police scattering for cover as they realized what wrath was descending upon them. It was almost comical.

Mulroy, a natural left-hander, stuck an Uzi pistol out the driver's-side window and slowed to sixty.

At thirty yards from the loose roadblock, the Vulture said, "Fire."

They unleashed the kind of firepower that the police could never have expected, antiaircraft shells targeting cruisers, blowing them into the air as automatic fire tore into rapidly fleeing police.

The intersection was on fire when they reached it. Knocking the hulk of a burning car out of the way, they skidded into a wide turn and raced into the hairpin twist of Mulholland Drive.

"Pull over first chance and steal a car," the Vulture said casually as he retreated into the car to sit. He reloaded. "I believe the police will have their hands too full now with an evacuation to worry about us."

"You've got a way out of here?" Mulroy asked.

The Vulture laughed. "Of course I have a way out," he said. "Unfortunately I can only take one person with me."

With that, he turned to the back seat and emptied his clip into a surprised Armon.

BOLAN JAMMED HIS FOOT on the brakes when the truck tipped over, skidding wildly as cruisers fishtailed past him. He looked to his right at the hillside's long slope, graded at forty-five degrees.

He had to take a chance.

He aimed his skid at the shoulder and left the road, airborne for several seconds before slamming on the hard-packed dirt of the hillside, choked with weeds and scrub oak.

The Mercedes careered downward and Bolan fought the wheel, trying to steer around rocks and gullies as he bounced wildly up and down, the car trying to buck him out.

As he sped down the long hillside, he could see

the Vulture destroying the intersection and skidding onto Mulholland a half mile away.

He reached bottom, slamming down hard on the access road running beside and below I-405, pieces of car clanking onto the road and thick black smoke pouring from under the hood.

But it was still running, and the Executioner gave it gas. The Mercedes wobbled along the access road bleeding thick black smoke. He got to Mulholland in a minute, the car unable to chug over twenty-five. Following Mulholland, he found the Vulture's Lincoln ten minutes later. It was abandoned, a dead man in the back seat with a surprised look on his face.

They'd changed cars.

Civil-defense warning horns were blaring loudly all through the hills. A chopper flew overhead, a godlike voice emerging from it to boom like thunder on the expensive houses below. "There is an extreme biohazard at the juncture of Mulholland and 405. You must evacuate the area. Evacuate now. Extreme biohazard. Evacuate now."

The Executioner climbed into the remnants of the convertible Mercedes and chugged away on Mulholland, putting distance between himself and the hot waste.

"Kurtzman," he said into the headset.

"Yeah," the man returned, dejected. "It's a horror show."

"On any of the chopper cams, did you see…?"

"Nothing," the man returned. "He got away clean. Maybe he won't be able to get out of the country."

"Right," Bolan said. "And maybe pigs can fly."

"What now?"

"If he won't stay in my yard, I'll just go to his."

"Switzerland?"

"If that's what it takes. I own that bastard and I intend to collect. It's all up to Hal at this point."

HAL BROGNOLA STUCK the small plugs in his ears as he walked up to the practice range at the FBI training center at Quantico, Virginia. He'd spent the better part of the entire day tracking down one Colonel Dan "Red" Mulligan, top of the organizational chart for Cove Stud and Operation Snowbank.

Mulligan was a difficult man to find, especially since he never, apparently, wanted to be found. There wasn't even a home address for him in the government files. There were endless phone numbers and fax machines and pagers Brognola could talk to instead, but the genuine article had continued to elude him.

But Brognola had learned patience long ago. He'd managed to methodically track down Mulligan's government license-plate number, then ran it through the computers to see if it was checked in anywhere. It turned up a positive on the firing range at Quantico and hadn't checked out yet, so he hustled over to catch the elusive Colonel Mulligan in person.

It was an outdoor range near the famous Hogan's Alley testing ground for FBI recruits. Concrete slabs separated each target area. The targets, bull's-eyes and silhouettes were suspended on wires and could be moved easily.

He found the man without difficulty, but not because he had red hair. In point of fact, he did not. But he was the only man on the range dressed in an Army colonel's uniform, the jacket off, folded neatly and hung over the concrete slab. It was nearly dark, and the range was already bright with artificial light.

The man wore mufflers on his ears and was firing what looked to be a nickel-plated Smith & Wesson 586. It was a prestige gun, called the Distinguished Combat Magnum. Flashy, but not noticeably ostentatious. It told him a lot about the colonel.

Having just emptied his chambers into a silhouette target, the colonel hit the button that returned it the fifty feet back to him.

"Colonel Mulligan!" the big Fed said loudly because of the man's mufflers.

The man turned around, pulling his mufflers down around his neck and removing the plastic goggles that protected his eyes from back-flash. "That's my name," he said. "What can I do for you?"

"My name's Brognola. I've been try—"

"Yeah," the man said, taking down the silhouette to study. "I know who you are."

"You're a tough man to track down."

"I'm surprised you were able to."

"I'm persistent."

"And connected."

"Not connected enough to have you return my calls." He walked up beside the man, who was ignoring him as he studied the silhouette, six shots all in the chest area. Brognola was impressed. "Nice pattern."

"I try and stay field-ready," the colonel replied. "How about you?"

Brognola shook his head. "I only come out to the range when I want to lose my hearing." He took off his rumpled seersucker jacket and threw it over his arm. "Nice gun—357 Magnum, right?"

"Right."

"Is that the six-inch barrel?"

"I don't like the accuracy of the four-inch," Mulligan replied, plunging the spent shells from the chambers and reloading by hand. No speedloader for Colonel Mulligan. He was a fastidious man, his hair combed and parted just so, his uniform crisp, as if he'd just put it on. He was one of those guys who could work construction all day and come home clean. He was short and reminded Brognola of a strutting banty rooster.

The man finished loading the gun and snapped the chamber shut. He held it loosely in his hand.

"Don't see a lot of revolvers out on the range anymore," Brognola said. "Everybody seems to want semiautos."

"Get to the point, *Mr.* Brognola," the colonel said, his tone both sharp and condescending. He still held the gun between them, which was intended to make Brognola feel uneasy. "This is about the affair in Switzerland, correct?"

"Of course that's what it's about." Brognola was already beginning to hate the man. "Have you seen the news from California?"

"Yep," the man replied, shifting the gun from hand to hand. "It's a shame your people fumbled on the goal line."

Hal felt the anger rise up his neck but held it in check. "There were a great many contributing factors," he said, surprised at the calm in his own voice. "The important thing now is that we not let him slip completely away. We need the help of your contact in Zurich."

"We are running an extremely delicate and important operation in Switzerland—"

"Snowbank," Hal said.

"—that really can't be tampered with on any level. My operative stumbled upon the information about the Vulture and, trying to be a good scout, turned it over to you bunglers."

The man fixed Brognola with hard eyes. "My operation has already been jeopardized enough. I will allow no more contact. Good day, Mr. Brognola. You've come a long way for nothing."

"There is nothing," the big Fed said, "that you could possibly be doing in Zurich that is more important than the capture of this madman. He has created a major ecological disaster in California, an environmental slate wiper. Hundreds of people have died since he entered this country, thousands more may die on the West Coast."

"Good day, Mr. Brognola," Mulligan repeated, and turned away.

"Rennie Dennison," Brognola said, and Mulligan swung back around, the gun pointed at waist level.

"Are you threatening me with that gun?" Brognola asked.

"This gun?" Mulligan said, suddenly bringing it up to target Brognola's forehead, a scowl on his face as he pulled back the hammer.

Just as suddenly it was gone, bingo, lying beside him on the loading table. "I'm not threatening anybody," he said. "I'm just trying to inform you of the fragility of our enterprise and hope that you have the good sense and foresight to appreciate our position."

"I want to contact Dennison. I want to find out the real name of the Vulture."

"And I'm saying no."

"Okay," Brognola said. "I wanted to appeal to your better nature, but you don't have one." The big Fed smiled slightly. Paybacks were great. "I know about Dennison, quite the computer hacker he was until getting forty years in a federal jail for selling stolen national secrets to the North Koreans. How did you manage to get him out? Some sort of executive order that wasn't really signed by the Chief Executive or even anybody close to him, I'd venture. The forms from Joliet are being faxed to my office right now. Do you really want me to go public with this?"

"That sounds like treason," Mulligan said, his eyes drifting to the gun on the table. "This all falls under the umbrella of national security."

The man was still looking at the gun. Brognola had had enough. "If you're thinking about picking up that gun again, you'd better be ready to drop the hammer on me, because otherwise I'm going to take it away from me and give you a tonsilectomy with the barrel. And I mean it, Colonel. You get my meaning?"

The man looked hard at him for a moment, then nodded.

"Now tell me how to contact Dennison."

Mulligan's shoulders drooped slightly. "We usually use a dead drop," he said, "but he's got a room in Zurich." He went resignedly into his jacket hanging on the slab and pulled out a phone log.

"I want you to okay contact," Brognola said, and Mulligan nodded again. "And don't do anything to get in the way of this or I'll see you busted down to washroom attendant. Thank you very much for the information. You're doing our country a great service. Good day, sir."

"Good day," Mulligan said.

Brognola started to walk off, then turned around and looked at the man. "Why do they call you Red?" he asked.

The man shrugged. "It just sounded like a good nickname so I started using it."

BOLAN PACED, his eyes glued to the motel television as he talked to Hal Brognola on the headset. "Aaron says there's nothing, no trace at all."

"He's skipped," Hal said.

"How soon can you get me out of here?"

"It's eleven now. First flight out is 7:00 a.m. California time."

"What's the time difference there?"

"Six hours later than Washington time."

"That'll have me arrive in the middle of the night."

He stared at the television, watching footage of FEMA crews in burn suits trying desperately to contain the spill until it could be cleaned up. All the while gamma rays from the high-energy decay of used plutonium rods were pulsing from the spill at the speed of light, disrupting every living cell they came in contact with, overpowering in their intensity. Invisible. Deadly. People were dying already of radiation poisoning and would be joined by more. The first emergency crews on the scene were unprepared for a radioactive spill, and their bodies were still being carted away from several miles of highway in both directions. He'd probably gotten a good dose himself.

People were on the move, being evacuated, and Bolan was in Fresno, two hundred miles to the north. Even he could hardly believe the Vulture's handiwork, even though this kind of possibility always existed.

"You know he's going to be dangerous on his own ground," Brognola warned. "You also know I can't predict how the agent in Zurich will work with you. If he's anything like his boss..."

"I know. Hal, I don't care. I'm going to end this and be done with it. He's a monster walking the earth in human form, and I'm going to stop it. Thanks for the address, buddy. I'm sure Mr. Dennison and I will get along just fine."

"I'm not going to tell you to be careful," Brognola said, "just smart. Don't let your own rage get in the way of your jungle sense."

"I'll get the job done," Bolan said. "One way or the other. See ya, Hal."

"Yeah."

They cut contact. On the screen the death count rose to over two hundred. Bolan's rage was cold and deliberate. Nothing would stop him.

CHAPTER ELEVEN

Castle von Maur, Swiss Alps
July 21, Sunset

The Vulture sat beside Mulroy as he drove the open-topped Bugatti up the winding, protected road to his "family" castle. Purchased ten years previously from the broke and dissolute heirs to the place, he had legitimately bought the family name along with its environs. His new name was Baron Karl von Maur. His status was that of a demigod, for the town could not exist except for the baron, who kept it busy working for him, either in his castle, his private army or in the small chemical-fertilizer plant on the edge of town.

Below him, several miles beneath the snow line, sat the town of Maur, the family's traditional barony. Just to the west, was the magnificent Saint Bernard Pass, where both the Roman Legions and Napoleon had driven their armies and where Napoleon's famous artillery pieces were transported over the snow-covered gorge by a system of pulleys the little Cor-

sican had invented himself. Even the von Maur castle
had begun as a Roman fortress, Octoduras, con-
structed by General Servius Galba under Julius Cae-
sar's orders.

The pass was no longer in use. The roadway system
now tunneled beneath, and the Saint Bernard dogs no
longer carried brandy casks to lost travelers. But the
Vulture felt himself the heir to a lineage of famous
warriors who'd conquered these hills. It was right and
fitting that he be their master.

They continued upward, beyond the trees surrounding Maur and into the altitudes where the snow never
melted. The chill air was bracing in the open car. Here
they passed the first checkpoint, one in a series of
fortified bunkers developed from the remnants of Galba's original stone fortifications that extended, at broken intervals, around the entire peak.

The sun was dipping low, the magnificent, snow-
covered Alps effused with a warm glow all around
him.

"I love it when we come home," the Vulture said,
waving to the armed guards at the checkpoint as they
passed.

"I wish we'd taken the chopper up," Mulroy said.
"It's too damned cold around here. Man, I'd take the
beach in Galveston any day."

"You know people live longer in cold climates than
in hot."

"That's because only the strong ones stay there,"

Mulroy answered. "You know, I'm not sure you're right about being set up. I mean, couldn't they have just been conducting some kind of normal checking or something—?"

"First of all," the Vulture said, "I don't make a habit of saying something I haven't thought through completely and know that I'm right. Secondly I wasn't selected randomly or indiscriminately. They were looking for my passport, and when they found it, half the police in America were waiting there to arrest me. No, Willy, unfortunately someone betrayed me. The question is—who?"

"Maybe it was someone in the platoon," Mulroy returned. "If so, we don't have to worry about it because they're all dead."

"My dear Willy. You're long on heart and loyalty but short on intelligence. A person doesn't snitch on his associate, then go out and die for that associate. The platoon proved its loyalty by dying to a man."

Mulroy shrugged. "I don't know, then."

"You'd better know. I'm making it your job to find out who it was, and I mean quickly. The wine festival is in three days. I don't want any trouble connected with it."

"What kind of trouble?"

"Whoever betrayed me, betrayed me first to someone in this country. We're going to find that person, too. This must be tidied up. Then there's the matter of the big man."

"The big man's dead," Mulroy said. "Shot and run over."

"Did the man who told you that ever show up at the motel?"

"No, but—"

"They know something about me. They'll come for me. *He'll* come for me." He laid two fingers to his temple, right beside the patch, rubbing gently. "I can feel him…here. I want you to hire more men."

The road narrowed, spiraling lazily upward around the rocky hillside, the distant peak of the Matterhorn coming into view ten miles to the east.

"It may not be possible to find the snitch and his contact in three days," Mulroy said.

"I have faith in you, Willy," the Vulture said, patting the man on the shoulder as they passed the second checkpoint, a siege line of sharpened logs and razor wire one hundred yards across, with fortified-iron gates. Fully a dozen men in the traditional Swiss mercenary uniform of red and white with a bearskin cap saluted as the gates were opened. Their laser-sighted automatic weapons, though, were anything but traditional.

The castle walls loomed ahead, tall and imposing with towering spires on three sides and bowman notches on the battlements. Thrusting itself out of solid rock, the castle merged with the peak like a magnificent sculpture by a cosmic artist.

Snow lay everywhere, snow and a stunning vista,

shrouded by darkness now. Mulroy shivered beside him. Even the Vulture felt the chill as they drove through the open castle gates and into the huge, wide courtyard with the chopper pad in the center.

Servants ran out to get their luggage when they pulled to a stop before the great hall. Light spilled from a mammoth cathedral doorway, silhouetting the troops milling about.

An old, stooped servant in red livery moved into the doorway, snifter in hand, to smile at his benefactor. "Welcome home, Baron. We have missed you."

"Thank you, Mr. Schwander." The Vulture stepped into the vestibule and took the brandy from the old man. "I can't tell you how good it is to be home."

"A successful trip, I hope?"

"Not especially."

They walked into the great hall where roaring fires spilled warmth from fireplaces at each end. Mulroy ran immediately to the west fireplace to warm himself. Dozens of sofas and chairs arranged in conversation groups filled half the hall, and the other half contained dining tables for up to one hundred people. Other rooms opened from the mezzanine above.

"You had a special-delivery package today," Mr. Schwander said as he followed his employer down the hall. "A very special package."

"Where?"

"The study, Baron."

The Vulture charged through the vaulted arches of

the side chambers and tore open the study door. A brown parcel rested on an easel in the center of the room.

The office was modern, with electronic communications equipment and a large mainframe computer featuring his own compiled data base on the governments and mercenaries of the world. Not even Interpol got near his knowledge base.

He ran to the large television next to his teak desk and turned it on. It was tuned to CNN news. The spill in California and the various details of assigning responsibility, the trail of counterfeit bills and customs involvement were hot on the agenda. What he didn't see was an arrest report on Verna Cassabian. Good.

He moved back to the package and carefully started to open it as U.S. government officials droned on about bringing the infamous "Vulture" to justice. He'd been hearing that for years. They even showed his New York mug shot on-screen. Unflattering.

What they'd never know was the true story—the story about using the shoddy lawyer to get word to his people to make the breakout spectacular. His real plans had ended the second he'd stepped off the plane at Kennedy Airport. Everything from the arrest on had been improvisation. If he couldn't succeed with the Iraqis on the money issue, at least he'd raise his market value by the scope of his audacious terrorism and the beauty of his escape—a seaplane waiting in Santa Barbara; quick flight to Santa Cruz Island's airstrip and the chartered Learjet; on to Midway Island, Tokyo and Bombay for refueling before landing in Zurich. He'd caught up on his sleep and was now totally refreshed and clear of mind. All in all, things could be much worse.

He gently pulled the paper from the package, his breath catching in his throat at the sight of the painting. It was his favorite Degas, *Foyer de la Danse,* all muted pastels and dramatic lighting in the artist's oft-used locale, the ballet. The Vulture was a sentimentalist at heart, and Degas's loving and generous approach to his subjects always touched him. He was the world's major collector of Impressionist art, the most exciting period of art history in the world to him—before the camera had been developed, forcing the artist to shun reality and invent interpretation.

Unfortunately very few people got to see his collection. Most of it was stolen from the great museums of the world. He'd commissioned this theft just two weeks before from the Louvre.

"It's beautiful, Baron," Mr. Schwander said.

"Yes," the Vulture whispered low. "How are the preparations for the festival gala coming?"

"While not as efficient as when the baron is on the premises, we have done our best to keep in step with the necessary arrangements. By the way, the English duchess and Count and Countess Wolfstein have accepted their invitations."

"Excellent."

"And there's one more thing," Mr. Schwander said. "Do you remember that American actress you met at Cannes last year—Kimberly Adams?"

"Oh, yes. I remember Miss Adams."

"She rang us up earlier today and said she'd been displaced by the nuclear spill in California and was, as she put it, 'looking for some place to escape to for a couple of days.' I took the liberty of extending your hospitality. She will arrive tomorrow."

The Vulture turned and smiled at the man. "How fitting," he said. "What irony."

"Sir?"

"Never mind. You always anticipate me, Mr. Schwander. I like that in an associate. Good initiative."

"Thank you, Baron."

"Not at all," the Vulture replied, letting the picture wash over his senses, almost smelling the perfume and sweat of the rehearsal studio circa 1872. He loved art. It breathed individual genius. Besides, paintings were portable assets not tied to any one currency. A good investment for someone in his position.

BOLAN PAID THE CABDRIVER in Swiss francs and emerged out of the small Peugeot onto the glittery street. It was almost 2:00 a.m., and the street crowds had started to thin out as late-night Zurich folded up.

He'd arrived at the downtown Hilton barely thirty minutes before, checked in, then come right over to the operator's address. Time was of the essence. If the Vulture had returned to Switzerland, he needed to be taken out and quick. If he hadn't returned, he needed to be ambushed when he did. Bolan was in the man's lair. Time was on *his* side now.

He wasn't armed. Stony Man had sent his harness and ordnance along in the diplomatic pouch, and he wouldn't be able to pick them up until the morning.

He walked Langstrasse, crowded with restaurants and bars. Like most cities, Zurich rose high and narrow, like the mountains. The six-story buildings were lined up right next to each other, and their narrowness heightened the densely built-up appearance. Langstrasse was the entertainment center for a city that basically rolled over and died at 4:30 p.m. every day when all the commuters left their city jobs and went home to the country.

There were Turkish delicatessens, Italian travel agencies and Hong Kong secondhand and shoe shops. The restaurants were exotic, and the bars looked very much like American discos of the seventies.

Hookers from every country of the world worked the streets, but they didn't approach Bolan. Street people always understood when someone else was on the street doing business. The limos of the pimps cruised slowly up and down, some of them nearly stopping beside him only to speed up and move along.

He found the small apartment block near the intersection with Hohistrasse. It was five stories of straight gray stone with ornamented wooden shutters painted a sky blue.

He looked up into the chill but comfortable night sky, seeing a light burning from a fourth-floor window. Dennison's address was 4-B.

Bolan moved through the doorway set on the side of the building and scanned the narrow stairs leading up to narrow landings. He moved catlike, the wooden stairs barely creaking beneath his light touch. On the fourth floor he walked to the first door he saw at the head of the stairs. It was 4-A. There were two apartments per floor. The light was coming from Dennison's flat.

He moved quietly down the hall to 4-B and knocked softly. "Dennison," he whispered, and the sliver of light shining under the door disappeared immediately. "Dennison. I'm from the colonel."

He listened but there was no answer.

"I know you're in there," he said. "I saw your light. I just want to talk. Mulligan has contacted you about me."

Again silence was the only response.

He reached out and touched the knob. It turned easily in his hand, and the door swung open to a dark room.

"Dennison," Bolan said, reaching around the door frame to find the light switch. "We don't have time for this."

He stepped partway in, switching on the light just

in time to see an iron bar blurring in an arc right toward his head.

GILA BEND, ARIZONA, WAS a dusty, sleepy town just off the interstate in the south part of the state, all flat desert and small clusters of mountains. It was a blinker—one blink and you could miss it completely.

Verna Cassabian, in a black wig, frowned at the 105-degree heat beating through the windshield of her rented car as she pulled into the parking lot of the Iguana Motel and turned off the engine.

She'd pulled her Ford Taurus right beside the maroon Cadillac, Ari's car, and hauled the suitcase and the briefcase out of the trunk, carrying them to the door.

It opened without her knocking. She hefted the bags inside room 130 of the one-story motel. It looked like just what the sign outside advertised—a ten-dollar-a-night room, complete with vibrating bed.

Ari smiled warmly at her from behind his large, black frame glasses. Tariz, bald and staid looking, perched uncomfortably watching a baseball game on the television. His eyes jumped quickly to the suitcase, then back to the television. The suitcase contained the twenty million dollars in counterfeit currency left behind by the Vulture, and in the briefcase was the million paid to Cassabian for her safehouse.

She'd cut a deal. If everything fell just right, she could come out of this on her feet, like a cat.

Ari had moved to the window to peer out into the parking lot and surrounding desert. Those were the only names she'd ever heard them called. First names, always. Nothing more. She wondered what their real names were.

"So, you've come to us," Ari said, "to return our money."

"To *fence* your money," Verna said. "And ten cents on the dollar for paper of this quality seems to be a wonderful deal for you, too."

"Indeed it is. More than fair. We can either use our own means to pass it or resell in bulk at a decent price."

"Get on with it," Tariz said, turning off the television with a remote. He walked to her and took the suitcase out of her hands to lay on the bed. "Ask her how she managed to get away."

"I was being questioned," she answered, looking at Ari, whose face was kind, gentle. "Everything was in a mess, cops and neighbors everywhere. They were trying to question me on the scene...I was busy playin' innocent victim, when the warning horns went off and the loudspeakers came on. Everybody scattered. I'd stashed the suitcase and valise when Charlie left. I just grabbed them and walked away. Then I called you. I had to cash a few of the bills for expenses."

"Why did the man leave the suitcase behind when he left?" Tariz asked. "He knew he was driving into an ambush. He wasn't coming back."

"I wondered about that," Cassabian said, perching on a chair. She nervously got a cigarette out of her handbag. "He knew it was counterfeit. Why take it?"

"For the same reasons we're standing here," Ari said, asserting authority. "Have you opened the bag?"

"Yeah. I'd seen the cash in it before, but I wanted to check and make sure it was still there. I grabbed a few bills, then shut it up and haven't opened it since. Honest. I only took...fifteen hundred. You can deduct that from my payment."

"I want you to open it again," Ari said softly.

"Sure." She shrugged, walking to the suitcase.

"Not yet," Ari instructed, and moved to the front door, Tariz hurrying out with him.

"Now," he said, and closed the door from the outside, leaving Verna alone in the room. She moved to the suitcase without further thought and opened it. It was still stuffed with banded hundred-dollar bills.

"Yoo-hoo!" she called. "You can come in now."

The door opened slowly as the men peered around it. They didn't come in until they saw the open suitcase on the bed.

They went up to it, staring down. "Amazing," Ari said. "It really has come back to us."

"Now, how about my payoff?" Verna asked.

"Your payoff," Ari said, and pulled the small .22 out of his shark-skin jacket. The silencer was already attached.

"I...I don't understand," Verna said, suddenly feeling extremely cold. She shivered.

Ari pointed the gun at her. "You have achieved a miraculous thing," he said. "You have brought this gift to us with no trail attached. No one will ever know about the money. It could be in the possession of the Vulture, it could have been confiscated and kept under wraps. Nobody knows. Except you. The paper trail ends with you, the only other logical person who could have also had it. If you disappear completely, and believe me you will, everyone who doesn't believe the other explanations will assume you took it and ran away. It's so perfect."

"But my husband...your friendship—"

"Your husband was scum, a liar with no honor," Ari said. "And I mean that with all due respect. He cheated us. I drowned him myself in your swimming pool."

Tariz, grinning broadly, looked into the case, stuck his hands in, fingers tracing down the stacks of bundled cash. "I still can't believe he left it behind," he said, grabbing out two handfuls of banded bills. "I still don't und—"

He felt return pressure on the wads of bills and looked down, too late, to see the trip wire.

There was a click, a small hum, then a flash of

tremendous intensity as the deadly barbed tentacles of the Vulture reached out and exacted vengeance on the Arizona desert in the middle of a scorching afternoon. Instant karma.

The bodies were vaporized and never identified.

CHAPTER TWELVE

Bolan ducked easily under the path of the iron bar, then came around with an elbow to the side of the head as the attacker's momentum carried him right past Bolan.

He connected solidly on the man's temple. The stunning blow sent him sprawling, the fight already out of him, to the floor. The man appeared to be in his early twenties, with shoulder-length hair, and his wire-rim glasses lay beside him from the fall.

"Please don't hurt me," he moaned, his arms wrapped around his head as Bolan bent down to pick up the weapon—a fireplace poker.

"You were trying to kill me," Bolan replied, touching the man's ribs with the poker. "Get up."

The man rolled away slightly, trying to keep some distance between himself and Bolan. He stood on shaky legs, the right side of his face all red and puffy. He'd have a hell of a bruise by morning.

The apartment looked narrow and deep. It was jammed full of sophisticated computer gear and transmission equipment, including a cryptophone. Bolan had definitely come to the right place.

"Where's Dennison?" Bolan asked, holding up the poker. "You've got about five seconds to tell me before I use this on you."

"I...I'm Dennison," the man said, gingerly rubbing his face. He sat at his small kitchen table on a wooden chair, offering the other to Bolan.

Bolan sat, leaning the poker up against the table. "If you're Dennison, why did you try and bash my brains in?"

"To get you out of my damned life," Dennison answered. "Believe me, killing you would be my only viable option in this situation."

"I think you've got some explaining to do."

"Do you mind if I make some coffee while we talk? I...need a cup."

"Go ahead," Bolan said.

Dennison got up and began working with an old-style percolator. "Where do you want me to start?"

"Start with Mulligan. I assume he got in touch with you."

"Over the scrambler."

"What did he tell you?"

"That someone from the Justice Department would be coming to my flat to talk about the Vulture."

"That's all he said?"

The man shrugged. "It was enough. Once my name got revealed, I was cooked. He's very powerful. That information will find its way back to him, and he'll kill me."

"The Vulture, you mean?"

"Yeah. And my work here's not even finished yet. Not that it matters now. I'm out of here first chance. I didn't hire on to get killed."

"No, you hired on to get out of prison. What, exactly, is your work?"

The percolator was already on the gas burner, and Dennison sat across the table from Bolan. "Kind of eclectic, really. I've been able to access the top five Zurich banks and eavesdrop a bit. All on the periphery. My machines listen in on and intercept electronic transfers of funds from America into the numbered accounts. As you know, the Swiss don't share their financial data with anyone willingly. So we use the back door. When unusually large amounts of cash start coming in, there is generally reason to suspect something illegal happening on the American side. It's kind of an investigative tool. Domestic branches use the information as a starting point in asking for federal wiretaps and surveillance."

Bolan sat back and stared at the man. He was looking at some lower-level computer nerd whose job was to sit in Zurich and try to drum up business for the FBI in America.

"What the hell does any of this have to do with the Vulture?"

"Absolutely nothing."

"Nothing," Bolan repeated. "Don't make me work for this, kid. How did you come up with your information?"

Dennison shrugged, looking at his glasses, now bent at an impossible angle. He twisted them back into shape and put them on his face, slightly askew. "I lead a solitary life," he said. "In this job…well, I guess you already understand the dangers of becoming too close to people."

The Executioner understood.

"I have no friends, no social life at all. I drink at a bar down the street, called Der Stein, occasionally make conversation with the regulars."

The coffee was perking dark brown now, and he jumped up to turn off the burner and pour them each a cup. "A few months back one of the regulars took a real liking to me and wanted to talk a lot. He's a printer, and it turns out he prints more than just restaurant menus."

Dennison paused to sip his coffee. "He has underworld connections and has a pretty good traffic in fake passports and identity cards. All hidden assets. The Swiss love hidden assets. He eventually took me into his confidence and told me he had just made a phony passport for the Vulture, one of his best clients. A few questions later I had all the pertinent data. It was serendipity."

"Why do you think he told you?"

"He's like me...lonely, friendless. When you've got hot news, you want to tell somebody."

"So, who is the Vulture?" Bolan asked, not quite believing the story. The printer-forger and his chance meeting with Dennison seemed too coincidental to be true. And if Dennison was as afraid of the Vulture as he acted, why had he turned the man in at all? There had to be something else, but Bolan decided to play along for a while.

"His real name, I don't know," Dennison said. "But if you promise to leave me alone after this, I'll tell you the name he 'owns' here in Switzerland."

"You're an NSC operative engaged in clandestine activity illegal in the country in which you are residing," Bolan said. "I'm not going to leave you alone. I might need your help."

"Go to hell."

Face set hard, Bolan grabbed Dennison's shirt and hauled him close. His blue eyes bored into the younger man with chilling coldness.

"I pretty well have a free hand when the stakes are this high. If you value your hide, you'd better tell what you know right now."

Dennison was convinced and went pale. He'd heard truth and determination in the voice. He nodded, and when Bolan released him, he slumped into his chair.

"Hey...sure man," Dennison said. "Anything you say."

"The Vulture, Rennie. Tell me about the Vulture."

"Sure...sure. Like I said, I don't know his real name, but he bought the lands and title of the von Maur family a number of years ago."

"The local authorities don't know who he really is?"

The man shrugged. "It doesn't matter whether they do or not. They wouldn't do anything to him anyway."

"Why not?"

"You don't know much about Switzerland's history, do you?"

"Chocolate," Bolan said. "Cuckoo clocks. Neutrality."

Dennison straightened his shirt, then once again tried to fix his glasses. "Because the Swiss are neutral, everyone assumes they are peaceful. But since the Middle Ages the Swiss have been a country of professional soldiers, and have fought for one side or the other in every major European war for the last thousand years without those wars touching them. Military service is mandatory here, and men can be called to active service up till the age of fifty."

"So they like mercs," Bolan said.

"It's always been a respectable profession to the people here."

"Where can I find him?"

"The city of Maur is south of here, in the Alps, a region they called the Valais. Castle von Maur is located on a high peak, within easy sight of Saint Bernard Pass."

"How far away is that?"

"Nothing's very far away in Switzerland. Something like 125 miles. They have a fine railway system running out of Zurich to most of the country. If you go down to the main station—"

"Do you have a car, Rennie?"

"I'm not going to lend you my car."

"How right you are. You're going to drive me."

Dennison stared at him. He may have been a jerk, but he was nobody's fool. Bolan could almost see the wheels turning behind his eyes and resolved to always keep a close eye on him.

"Look, I'm just a hacker...what should I call you?"

"Belasko. Mike Belasko."

"I'm a hacker, Mike. One of those guys in high school who always wore glasses and had pocket protectors for their twenty pens. I've never fired a gun in my life...hell, I've never even been in a fight."

"Except for tonight."

The man put a hand to the rapidly darkening welt on his right temple, wincing with the pain.

"You should get some ice on that," Bolan said. "It'll help."

"*I'll* be on ice if you drag me along," Dennison said. "You look in my eyes, check me out and listen to me. I'm a coward. I have no desire or intention of involving myself in a military operation. How many men have you got?"

"It's just you and me."

"Just you and me," Dennison repeated softly, his eyes locked on the Executioner's.

"I went to Maur for the wine festival last year," Dennison said. "A holiday, just getting away for a couple of days. You can see von Maur's castle quite well from the village. It's an operational fortress guarded by a private army that sits at the top of a mountain."

"I've always liked the Alps," Bolan replied, now seeing nothing but honesty coming from the kid's eyes. "And everybody's a coward, Rennie. It's situations that force us to be otherwise, self-preservation and all that."

"I don't believe in any of this. It's not my concern."

"I don't care."

"You won't be able to depend on me. I might freeze up or run or something."

"Remember your own theories," Bolan said. He moved toward the door. "The Vulture will not let you get out of the country alive. He'll have his people watching all the booked flights, looking for somebody who doesn't belong. Like you said, Rennie— He's going to get you...*unless* I can get to him first. Where are you parked?"

"Down the block. I—"

"Let's go then," Bolan said, and was out the door and down the stairs.

The man was right: he'd be no good to Bolan in a combat situation, but he wasn't ready to turn the man loose yet. There were still secrets, pieces that didn't match up. For example, given the nature of Rennie Dennison, he would have never jeopardized himself and turned in the Vulture to begin with. He was, after all, a man who had sold national secrets for money to an enemy of the United States.

No, there was something more at work here, something more complex.

THEY'D DRIVEN National Highway 9 in a cramped Alfa Romeo all the way to Sion, the canton's capital, then took the small local roads from there for the short trip to Maur. The Valais, Latin for "valley," eighty miles long, was nestled in the chain formed by the Valaisan and Bernese Alps.

Mountains surrounded them everywhere on their drive, fifty one of them soaring over fourteen thousand feet. It was beautiful but claustrophobic.

They pulled into Maur just before nine in the morning as early light was beginning to wink over the mountains. Maur was a typical medieval town of stone houses and narrow, winding streets meant to confound and contain enemy attacks. It was backed up against a mountain and would have looked forboding had it not been for the Swiss practice of using brightly decorated window shutters with flower boxes attached.

"I'll give you a notion of the people here," Dennison said. The whole right side of his face was an ugly purple-and-yellow bruise. "The local hero around here is a guy named Farinet who decided the government had no right to monopolize the money supply and started counterfeiting his own. He was killed in a hail of police bullets. They write songs and books about him. This is a different world, Belasko."

"Pull over," Bolan directed just before they entered the center of the town.

Dennison complied, pulling the Alfa into the weed-choked shoulder of the one-lane country road.

The mountain rose majestically above the city, and atop it, thousands of feet above them and covered in snow, loomed a fantasyland castle of towering spires and vast battlements. It fairly glowed in the first rosy glow of morning light.

"That's it," Dennison said. "That's the Vulture's aerie. He and a couple hundred of his closest armed associates enjoy all the comforts of home there."

Bolan shook his head. Here was a monster for whose life a sewer would be a much better metaphor, yet he had been granted seemingly unassailable heights.

"Looks like your buddy is home, too," Dennison said.

"How do you know that?"

"See the flag flying atop the highest spire?"

Bolan pulled Dennison's binoculars from the glove box, wishing he'd have waited a few extra hours before making the trip to Maur. He still hadn't retrieved his gear from the consulate. He focused on the tall spire.

The flag was huge, maybe as big as a house, and rippled stiffly in the hard wind that blew up that high. The flag was black, its center icon a clenched fist.

"Whenever the baron is in," Dennison said, "the flag is flown. Kind of like the Queen of England."

"I'll be a son of a bitch," Bolan whispered. "The man's arrogance has no boundaries."

"And why not?" Dennison chortled. "Even Swiss television is dominated by the nuclear spill. Not one of those idiots we call servants of the people back home was able to stop him."

Bolan slowly lowered the glasses and turned his head toward a grinning Dennison. "I'm about thirty seconds away from the end of my patience."

The man began to speak, stopped, his eyes widening in sudden understanding. "I didn't mean anything personal, you know. If you were involved with the attempt at...you know, capturing... I mean, you've got to kind of respect somebody who can get away with what he got away with, no reflection on any *one* individual intended."

Bolan grabbed the man's lapels and pulled him

close. "He hasn't gotten away with anything," he snarled.

"That flag tells me different."

"That flag tells me I'm only a mile or two from that other eye," the Executioner said, shoving Dennison away from him.

Dennison straightened himself out. "I assume when you talk about the other eye, you mean it just as a...symbol, right?"

Bolan just stared at the man.

"Oh, my God," Dennison whispered. "What have I gotten myself into?"

"You should have asked yourself that question the day you decided to break into Department of Defense computers," Bolan said. "I want a closer look."

"You're the boss," Dennison said, driving off down to the cobbled street entering the city. It was barely wide enough for the car to squeeze through.

There seemed to be a lot of people in the streets, a lot of cars blocking progress. The town square was full of people when they reached it, with long tables set up outside. Dennison parked near the city's one church, its steeple tall, its Gothic origins in keeping with the rest of the town.

"I think we can get a pretty good look just on the other side of town," Dennison said. "I seem to recall a field that gives an unobstructed—"

"I want closer than that, higher."

"You ever do any climbing?"

"Some. I know the rudiments. How about you?"

"I've been here two years," the man answered. "You learn to do everything Swiss in two years. We'll need gear. You got money?"

Bolan nodded. "Where are we going to make the climb?"

"I'll show you," Dennison replied. "Let's get out."

"What's going on around here?" Bolan asked as they climbed out of the car. "Seems busy."

"Remember I talked about the wine festival? It starts in a couple of days. It's the biggest time of the year in Maur. The baron throws a big party for the town, then has his own private party in the castle. It's a good time."

"I'm so glad you enjoy it," Bolan said, frowning. "It might be a good cover for us, though."

"For *us*?"

"Yeah," Bolan said, walking off. "Show me where we're going to climb."

Dennison hurried to catch up to him. "A couple of things before we get into this," he said, getting beside Bolan. "First be careful what you say and who you say it to. Quite frankly your nemesis owns this town and everybody in it. Anyone here would turn you in without a second thought. We're lucky, in fact, that it's festival time. There'll be a lot of strangers in town, and people won't be so suspicious."

"What else?"

"They call themselves independent in the Valais, which gives them a certain license. They'll say or do anything they choose. If you tell them you love Zurich, they'll tell you what's wrong with it. If you tell them you hate Zurich, they'll tell you how wonderful it is. But don't let that make you think they're free thinkers. The people of this village have lived off the welfare of the von Maurs for six hundred years. Being owned is part of their heritage. Get it?"

"Yeah," Bolan said, shaking his head. "I get it."

He was following Dennison now, who was leading him out of town and a half mile into the countryside into a field of millet. They got a different angle, and were approaching a piece of the large mountain that had splintered off hundreds of millions of years ago and now sat nearly a mile from its larger cousin. It wasn't quite as tall, but almost, and seemed easily scaleable.

"They call it the Little Madam. It's a favorite of beginning climbers in the area because you can take it in various degrees of difficulty. The side we're looking at slopes upward before the real climbing starts. The other side of the Little Madam is a sheer wall of rock."

"Let's take the easy way up," Bolan said, knowing that nothing was easy.

"Fine," the man replied. "Why don't you stay here and I'll go to town and purchase our gear?"

Bolan shook his head. "No way, partner. Until I'm through with you, we're joined at the hip."

"You worry too much. If I want to get rid of you, I'll just let you fall off the mountain."

CHAPTER THIRTEEN

The mountain was a lot taller than it had looked from the ground, and climbing had become a lot more difficult once they'd hit the snow line. The slope was steeper, handholds nonexistent.

"Hurry it up!" Dennison called from thirty feet below, dangling from the tether line holding them together. "I want to get up there before I'm old enough to collect social security."

"Dead men can't collect anything," Bolan responded.

They were nearly to the peak. Bolan was kicking out hard, the metal spikes of the crampons attached to his climbing boots digging in hard. "We're getting there," he called back. "Be patient."

"No worries there, chum. I'm protecting some hot property with these pants. Speaking of hot...I wish we had some coffee."

Bolan smiled despite himself. For all the man's obnoxiousness, he was an excellent climber and worked well in the teamwork situation, willing to let them move at a safe, if a bit slow, pace.

Bolan used the snow ax to chip away at the ice just beside his head. It was solid. He pulled out a ringed piton, hammered it to get it started, then screwed it into the solid ice until just the ringed end was exposed. Then he clicked a snap link onto the piton and made sure the rope attached to the snap link was pulled taut.

"Come on up!" he called.

Dennison immediately kicked out from the ice and climbed it in huge leaps, feeding rope back through to dangle beneath him. He was beside Bolan in seconds.

"Are we having fun yet?" he asked.

"How long to the top?" Bolan asked, looking up, his masked and goggled face peering up at what still seemed an endless expanse of ice. It was cold, numbing even through four layers of clothing.

"Fifteen minutes," Dennison said, smiling, enjoying being in control. "I'll go ahead and scramble up from here. We're getting a nice inward slope now. I'll throw you back a line."

"I'm going up with you," Bolan said, and they retrieved their ropes and wrapped them around their shoulders. Using nothing but ax and crampons, they scurried up the long wall of ice, Bolan feeling the fatigue in his thighs and upper arms.

Just when it was becoming unbearable, they crested

the peak to stand on a broad plain several hundred yards wide, broken by minipeaks and gullies. Bolan was amazed to find a crude stone hut sitting on the castle side of the peak.

"What's that?"

"Did you think you were the first person to climb the Little Madam?" Dennison asked, sitting atop a rock and taking a long breath. "This is a beginners' peak, remember? The house is for people like us who take too long to climb up and have to spend the night like we're going to have to do."

"Good," Bolan said, walking in that direction, mesmerized by what he saw beyond.

Castle von Maur sat barely a mile away, only slightly more elevated. It was huge, massive, its high walls seemingly a part of the mountain itself.

He dug through his backpack and brought out the binoculars, focusing on the walls. They teemed with activity, guards with automatic weapons. The spires were topped by rooms, but he couldn't see within them well enough to know if they were defensive bunkers or simply real estate.

He glanced quickly at his watch. Barely 5:00 p.m. "It gets dark so quick," he said.

"Listen," Dennison said, "there are towns in these hills that are in shade nearly ten months a year because of the mountains. Think about that."

Bolan continued to scan the target area, deepening the focus to examine the main hall, located in the rear of the castle grounds and built into the face of the hill.

The top of the main hall had balconies that overlooked the city below. One of the balconies was occupied. He hit the focus, and the face of the Vulture sharpened into definition. The man stood casually, in suit and tie, holding a brandy snifter in his hand. He was gazing down at the village below.

All at once he jerked, his head snapping to look across at the sister peak. He stared hard, and if the Executioner's binoculars had been a rifle scope, he would have shot the man right between the eyes.

THE VULTURE HAD FELT the pain stab straight through his eye and into his brain as he stood in his favorite spot on the balcony. It sent a spasm through him, and he looked at the Little Madam. From there. The pain came from there. Could it be? Could the big man actually be this close already?

"This is beautiful, Baron," came the female voice from his study.

He turned, forcing the pain into the back of his mind and walked in from the balcony, a smile on his face. The actress was studying his Degas. She wore a clinging red gown, subtle red, that showed off the highlights of her strawberry blond hair. In fact it showed off a lot of highlights.

"An amazing man, Degas." The Vulture moved up beside her, their bodies barely touching, giving off heat. "He's a link between static Classicism and the movement of modern art. You see here, we have what would be a scene of action—the musician, the dance instructor, the ballerina—yet they have stopped their motion, the instructor halting things in midaction to make a criticism. Static action. Fascinating."

"I don't understand a thing you just said," Kimberly Adams replied, "but I just love the soft emotions of the thing."

"I, also," he said, lifting his drink. "Allow me to make a toast—to the most beautiful woman who has ever gazed upon this painting."

"How romantic." The woman smiled, catlike, and raised her glass of white wine.

"I've been thinking about you since Cannes last year," she said.

"I'm flattered," the Vulture replied. "You, also, have occupied my thoughts on many sleepless nights. It gets very lonely up here sometimes."

"I don't see how." She moved around the office, walking out onto the balcony herself. "It's like a storybook here. This is the most spectacular view I've ever seen. I think if I lived here I'd feel like a princess every morning when I woke up. Isn't it strange that it took a tragedy to bring us together?"

He joined her on the balcony, the pain hitting him the moment he walked out of the safety of his office. "A wise man turns chance into good fortune," he replied, slipping an arm around her waist.

She turned to him, fitting herself against him. "I don't know if I've ever thanked you properly for taking me in."

"Well, you know we believe in being proper here in the Alps," the Vulture responded, his eye socket throbbing painfully. The big man *was* here. He was!

She took his face in her hands and brought his lips to hers, a long, lingering kiss.

It would come down to a confrontation, man to man, and in Maur, a new legend would be born.

He pulled her fiercely to him, grinding his lips against hers, his pain and madness and passion flowing from one to the other. The woman, eyes wide, pushed herself away from him.

"Whoa, tiger," she said. "I'm hot to trot, but I like to be warmed up first. Let's notch it down a frame or two, okay?"

"I fear my passion for you overtook me," he said. "You now know just how much I've thought about you since Cannes. My sincerest apologies."

"Baron—"

"'Karl'...please."

She nodded. "Don't worry, Karl," she said, eyes flashing. "I *like* dangerous men, and you are nothing if not dangerous. It should be an interesting few days."

"My thoughts exactly," he replied, then turned to see Mr. Schwander standing in the doorway, something in his hand. "What is it?"

"Miss Adams's arrival made me realize that your passport has expired," he said, holding up the small booklet. "You'll need to renew if you plan on going to Cannes again."

The Vulture rolled his eye. "Give it to Mulroy. We have a man in Zurich who takes—" He stopped talking, his mind moving to Zurich and Jost Sprecher, the best forger he'd ever seen. And the worst drunk. Drunks talk.

"Get me Mulroy immediately," he snapped, then turned to the woman. "Kimberly...as much as I hate to say it, I've got some business to attend to. If you wish to wait in the library or the game room..."

She stood on tiptoe and gave him a peck on the lips. "Don't be too long," she said, then hurried from the room.

Sprecher. Sprecher. Why hadn't he thought of it before? He was the only man outside of the regiment's inner circle who knew about the passport the Vulture was using for the American run. He could have told anyone. He could have told hundreds of people.

"You want me, Baron?" Mulroy, dressed in fatigues, said from the doorway.

"I've got a name for you. Jost Sprecher."

"Sprecher," Mulroy said, coming inside the office. "It's got to be. I'll go down there tonight and see to it."

"No," the Vulture said. "Send someone else. I've got other work for you. Come here."

Mulroy followed him out onto the balcony. Night had descended fully on the mountain, and the lights of the village below were bright and festive. The Vulture pointed to the dark bulk of the Little Madam. "I think someone's up there," he said.

"Lots of people climb—"

"I think *he's* up there. I want you to check it...now! And I want a squad positioned on the peak for the duration of the festival."

"Yes, sir!" The man executed a sharp, military turn and moved swiftly toward the door.

"And Willy?" the Vulture called. "Whoever you send to speak with Mr. Sprecher...make sure they get every bit of information he has. I'm sure you understand what I mean."

"Count on it," Mulroy said, and smiled wide.

BOLAN AND DENNISON sat on their still-rolled sleeping bags and ate beef stew from cans. Dennison greedily drank from a large thermos full of coffee he'd brought up with his gear.

They'd covered the outside of the hut with blankets to block the wind that was whistling through the cracks. The small heater worked well.

A small window looked out at the castle, lost in darkness now except for the lights on the parapets and in the main hall. Bolan pulled aside the blanket covering the window and stared.

"You going to do it tomorrow?" Dennison asked.

"Yeah," the Executioner replied. "We'll haul it out of here in the morning. Will I have to go all the way back to Zurich to get a high-powered rifle?"

The man laughed. "Switzerland is the land of high-powered rifles. People love their guns here as much as we do back home, and the rifle is the weapon of choice. Ask anyone in town tomorrow. If you can haggle, you can get any kind of rifle you want."

"Good. We'll just climb back up, and I'll take him first opportunity."

"Correction. *We* won't be doing anything. I'll stick with you through the gun purchase. After that we split. You're up the mountain, and I'm on a flight back to Zone Interior. You don't need me to get back up the mountain."

Bolan nodded. "Fair enough."

It was almost too good to be true. With luck he could finish off the monster quietly, without the man's usual collateral fanfare of death and destruction. A day after that he could be back home, the Vulture just grim memory.

A mechanical sound drifted lightly from the direction of the castle. Bolan lifted the blanket again to take a look. A chopper was just clearing the castle walls, a bright spotlight shining from its bottom. He waited for it to angle down to Maur, as it had done many times that day, but instead, it turned, gained altitude and headed right for them.

"We got trouble," Bolan said as Dennison crawled through the small hut to gaze out the window.

"Here we go," Dennison moaned as he slid dejectedly into a sitting position. "I wish I'd have killed you in my flat last night. I could have been halfway home by now."

They had about a minute before the chopper would reach them. There was nowhere to hide on the peak. The spotlight would capture them soon enough. They had to take decisive action. "I don't suppose you've got a gun?" Bolan said.

The man just turned and stared blankly at him. "You're the killer," he said. "You're the one who's supposed to have the guns."

Bright light illuminated the window space, blinding light. "Get your crampons on," he said. "Hurry. They're almost here."

"Why should I—"

"Do it! Quick!"

The man slipped the heavy spikes over his new climbing boots. "I'm going to draw their fire," the Executioner said, moving to the covered doorway of the hut. "When I get them past here, I want you to grab a handful of snow screws and make your way up the jagged edge of the peak, the highest point. See it?"

The man looked out the door. His face was set but

fearful. They could hear the chopper above them, snow blowing crazily under the winds from the rotor.

"I'll lead them there," Bolan said. "Try and make them come down low. When they do, start chunking the pitons at the tail rotor, the small one. It's their stabilizer."

"This isn't happening," Dennison said.

"Brother," Bolan growled, "it is happening, and if you don't back me up on this we're both dead...as in really dead. Now go!"

He raced out of the hut. The chopper was hovering thirty feet overhead, its spotlight racing over the ground around him. It was an old Huey Iroquois in pristine shape and loaded for bear—a 7.62 multibarrel Minigun, a 20 mm six-barrel cannon. The thing could ultimately hold over seventy rockets. There was an M-60 placement mounted in the open bay.

He ran.

Dodging between the jagged rocks that dotted the summit, thrusting out of the snow, Bolan put distance between himself and the chopper, knowing the movement would catch their eye more quickly.

He turned behind him and looked, afraid that Dennison might simply lie low and hope they were satisfied killing him, but as soon as the bright circle of the spotlight passed the hut, the man dodged out and ran rock to rock, staying behind the slow-stalking chopper, moving to the same place Bolan was—a jagged section of ice and rock that rose forty feet above the actual summit.

The spotlight caught Bolan as he was reaching the outcropping. The night was absolutely clear around him, inky black, brilliant stars. Death.

The chopper's Minigun rattled, and he dodged right. The big slugs slammed into rock, blasting stone shrapnel at Bolan, who dived and rolled, watching icy snow bursting under heavy fire across the ground toward him.

Jumping to his feet, he charged back the other way and dived behind a rock pile the size of a phone booth. There was a second of silence, then Bolan thought he heard the tinkle of distant laughter mixed with the swirling prop wash of the Huey's rotor.

Then the Minigun was firing, staccato, like a slowly throttling engine. Orange fire shook the plain as rock and ice ripped to pieces in a constant chain of explosions.

His rock pile crumbled, and Bolan went down hard under the debris, covering his head. Pain flashed, was lost in the adrenaline rush. He struggled out and ran left, not wanting to distance himself from the upper peak, where he hoped Dennison was getting into position.

The M-60 cut loose from the bay right in front of him, the snow churning angrily. He jerked, then turned back, the ground exploding before him. Boxed in, he stopped, looking up to where the Huey hovered not twenty feet above him. Mulroy hung out of the bay, grinning that country-boy grin.

"Hey, Paraguay!" he called. "How ya doin'?"

"I've been better!" Bolan called back. "How about you?"

"Can't complain! You're harder to kill than a tick!"

Bolan shrugged, watching past them as Dennison made it to an ice peak on a direct line with their tail rotor.

"Just lucky!" Bolan said. "I see you're still playing soldier boy even though you washed out!"

"Where are your guns, cuz?"

"I'm just here for the wine festival!"

Dennison was balanced precariously on the jagged peak and was fumbling in the pockets of his heavy coat.

"Normally I'd think about taking you in for debriefing!" Mulroy called. "But you'd just cause some kind of ruckus. I'm gonna do you now, pard!"

"No, you're not!" Bolan called back. "I was right about you in Paraguay. You don't have the goods. You forgot rule number one—cover your ass!"

At that moment Dennison threw a handful of pitons at the chopper's tail, followed by metallic pings, then quickly another handful, and this time there was the screeching rend of metal on metal as the rotor blade twisted back onto the tail, tearing a section of it out.

The chopper immediately lost balance, jerking in

the air, wobbling as the pilot tried to regain altitude. The gunner tumbled out of the bay, but Mulroy managed to cling to the door as Bolan charged the man who fell.

He was groaning, trying to rise, as the Executioner reached him, knocking him over onto his back, a knee coming full weight on the man's throat, crushing it.

Bolan ripped the man's coat open as he lay, thrashing, suffocating in the death agonies. The chopper had climbed and was swaying wildly, trying to make it back to the castle.

The dying man was wearing a side arm, a Glock 17, 9 mm semiauto. Bolan tore it out of the holster and snapped a round into the chamber.

He raced to the edge of the precipice, watching the distant form of Willy Mulroy scrambling back into the bay. The chopper wasn't going to make the castle. Rather, it was going to ditch in a snowy hillside within the estate's peripheral defenses.

Any shot he'd make would be a waste of a bullet, a bullet they'd desperately need in a few minutes. Instead Bolan walked quickly back to the now-dead gunner.

He went through the man's clothes and found one extra 13-round clip. He stuck it in his pocket.

"Now what?" Dennison asked.

"Now we see how quickly we can get down that mountain."

"In the dark?"

He pointed to the distant chopper. "You want to wait around for their friends to join us?"

Dennison was gone in a flash, grabbing the rest of the gear as Bolan jogged to the section of the Huey's tail that had been chopped off by the broken rotor. He heard Mulroy's chopper hit ground with a loud rending. No explosion.

The piece of tail was about three feet by five feet. Bolan dragged it to their ascent point as Dennison charged up with their gear. Bolan fixed the spikes to his boots.

They tied the tail section to Bolan's back and went down the way they'd come up, finding their old crampon holes from the afternoon, trying to use the pitons they'd already screwed into the ice.

Troops would have already been deployed by this time, probably a lot of troops. They'd ring the peak and move relentlessly forward until finding Bolan and Dennison. Timing was everything at this point.

They reached the series of pitons and clamped them, sliding down their lines from piton to piton. In the rush of excitement, neither man spoke, and neither felt the cold or the pain in their arms and legs.

Bolan sneaked a look down. They were nearing the point where the Little Madam was a long downward slope of snow, walkable all the way to the tree line a mile farther down. He could see the dark forms of men charging up from ground level, moving through the trees.

Gunfire from below gouged the rock and ice beside them. Two hits ricocheted off the sheet metal strapped to Bolan's back.

"Got some marksmen down there," Bolan said, unclipping from the rope, then working the crampons. They were on solid ground, looking at a long, sloping hillside, then trees.

"They're *all* marksmen here!" Dennison yelled as another shot took a large chunk of ice right beside his head. "We're sunk."

"Maybe," Bolan hedged, unstrapping the heavy piece of metal from his back.

"They're making a contest of it," Dennison said. "Taking turns."

"Their problem," Bolan returned. "You ever toboggan?"

The man smiled down at the three-by-five-foot piece of sheet metal. "An idea man," he said. "Cool. For a G.I. Joe, you're okay."

"I'll take the front," Bolan said, pulling out the Glock. "You sit behind and try to steer by pulling on the sides."

Both men positioned quickly as more shots resounded around them.

Bolan braced in the front, then Dennison gave a shove from the rear and jumped behind.

"Try and serpentine," Bolan called over his shoulder. "It'll take a little longer to get down, but they won't know where to try and converge on us."

"You're the man," Dennison called.

The wind was whistling hard, whooshing, stinging their faces as they picked up more speed. Shots rang from all through the tree line now, flashes like fireflies, bursting everywhere, and bullets whizzing past them.

"Left!" Dennison yelled.

Both men leaned as Dennison pulled up on the metal. The sled arced wide left, and shouts came from below as men ran in that direction.

"Right!" Dennison yelled, then "Left!" as soon as they'd started the turn.

Directly to their left, as the tree line rushed toward them, several men had broken into the open to fire at them. Bolan held on with one hand, firing single shots into the small crowd with the other hand.

Two fell, rolling down the mountain, the others scattering.

"Right!" Dennison called.

They were flying, everything a blur except the trees. They were close.

More shots came from close by, and Bolan swung the Glock to the right to take out two more men with chest shots.

"We're running out of snow!" Dennison called.

"Aim for open space!" Bolan yelled as they hit the tree line.

The toboggan jerked to a dead stop once it ran out

of snow, and Bolan and Dennison were propelled at forty miles per hour into a pine forest.

They traveled in the air before crashing hard onto near-frozen ground. Bolan tucked and rolled with the impact, finally stopping when he tumbled hard into a tree, blacking out for a second before shaking it off and rising on wobbly legs.

Darkness and tall trees surrounded him, with the sound of many voices farther up the hillside. The sled had thrown them past their assailants.

Where was Dennison?

He turned a full circle, trying to see in starlight. He heard movement ahead. Wiping dirt and pine needles from the Glock, he moved in the direction of the sound, finding the NSC man wandering aimlessly, dazed.

"Come on," Bolan whispered, taking him by the arm, leading him down.

"Where...what...?"

The man was incoherent but docile as Bolan pulled him along.

Voices from behind called out in Valais German. They'd been spotted!

Bolan turned Dennison to face him and slapped the man as hard as he could. The man's eyes slowly focused.

"What?" he said.

"Run like hell," Bolan replied, and took off to the sound of gunfire from behind.

Dennison was beside him within seconds. "I could have been home," he kept saying. "I could have killed you and gone home."

Bolan ignored him and turned to fire over his shoulder at thrashing in the thicket beside them. A grunt and a crash to the ground rewarded his effort.

Suddenly they broke from the tree line, reaching the valley floor. The millet field was full of cars and transports, and men rushed from the forest all around the peak.

They were being charged from all directions as they hurried into the makeshift car lot, frantically checking cars for keys left behind.

"Here!" Dennison yelled, pointing to an ugly yellow Volvo.

Any port in the storm. The man was already behind the wheel as Bolan ran to the passenger side.

"Go!" he yelled as he climbed in, firing over the fender of a truck parked beside.

A man in a red-and-white uniform sprawled over the hood in a spurting haze of blood.

Dennison popped it into gear and bounced off the English Ford parked on the other side, then gained control and aimed toward town, passing a long line of cars and trucks.

Two men in white snow fatigues jumped into their path fifty feet ahead, firing rifles, shattering their windshield. Bolan leaned out the window and emptied the rest of the clip into them. Their white uniforms drooled red as one spun away, the other plowed under them, the Volvo bouncing high as it ground up the body.

They bounced from the field onto the roadway, and Dennison floored it as other vehicles were starting up to give chase. Bolan dropped the empty clip and reloaded.

"Just get to the town square," Bolan said. "We can make it on foot to your car from there, get away in the confusion."

"Okay," Dennison replied, humping it into town as Bolan went through the car, looking for weapons. He found a fully loaded AK-47 under the passenger seat.

They roared into town. A huge dance was in progress in the square. The townspeople were dressed in bright red-and-yellow traditional costumes, laughing and singing, quaffing huge steins of beer. More of the red-and-white mercenary uniforms were evident amid the merrymakers.

They pulled up in the middle of the street and just left the car. Bolan stuck the pistol in his pocket and carried the Kalashnikov out in the open. Nobody noticed. Most of the men were carrying their weapons.

They were halfway through the crowd when other cars squealed up to the square. Men jumped out of the vehicles and charged into the crowd, causing more confusion as Bolan and Dennison made their way to the Gothic church and the small Alfa they'd left parked there that morning, a million years ago.

They made the car and pulled quietly down side streets, Dennison continually checking the rearview.

"First chance you get, step on it," Bolan said.

"To where?"

"Zurich. We've got to get to your forger friend before the Vulture does."

"Oh, my God," Dennison said. "Sprecher could tell them my name!"

He hit the gas, and they were off.

CHAPTER FOURTEEN

Zurich
July 23, 4:00 a.m.

Dennison drove Bolan slowly through the dead-of-night city, taking Lagerstrasse, just south of the railway lines, where Zurich's slums existed side by side with the opulence of the world's financial capital. Once the refuge of Catholics from neighboring cantons escaping the medieval Reformation, the area was now comprised of shabby, gloomy blocks of flats that housed the cheap labor pool of the money barons.

"You were so close...that close," Dennison said, holding a thumb and forefinger an inch apart. "How did he know we were there?"

"Maybe someone from the town dropped a dime," Bolan said, unconcerned with what was already past. He had the immediate future to deal with.

"No, there was nothing suspicious. People climb there all the time—it's one of the reasons people come to Maur, for God's sake."

"He's tough," Bolan said. "We'll have to be tougher."

"This is a wash, man. Over. There's no way you can take him."

"There's always a way," Bolan replied. "How far to the printer's?"

"A block farther up...on the left."

"Pull over here. On the other side of the street."

Dennison did as he was told. Bolan brought the AK-47 with him, and the Glock was snuggled in his coat pocket. They climbed from the car and walked the street slowly, staying in the shadows of the side opposite the shop.

"There," Dennison said quietly, pointing across the street to a narrow store on ground level with housing for the owner above. There were no lights on in the structure. All seemed quiet, except that a black Peugeot was parked partway on the sidewalk in front of the building.

"Der Stein is a block down," Dennison said, pointing, "my place a block farther on from there."

"What kind of car does Sprecher drive?" Bolan asked.

"Herr Sprecher does not drive," Dennison said. "He has never driven."

Bolan primed the AK-47 and handed it to Dennison. "You know how to use this?"

"No," the man returned. "And I don't want to learn."

"It's set for single shot. You point and pull the trigger. Don't shoot unless you've got something to shoot at. And if I'm in front of you, don't point that thing at my back."

"It's a thought, isn't it?"

Suddenly the apartment above the print shop flashed brilliantly to light—three times in rapid succession.

They were too late.

"Come on!" Bolan said, charging across the street, the gun out of his pocket, Dennison hanging way back. He was only fast when they were running away.

Bolan jumped the sidewalk and hit the front door of the shop on a dead run. The door had already been crowbarred open at the latch. The place was dark, filled with lumpy shapes that must have been machinery. He could barely see. He primed the Glock. There were thirteen shots in the magazine.

In the back of the shop, he could hear the sound of feet rumbling down stairs and could see the dancing spot of a flashlight. They were coming and didn't know they had company. He moved to position himself behind a printing press. With surprise on his side, he could take them easy.

The room exploded with light, Dennison standing wide-eyed at the switch. "Hey, I—"

"Down, you idiot!" Bolan yelled as four men on the wooden staircase opened up with automatics to a deafening roar. The place was jammed full of beehives of typefaces—no computers here—and low-hanging lights, and everything inside the small shop jumped, danced, under a hail of fiery death.

He looked to see Dennison, down behind a huge linotype machine, shrugging at Bolan, his weapon lying on the floor.

"Pick it up!" Bolan yelled, standing to fire at the four men, who'd jumped the stairs and were charging.

He took out the first man with a head shot and was already drawing a bead on the second as the first crashed into a stack of print drawers, sending little wooden cubes flying everywhere.

He plugged the second man through the chest and throat. His momentum keeping him running right past Bolan, a hand to his neck, blood leaking between his fingers.

The other two were on him, and Bolan had to dive and roll as Dennison pulled the trigger from his side of the room, over and over, wasting ammo but managing to hit one of the men in the arm.

But it drove the men out, and the assassins crashed through the glass remaining in the front door to make the street. Bolan was up, giving chase. The guy he shot through the neck was standing, leaning against the door frame—dead—his hand still holding his throat.

The Executioner jumped through the glass space in the door and shot at the man Dennison had wounded. He hit him in the back of the neck, and the man staggered forward several more steps before he plunged headfirst to the cobblestones.

The fourth man had climbed into the car and was starting the engine. Bolan charged at the car.

It started with a roar and lurched off the curb, but the Executioner was already digging for the driver's door even as it picked up speed down the street.

He ran hard and came abreast of the driver's-side window. The driver looked over at him, surprised, as he put two bullets through his forehead.

Bolan stopped running, and the car continued on, picking up speed. It traveled on, straight and true, for three more blocks before swerving hard right at eighty miles per hour. It flipped, end over end, before crashing into the brick facade of a boutique and exploding.

Dennison was walking out of the print shop, dragging the AK-47 by the barrel. He moved to stand over the man he'd shot, frowning down at the body. Bolan jogged to him as the sound of distant sirens filled the night. People were beginning to poke their heads out of windows.

"Come on," Bolan said. "The first one's always the hardest."

"This man, he…he…"

"It's meat," Bolan said. "Let's go!"

"What about Sprecher?"

"He's gone."

They hurried back down the block to the Alfa,

climbing in and sinking down in the seats just as several police cars screeched by, the sirens bleating like sheep.

"We've got to assume they called the Vulture on you," Bolan said. "You can't go home."

"What about your hotel?"

"Yeah…right. After my little run-in with Mulroy tonight, we'd never make it out of the parking lot of the Hilton. We need someplace else to stay. Where?"

"Another hotel?"

"Forget the hotels and the airport. You must know something about this place after two years."

"I told you, I have no friends, I— No, never mind."

"What? You were going to say something."

"There's a…a girl," Dennison said.

"There's always a girl," Bolan returned. "Could she also be connected to the Vulture?"

"No, no. That's not the problem. We're not… together anymore. Marta Kleppe broke up with me because I'm too weird."

"Sensible lady. Let's go."

Dennison started the Alfa and pulled slowly away from the curb as vehicles and citizens filled the streets before the print shop. There was a confusion of lights and noise. Some things were the same everywhere around the world.

As they drove out of the city, Dennison was unusually quiet after the firefight. The man he'd run over in Maur had been happenstance, unavoidable, but in the print shop he'd had to make the decision to pull the trigger. It's not one that everybody could make. He hadn't done well, but he'd tasted blood. They drove for thirty minutes, then finally Dennison pulled into a subdivision of chalets built into a hillside. They were new, all fake gingerbread, meant to mimic the world's perception of Switzerland, all A-frame and wooden decks.

They pulled up to a house halfway up the four-hundred-foot hill and climbed out.

"What am I supposed to say to her? It's been six months...."

"Tell her you have a business proposition for her, that you need lodging for one night, no questions asked."

They were moving up the stairs, and Dennison was shaking his head. "It's not going to be that easy. It's—"

Bolan interrupted him by knocking on the door persistently, enough to wake someone without rousing the neighborhood.

A few minutes later a slightly fearful female voice sounded from the other side of the door. "Who is it? Who's there?"

"Marta," Dennison said softly. "Marta. It's me, Rennie."

"Go away."

The man looked at Bolan, who prodded him, nodding toward the door. "I...I must talk to you. I have a...business proposition to offer."

"What sort of business?" she said, the door still closed tight.

Bolan reached into his pocket and took out a thousand-franc note, shoving it under the door. Fifteen seconds later they were standing in the vestibule of a cozy little house with a loft bedroom.

It would do. The Executioner was beginning to understand the thinking of some Swiss citizens.

WILLY MULROY, in pleated pants and a baggy shirt with a sports jacket, wandered down the length of Langstrasse. The smells of the bakeries and delis cranking up for the day made him realize he hadn't eaten since the previous night.

That guy from Paraguay could screw up anything. Mulroy was lucky to be alive after going down with the chopper. The pilot hadn't been so fortunate.

He moved up, getting across the street from the police barricades. Crowds of tourists and locals gathered around, and a separate but similar show was taking place down the street where that idiot Heller had crashed.

Sprecher had apparently had no phone, not even a business phone; Heller had stupidly forgotten to take a cell phone along to pass information.

Now it was gone, lost with the printer and Heller.

The big man had put Mulroy's butt in the wringer again.

He kept walking, looking. Sprecher had spent his years on this street and had probably done his drinking here, as well. Mulroy was looking for a place a loser like the forger would frequent.

He didn't have to look far. Barely half a block from Sprecher's tiny business, he came across a neighborhood bar called Der Stein. It was a working-class place, cheap booze, cheaper conversation, unlike the discos and retro sixties clubs that filled the rest of Langstrasse.

A small man in an apron with a huge handlebar mustache was sweeping the sidewalk in front of Der Stein. Mulroy sidled up to him and put on his good-old-boy smile.

"Howdy!" he said, loud. The man looked up and smiled distractedly. "You speak English?" Mulroy asked.

"Impossible to have a business on Langstrasse without speaking English. How may I help you?"

"I'm just passin' through, on vacation," Mulroy said, moving closer to the man. "I was just wonderin' what happened over there across the street. Somebody get shot or something?"

"Five people shot," the man said, holding up five fingers. "It was horrible. They shot poor Mr. Sprecher, then shot among themselves...I don't know what was going on."

"You saw it?"

"I saw the end of it…the last. All the guns, they woke me up. I looked out the window and saw men shot in the street, a man trying to drive away. This big man chased down the car and shot the driver right through the window. Then another man came out of the building and ran away with the big man."

"Another man," Mulroy said, not a question. "Did you tell the police about it?"

The man laughed. "The police?" he said, and spit on the ground. "They can all go to hell, you know? They've done me no favors."

"Boy, I hear you. Hey, you said, 'poor Mr. Sprecher.' Did you know him?"

"He was my best customer," the tavern owner said sadly. "It's going to make a difference in my business. I always worried about something happening to him. He was a petty criminal."

"Really?" Both men stood for a moment, staring over at the crowds and the police tracking blood trails on the sidewalk and streets, trying to reconstruct the action. "If Sprecher was here all the time, I guess there's a lot of people who'll miss him."

The man tugged on his mustache, his eyes narrowing just a touch. "He kept to himself," he said. "No friends, really, except for the young American fellow, a long-hair who did something with computers."

"Computers," Mulroy said. Things just kept getting stranger. "Did the young man live around here, too?"

"Why would you want to know these things?"

"I'm just a curious guy."

"Well, I'm very busy and must get back to getting my place open. If you want any more of my time, you'll have to pay for it."

"How much?"

"Five hundred francs."

Mulroy had the money in the man's hands in seconds.

"His name is Rennie Dennison," the man said quietly. "He lives in an apartment at the corner of the next block. I returned a book to him there once. The number is 4-B. That's all I can tell you."

The man turned abruptly and moved into the tavern, locking the door behind him.

Mulroy, whistling happily, went down the block, finding the apartments without much trouble. He made it quietly up the stairs, tapping gently on 4-B to no response.

The lock jimmied easily with Mulroy's Swiss Army knife, and he walked into a computer nerd's wet dream. Computers and telephones were everywhere, screens running continual data. He walked around, trying to put something together, when he saw the scrambler.

Willy Mulroy was no genius, but he knew a scrambler phone when he saw one. A scrambler phone meant covert activity. The guy at the bar had said the man here was an American. A spy! He'd also said the big man had had an accomplice last night.

He smiled, walking out the door and latching it back up tight. The American spy and Belasko were working together. With all of his equipment here, the American would come back. All Mulroy had to do was wait, and the big guy would be delivered to him.

He took his cell phone off his belt and dialed up the security number at the castle. The baron himself answered after two rings.

"I've got him pegged," Mulroy said. "Just waitin' for him to return to the roost."

"I've been very disappointed in you lately, Willy," the Vulture said. "I hope you've got control of the situation this time."

"We need to keep a watch on 817 Langstrasse," Mulroy said. "Surveillance. It'll pay off, I promise. Send me some men, too."

"How many?"

"Thirty should do it."

CHAPTER FIFTEEN

The inspector's name was Stiler. He was very precise, very neat. His hair was short, slicked down, his mustache clipped to a pencil line, his wire glasses small and round. He held Bolan's passport in one hand and the photo of the Vulture in the other.

"Now, you say, Mr. Belasko," he said in precise English, "that you saw this man—" he held up the photo "—in our airport when you got off the plane, and that this man is the international terrorist, the Vulture?"

"Yes," Bolan said, taking a desperate stab at getting something going.

"May I ask where you acquired his photo?"

"They were handed out in the airport when I came over here on vacation."

"And you saw—" he turned the photo to Bolan's face "—this man when you got off the plane?"

"Yes. I've already told you that. And I heard the custom's man say, 'Welcome home, Baron von Maur.'"

"I see," Stiler said, handing the photo back to Bolan. "Well, we'll…look into it, Mr. Belasko." He handed back the passport.

"You're not going to do anything, are you?"

"Mr. Belasko, Baron von Maur is a very famous man in my country, like…Elvis, huh? He's a world-renowned art historian and critic, and is a benefactor to many. I do not believe he is the Vulture. Their resemblance ends at the eye patch."

"He's a vicious, sadistic killer," Bolan said.

"Thank you, Mr. Belasko," Stiler said. "Enjoy your stay in our country."

"I'm afraid, Inspector, that you will come to regret this decision."

In response, the man swiveled his chair, showing only its tall back. Bolan picked up his passport and left, not saying everything he wanted to say.

It was destined to fall on his shoulders, and he was probably foolish to think it otherwise. Now he knew for sure. Private army or not, he was going to have to go up that mountain alone and kill Baron Karl von Maur, the Vulture. He could count on nothing from Dennison—the man wasn't any good in a firefight. The best he could hope for would be some help in getting himself there and ready. And he would insist on that.

He left the modern glass-and-steel building and took a cab back to Rapperswil, where they'd spent the night with Marta who worked at a diamond-brokerage firm in Zurich. She'd let them stay, for a thousand francs a day, only because she was leaving town for vacation. Bolan had driven into Zurich with her this morning, picking up his combat harness at the consulate; the war drums would beat any time, and he'd best be prepared.

The bustling metropolis of nearly a million people slid past his window, all swiftly gliding trams and gray stone banking houses. There were cosmopolitan restaurants on the great stone banks of the fast-moving Limmat River. Zurich was a city of jeweled escarpments and refugees of all kinds.

In many senses Switzerland was like much of America—hardball business and plainspoken common folk. No nonsense. But in some ways it was completely different, the citizen's loyalties tied more directly to his locale than his nation, the confusion of nineteen languages and dialects politically and socially daunting even to the Swiss.

The picturesque trip passed quickly, with Bolan's mind centering on getting up the mountain. He'd seen two defensive lines, plus the castle walls themselves. Fifty to sixty feet high, they were an obstacle to be reckoned with. He had enough confidence in himself to figure if he was able to get inside the walls, he could get to the Vulture. But part of being good was being honest, and getting past those walls was going to be a problem—unless he could bypass the defenses completely.

After spending the day in Maur, he'd had a chance to observe the comings and goings of the castle. There were two choppers that he knew about. One of them he'd taken out of commission on the Little Madam the night before. It had been a part of their perimeter defense, making a sweep around the mountain every two hours.

But there'd been another chopper, one that was used to ferry guests up to the castle, since the car ride up was picturesque but dangerous and time consuming. The old Navy Chinook had a landing pad near the town square, but was never left in town. It always went back up the mountain after making a pickup or delivery in town.

If he could scheme his way onto the chopper, the job was three quarters done. All he'd need from Dennison would be a diversion once he'd gotten inside.

They pulled up to the fake-rustic subdivision and took the winding hill up to Marta's chalet. The rest of the hillside sprouted identical houses to Marta's. They were like mushrooms.

He got out and paid the cabdriver, then moved cautiously up to the house, checking through the front window before entering. Holding a coffee mug, Dennison was gathering notes together.

"And how goes the grand scheme?" Dennison

asked as he put down his coffee cup and stacked his notes neatly on the dining-room table.

"Everything's simple to me. I've got some notions."

"So do I," Dennison replied. "I've been ordered out."

"I give the orders."

"I spoke with Mulligan this morning," he said, "and was told that the operation has been contaminated and that I should shut it down completely and return as quickly as possible. You may be pulling on my chain, Belasko, but the U.S. government owns my ass. This is NSC. Top priority. What the hell am I supposed to do?"

Bolan just stared at him, wondering what the notes were all about.

"I have also been ordered to offer you a deal. And I have to say that I hope you don't take it."

"What deal?" Bolan asked, sitting at the dining table.

"When I shut down operations, we'll lose all of our contact with the bank accounts. But there is a bug I can plant at the source that will do the job without needing somebody like me to watch it."

"So?"

"So...if you can help me plant the bug, I can give you a hand getting to your destination and getting you set for your run up the hill. I'll then just take the Saint

Bernard Pass and *drive* into Italy. I'll fly out from there."

"What kind of help do you need from me in planting a bug?" Bolan asked.

"Well, we've got to…get in, you know, after hours to do it. I thought that with your vast experience—"

"You want me to break into the Zurich banks for you?"

"Just one…Bank Leu. That's where the majority of our leads come from. It won't take long once we get in."

Bolan pointed to the phone. "Call your boss back," he said. "I want to talk to him."

"I can't call him on a regular line," Dennison said. "He won't accept anything other than scrambled contact from the field."

"Where did you call him from before?"

"My flat. I—"

"You went back there?" Bolan said, running to a window and twitching the curtain aside. "I told you not to go back there."

"It's cool. I didn't see anybody or anything."

Through the window Bolan saw carloads of men dispersing through the development. They were deploying rapidly, surrounding Marta's house.

"They're here," the Executioner said. "We've got to move now!" The Glock was lying on the table. Bolan ran to it, priming it and handing it to a pale, shaken Dennison.

"What do you mean, they're here?"

Bolan ran back to the door, dragging the man with him. "You've got seven shots left in the clip," he said, unholstering the Beretta and snapping one into the chamber. "Don't fire unless you've got a sure target or need to push somebody back. Sight down your finger, just point and shoot."

Bolan opened the door. "If they get set, we're dead. Got the car keys?"

"Yeah!"

"You drive. Let's go!"

Bolan charged out of the house, Dennison right with him, as usual, as they sprinted away. They ran around the wooden deck to the back, with gunfire crackling from nearby, wood chips flying beside their feet.

They vaulted the back rail for the Alfa, which was parked on a small driveway right beside it. Bullets whizzed around them, and Bolan fired at a man armed with a rifle who was jumping over a hedgerow across the street, hitting him in the groin in midleap. The thug went down in agony amid the bushes. Bolan swung immediately to the side of the house right next door, using a head shot to take out a gunman aiming around the corner.

Bullets thudded into the Alfa as Dennison got behind the wheel and started the engine, then Bolan was next to him in the passenger seat.

"Go! Go!" Bolan said, jamming his foot atop Dennison's on the gas pedal. The car surged out of the driveway just as Bolan heard the whoosh of a mortar rocket.

Marta's chalet went up in an orange ball of fire just behind them, sending burning debris falling all over the street, bouncing off the car.

"Ignore it!" Bolan yelled, grabbing the wheel from the reluctant man and jamming his foot down again. Another mortar took out the street right behind them. The car jumped, coughing, but still on line.

"Keep moving downward," Bolan said. The streets all around them were crisscrossed with enemy vehicles, men with guns everywhere. The windshield went a second later, and Bolan cleared out the shattered glass with a well-placed elbow. "Always down, even if you have to go overland."

He rolled down the window as they sped toward an intersection with cars racing to block them off. Dennison swerved wide as the intersection filled with cars. The Alfa went up on two wheels as Bolan emptied the Beretta into the roadblock, several men going down hard, a car catching fire.

The Alfa bounced back to four wheels only to jump the curb and fishtail through someone's yard. They banged the chalet's deck on the way past, the support columns snapping to dump outdoor furniture into the streets, and the Alfa was bleeding black, oily smoke from beneath the hood.

"Damn!"

"Keep driving...don't stop!"

Bolan dropped the clip from the Beretta and reloaded, bringing out the .44 at the same time. He primed it and prepared for Armageddon. They were still blocks from the bottom of the hill, careering downward at a forty-five degree angle, and the noose was pulling tighter around them, choking off their avenues of escape.

As they bounced back onto the street, the engine sputtered loudly, wanting to quit.

"This damned—" Dennison began, but the explosions cut him off.

Mortars went up all around—ground, streets, houses—and a holocaust of fire and smoke and shrapnel blinded them as the ground buckled in front of them. The Alfa jumped high, and Bolan braced himself for impact.

They came down sideways and rolled through burning debris and smoke, then the car landed upright, all four wheels splayed out on the ground, the hood popped open to churning smoke.

Bolan pulled himself up from the floorboards and kicked open the busted passenger door. Dennison was moaning beside him, blood pouring down the side of his face.

"Come on!" Bolan growled, rolling out of the car and onto the twisted street. "Don't lose your weapon!"

The man was out of the car immediately, survival instinct overcoming all else.

They ran.

The chalets were spaced fifty feet apart on a rolling hillside of thick grass. Bolan took them into open fields, through the yards. They were less than a quarter mile from the bottom of the hillside, but several streets and houses still separated them from escaping the jaws of the trap.

He looked around. A confusion of men on foot was trying to bring them down on the hoof.

Bolan and Dennison pumped hard in a losing cause. The noose drew taut as loose lines of men and machines were cutting them off in all directions.

The men on foot charged. The last chalet between Bolan and freedom lay to his right.

"The house!" he shouted.

Dennison turned with him, and both of them charged the chalet as their assailants opened up from mere dozens of paces away.

The Executioner sprang onto the porch and dived through a picture window to roll and jump back to his feet, both guns, fully loaded and primed, out before him.

All the glass inside the house began shattering under relentless fire. Dennison rolled through the window space, turning to fire behind him, knocking down a man in a small fedora with a shotgun.

"Windows!" Bolan yelled as the Vulture's men charged the house, reaching it on all sides at once.

He reacted with pure warrior's instinct. Guns up and ready, he turned a circle, firing at anything that moved, both barrels blazing away.

One man on the porch...two. He knocked them off, then blew both barrels at a large form lunging through the doorway, taking his eyes out to a strangled scream as Dennison fired at the two windows facing out.

Bolan swung the other way, firing four shots at two men coming from the back of the house. He hit them both twice, chest high, the men spinning a ballet of death in the kitchen doorway before flopping to the polished wood floors.

"Come on!" Bolan urged, moving toward the kitchen area, swinging back to take another man in the doorway and one more at the front-porch window. Bodies were falling atop one another, piling up, but a deafening racket of automatic-weapons fire still filled the house.

In a crouch Dennison hurried to him, firing once more at the window until the slide snapped back, empty.

Bolan dropped the clip from the Beretta and with the Desert Eagle he took out a man coming through the kitchen door. He jammed another clip into the bottom of the gun and tossed it to Dennison, who fired three shots through the porch window. A man fell inside, yelling in pain, his screams eerie amid the jangling gunfire.

The Executioner reloaded the .44 and shot another man at the back door. "We go through the back!" he yelled. "Take the closest car to us!"

"Okay! Okay!"

They moved to the kitchen, where wood paneling exploded all around them. A small hall separated living from kitchen areas. Bolan swung quickly into it and dived forward as bullets whizzed just over his head. Returning fire, he nailed one gunner in the head and another twice in the chest. The man shot in the head wandered blindly into a back room, where gunfire threw him back into the hallway, his body chewed up.

The man was still screaming in the living room as Dennison took an extra shot to target a man in the doorway who'd stumbled over the bodies of his associates.

Bolan grabbed him and pulled him into the kitchen, shooting a man off the back porch.

"Ready?" Bolan asked.

"Would it make a difference if I said no?"

"Now!"

They charged through the open back door just as a grenade blew up the living room behind them. A black BMW was parked just beneath the porch railing. One leaping step and they jumped onto the top of the car, leaning down to fire right through the windows, blasting the three occupants to hell, brain tissue and blood running down the windows.

They jumped to the ground.

Bolan was on the driver's side. He pulled his man out to tumble on the grass, straightening to fire at two men rounding the corner. He got the first, and the second ducked back.

He climbed behind the wheel and Dennison climbed in beside him. Bolan hit the gas before the man even had his door shut.

The car lurched into the street at the bottom of the hillside. Dennison rested his arm at the bottom of the window and fired the rest of the clip at the men on that side of the house, forcing them to cover.

"Good boy!" Bolan shouted, firing the Desert Eagle from his window, knocking over two men who were chasing on foot, and a third man tumbled over the other two, bouncing hard on the pavement.

The Executioner squealed hard into gear, leaving a strip of rubber on the road behind them. In the rearview mirror, the picture-perfect development was a nightmare of burning houses and twisted metal, bodies all over the streets. Behind them the Vulture's men were running back to their vehicles.

They were entering the town proper and its narrow, twisting medieval streets. "Turn right here," Dennison said. "When I dated Marta, I got to know this town pretty well. We need to get past the bus station."

The narrow street twisted wildly, then opened up

straight to the square. The bus station was on the other side.

"Take the dirt road," Dennison said.

Bolan bounced onto an old wagon path leading into stands of tall bushes, and the roadway, then the town, disappeared behind them.

They crossed a rickety bridge over a small, quiet stream, and Bolan pulled up behind a stand of holly bushes tall enough to cover the car entirely.

He sat back, getting a breath, as they listened to the sounds of squealing tires and honking horns. It could have been in another universe. They were sitting in a beautiful field of waving grass and grazing cattle, a tiny farmhouse in the distance. They could have been five hundred years back in time.

"Marta and I used to picnic here," Dennison said. "Now her house is blown up."

"Happens," Bolan said, holstering the Desert Eagle and taking the Beretta back from the man. "I've been thinking about Mulligan's proposition."

"Yeah?"

"I will help you break into Bank Leu tonight if you help me tomorrow."

"Great," the man said dejectedly. "The fun never ends."

"THIS ISN'T EXACTLY what I had in mind," Rennie Dennison said as he and the Executioner stood on the toilet seat in the executive washroom of Bank Leu so their feet wouldn't show through the bottom of the stall.

"Simplest is always the best," Bolan answered. "I'm sure better men than me have tried to break in here. We'll just skip that part." He was looking up. "Those are movable ceiling panels."

Dennison pointed just beside Bolan's head. "That's a main support beam right there," he said. "It'll hold our weight easily."

"How do you know that?"

"I've done some carpentry."

"How strong are your shoulders?"

"I'm not anemic or anything, if that's what you mean."

"Sit on the back of the bowl. I'm going to climb onto your shoulders and see if I can hoist myself up."

Bolan climbed onto Dennison's shoulders and pushed the ceiling panel out of the way. Straightening, he was shoulder high in the spacious ceiling. Dennison had been right; a long support beam ran through the entire structure. Bolan grabbed hold of it and hauled himself up. Once he was positioned on the support, he reached down and pulled Dennison up behind him. They replaced the ceiling tile and sat on the beam.

They had about three feet of space to work with between the fake ceiling and the real one, which was older. Much older. Cold stone. Light sliced up into their aerie through tiny cracks in the tiles, like thin walls of light.

They'd cleaned up as best they could in a public restroom, getting blood out of Dennison's hair and combing it over the large cuts on the side of his face where his car window had shattered all over him.

"Where do you want to be?" Bolan asked as they listened to the sounds of people leaving below them. It was four-thirty.

"Any office that has a working terminal," the man replied.

"You have a device to plant?"

"No. It's a string of commands that leads into a lot of strange places before getting to the part where their electronic data is retransmitted back to the Comstar satellite and then Mulligan's office. It will go out with scheduled transmissions. It's a beautiful system, if I do say so myself. I designed it."

"Good for you."

"You know, this is a really stupid way to break into a bank. I could have thought of it myself."

"But you didn't. And now you're stuck with me."

"How long should we wait?"

"Hour. Hour and a half."

"I can't believe I'm doing this."

Something in Dennison's expression made Bolan look hard at him. There was something in the man's eyes he didn't trust. Maybe it was the glow in the near-darkness, just shadows. Tricks of the dim lighting. Whatever it was, confirmed his first impression of the man and made him uneasy. Bolan never ignored that particular feeling.

They waited for a full hour and a half before hearing the place settle down to the shuffling feet of an all-night guard and a janitor. The security cameras were located in the lobby and vault areas, which meant they were bypassing them completely by going directly into the offices off the lobby.

This could work.

They stayed on the main beam, lifting ceiling panels aside to check their position. They found a back-corner office, far from the main business of the bank, then removed the panel and dropped quietly to the office itself.

He watched Dennison move right to the terminal and slide out the extra desk panel above the left-hand drawer and look beneath it. He closed that and opened the top drawer, checking under that, too. Bolan knew what he was doing—the old safe-combination trick. People who couldn't remember safe combinations or computer passwords usually taped them to the bottom of a drawer or the sliding desk space.

The man chuckled, then logged on to the terminal with the password he'd discovered. He slid into the system like eggs on Teflon.

"This is going to take a while," he said, his hands busy with the keyboard. "Maybe you could go out and check on the guard and the janitor. I'll work better if I know you're monitoring the situation out there."

Bolan knew the bum's rush when he saw it. "Time to make a sweep anyway," he said in agreement.

The offices were wood-paneled cubicles with glass fronting onto the hallway and a wooden door. The offices were elegant in a way he could only describe as old-world. He moved out into the hall, which was all offices on both sides and led back to the large, open, high-ceilinged lobby area. He went to the end of the hall and peered into the lobby.

The guard had a small station near the front door where he drank coffee, read magazines, watched the monitors of the security cameras and occasionally dozed.

He could hear the janitor in the west wing, down a hallway like this one on the other side of the lobby. He'd be there for hours.

Bolan walked into another luxurious office and sat behind the desk in a plush leather chair. A computer sat in front of him, the screen saver flying dollar, pound, mark and franc signs. He pulled his headset out of the harness and put it on, getting on the satellite system to reach Stony Man. As the connection went through, he peered under the pull-out and scored the password on the first try.

He logged himself on to the system as the phone rang at Stony Man.

Kurtzman answered immediately. "Where are you?"

"That's what I want to talk about," Bolan said, "I'm in Bank Leu."

"No, you're not. I've got a clock here set to Zurich time, and Bank Leu has been closed for two hours."

"That's what I want to talk about."

"You're really in Bank Leu?"

"Yep."

"Be careful. They treat money thieves like the Old West used to treat horse thieves."

"The NSC guy cut a deal with me for this," Bolan said. The computer screen in front of him offered a large menu of choices, none of them what he was looking for. "He says that he's invading the bank's systems in order to retransmit their electronic funds transfers back to America for study. Does that make sense?"

"Maybe, though I believe it's possible to do it from the outside. Is he on the machine now?"

"Yeah. I'd really like to see his screen."

"Possible to do," Kurtzman said. "I'm sure they're internally linked and probably use a Unix-based system. No reason our machines can't chat. Have you got their modem number?"

"Yeah, its here on the machine." Bolan gave him the number, and Kurtzman went off the line but left it open. Within minutes his console began bleeping, and Kurtzman was back on the headset.

"We're contacting the master unit at the bank—everything else slaves from that one. Once we get the master, we can give you the screen. I can work it from my end."

Bolan sat and watched commands and responses flash quickly on the screen. A minute later Bolan was watching Dennison's work on the computer in progress.

"Are you watching this, too?" Bolan asked.

"Yes," Kurtzman replied. "We're looking at a lot of transit numbers, something being moved around a lot."

"That's the diverting tactics he talked about," Bolan said.

"I don't think so," Kurtzman replied. "Those transit numbers are connected directly to inner bank codes, which have the exact same number of digits as numbered accounts. Those are then attached to amounts right…there. Bingo! Checkmate."

"What?"

"Funds transfer," Kurtzman said, "from one numbered account to fifteen others, finally ending up in a sixteenth numbered account in Geneva. Give me a minute to total the amounts in American money. There. In case you haven't figured it out yet, Mack, you are in the process of stealing fifty million dollars from a Bank Leu account. I hear Swiss jails get very cold."

"Son of a bitch," Bolan said, immediately printing a copy of the screen.

"Buddy, you're playing the rear end of the horse, and I suggest you get yourself out of there as quickly as you can."

"My thoughts exactly," Bolan replied, ripping the hard copy out of the printer and sticking it in his pocket. "Thanks."

He broke contact and put the headset away. He moved out into the hall and down to the corner office. Dennison stuck his head out just as he reached it.

"Okay, I'm done," he said. "I guess it's back into the ceiling until the morning, huh?"

"Naw," Bolan said, saving the anger. "I think we should be really creative. Here's a nice overcoat and hat, for instance. I saw a briefcase in one of the offices. Let's fix ourselves up."

They moved rapidly from office to office, picking up odds and ends, finally gathering enough clothes and accoutrements to look like distinguished bankers. Well, close.

Bolan picked up the phone and handed it to Dennison. "Dial zero. When the guard answers, ask him to come down here and escort the auditors out of the building."

As the man did as he was told, Bolan walked to the door and turned the lights on. Then he gave one of the laminated ID badges he'd found in desk drawers to Dennison and clipped one to the dapper trench coat he'd just acquired. He wore a small homburg hat and carried his umbrella and his briefcase in the same hand, the way he'd seen the bankers do earlier.

The guard showed up and made a slight fuss, Dennison doing all the talking.

Then they all left, Bolan turning the lights out behind him. When they went to the front desk to sign out, the guard glanced at their badges and merely bobbed his head in approval.

They were on the streets in minutes, the guard smiling and waving at them as he let them out. Twilight was descending upon the deserted financial heart of the city, and a chill breeze swept through the stone-and-steel canyons. Bolan turned up the collar of his trench coat.

"We just walked out of there!" Dennison said gleefully. "Man, oh man! You pulled that like you do it all the time!"

"Comes with the territory," Bolan replied as he flagged a cab.

Dennison climbed in first. "I'm starved. Let's get something to eat."

"Good idea," Bolan said, and listened while Dennison gave directions to the cabbie.

When they stopped, Bolan spied a narrow alley close by, flanked by blank gray stone that rose six stories. He gently steered Dennison into the alley, then released his arm and pulled the Beretta from the harness.

"You've got ten seconds to tell me the truth," he said, leveling the Beretta. "I wouldn't think twice about leaving you dead in this alley."

"T-truth?" Dennison returned.

"Yeah...like about the fifty million I just helped you steal. Truth like that. Truth like what your real connection to Sprecher was."

"I sought Sprecher out," the man replied immediately, unwilling to challenge Bolan. "I was looking for a forger. I got to know the owner of Der Stein pretty well and thought he could recommend someone. Sprecher's number came up."

"You wanted to create a new identity," Bolan said, working the puzzle pieces himself.

"Sure." The man shrugged. "So would you in my place. Prison is constantly dangled over my head. I didn't want to live under Mulligan's thumb for the rest of my life. I found I enjoyed living in Europe. So I figured that if I could create a new identity for myself through forged papers, I could slip away one day and simply be gone."

"What about the money?"

"Once Sprecher had done the job for me, he began trusting me with all his knowledge. The money scheme was born the day he told me about von Maur. I thought, here's this jerk with all this money. I decided to turn him in and let you people take care of him, then to take as much of his money as I could get. Who would care, you know? But I never could crack their systems from the outside. Then you came along."

"That's the Vulture's money you stole?"

"Yeah. Got close to cleaning him out. Do you want to give it back to him?"

"I don't think I'm going to make a decision about that right now."

"What do you mean?"

"It strikes me that you really need for me to take down the Vulture or spend the rest of your life looking over your shoulder. Maybe I'll decide what to do after I see how you do tomorrow at the castle."

The man's face fell, and Bolan put away the Beretta.

"Okay, it's chow time," Bolan said, "fuel up for tomorrow. There's hope for you yet—you didn't do quite as bad as expected."

CHAPTER SIXTEEN

Zurich
July 24, 6:23 a.m.

Bolan moved quickly and quietly along Langstrasse until he came to Sprecher's print shop. There were a few sawhorse barricades around the front, and the busted-out door and window were boarded over. He slipped around the barricades and did some judicious prying with a pocket knife, removing enough boards to slip inside.

He walked into the gray glow of the print shop, whose diffuse light was supplied by cracks in the boarded window. Most of the equipment was shot up, wrecked, blood splattered everywhere. The silhouette outlines of the men he'd killed were chalk outlines on the floor.

Very little of any interest was visible up front, but Bolan couldn't help but wonder if Sprecher didn't keep his seamier side out of view.

He moved quickly to the back of the shop and

found the sliding panel under the stairs quickly enough. It led into another print shop, a small one, with cameras and fingerprint equipment and stacks of official-looking Swiss government stationery. There were rows of hundreds of rubber stamps and various seals. A large laminating machine sat in the corner. He pulled the printout from his pocket and rechecked the information.

Bolan flipped the light switch, relieved to find the electricity still operational. He moved to the passport-photo booth immediately, setting the auto timer and moving against the white background. The flash went off.

THE VULTURE STOOD atop the battlements, the binoculars glued to his face as he swept them slowly across the wide breadth of the lower mountain and his defenses.

His troop ranks had swelled to over 120 thanks to some successful recruitment. They were out in force and would remain so, and the Vulture had brought thirty .50-caliber machine guns out of storage for an extra measure of safety. Two surplus American M-1 tanks prowled the snow-covered hills between the first and second battlements.

The town lay far below, already crowded with strangers. Could Belasko be among them? The Chinook was just taking off from the square, weaving its way around a half-dozen hot-air balloons that floated lazily through the morning sky. The partiers were ar- riving also, the cream of European society paying homage to one of their own. For the moment he would let Kimberly entertain them. Kimberly was a very entertaining woman.

"Baron!" Barbaro called from the nearby parapet. The man's Neanderthal face, thick with black beard, poked from the bow slot. "We are ready for you."

The Vulture nodded, removing his binoculars and putting them in the case slung over his shoulder. He wore a black tuxedo with a miniature red rose, pro- vided by Kimberly, in his lapel.

He moved along the narrow ledge. The courtyard, cleared of last night's snowfall, was fifty feet below. The drop-off on the other side was hundreds of feet. The sky was huge around him, the bright sun parting gray clouds, Nature's vast panorama a present just for him.

His eye began to throb as he moved into the cir- cular tower to climb the spiraling stairs set against the outer wall.

The big man would not ruin his festival. The castle could not be penetrated.

The stone stairs led into a tower chamber, which was now fixed with three of the heavy machine guns sticking through the slots and sandbagged all around. The other two towers were similarly buttressed. But that wasn't what Barbaro wanted to see him about.

Willy Mulroy, stripped to the waist with arms

spread wide, was chained to the wall. Ugly welts covered his torso—burns and the bloody tracks and grooves of flailing. The weighted leather cattails, dripping blood, were on a side bench.

The man's eyes were wide, wild things. Nearly inured to the pain by now, Mulroy had to be living in a pristine mental state, adrenaline flowing, endorphins pumping through his system to narcotize the pain. His mind was probably clearer than it had ever been, as it should be. He was dealing with the issue of continued existence on a very personal and immediate level.

Barbaro was over by the bench, going through a leather pouch full of what looked like dental and carpenter tools. Barbaro had been with the Vulture for many years. He was the point maker, the man who took over when civilized methods no longer helped. He was very talented and believed in using his talents. He'd lusted after Mulroy for a long time and had finally gotten him. The Vulture believed in rewarding good service.

"Willy," the Vulture said, "how it pains me to see you in such a situation."

"Don't kill me," Mulroy rasped.

The Vulture walked up, grabbed him hard by the jawline and squeezed, watching his eyes. There was fear there, pain, questions—but no blinding hatred. He had acted as a mentor and tutor to Mulroy since Paraguay. The loyalty it had engendered was obviously total. Fine. When all else failed, loyal sacrifice was usually dependable.

He heard the match strike, and both his and Mulroy's eyes darted to the candle Barbaro was lighting on the bench.

"Don't worry, dear friend, no more burning."

"Please don't kill me," Mulroy said. "I can still get him."

"The question of what to do with you has been most perplexing," the Vulture said. "You are so wonderfully, doggedly loyal on one hand and so fecklessly stupid on the other."

He walked to the bench and took Belasko's knife from his pocket, tripping the spring that opened the blade. He walked to the candle and dipped the blade into the flame, holding it there.

"What are you going to do?" Mulroy asked, watching the blade as Barbaro moved to his left, a pair of garden clippers in his hand.

"I came to the conclusion that no one is stupid," the Vulture declared, ignoring the question, "that the kind of irresponsible ignorance you have displayed is simply the result of shabby thinking and that it can be corrected."

"Don't kill me."

"I'm *not* going to kill you. I love you. But sometimes you have to hurt the ones you love in order to teach them the proper lessons in life." He looked at Barbaro. "Cut off a finger."

"No!" Mulroy yelled, struggling against the chains that held him fast.

"Which one?" the dark man asked.

"He still needs to be able to shoot and fight. Just a little finger."

"Baron, please!" Mulroy screamed to no avail.

Barbaro smiled slightly as he snipped off the digit, bone crunching beneath the onslaught of the clippers, Mulroy's eyes bugged out of his head as he stared at the bloody stump where a little finger had been.

He screamed.

"Here," the Vulture said. "Let me help you."

He jerked the knife out of the flame and walked to Mulroy's hand, laying the edge of the blade on the open wound to cauterize it. The smell of burning flesh made the gunners turn around and wince.

Mulroy swooned in his chains, but the Vulture slapped him and brought him around. "I'm giving you one more chance," he said. "Do you understand me?"

"Yes...yes," the man said.

"I want you to make sure that Mr. Belasko does not interfere with the festival. Will you do that?"

"Yes...please..."

"If you fail, I will cut you apart a piece at a time...a little piece at a time. Clear?"

He shared a long look with the man and could see absolute understanding between them, true communication.

He looked at Barbaro. "Clean and dress his wounds. Willy is going back to work. He has a job to do."

Barbaro held up the finger. "And this?"

"Put it on a string and hang it around Willy's neck. In case he forgets."

THE FAKE BEARD ITCHED but Bolan was willing to tolerate it because he could hide behind it so nobody would see who was wearing the leather shorts with suspenders that Dennison called "traditional" and the little Alpine hat with the feather in it.

And in fact he blended right in with the rest of the shoulder-to-shoulder crowd, none of them embarrassed about being dressed as they were. Soon enough it felt normal, and Bolan didn't think about it anymore.

Dennison was gone in his cute little outfit, checking with some of the balloon owners to see if they were rentable. Bolan was improvising as he went along.

Heavily armed men with roving eyes were everywhere, all of them looking for him. It was what made such serious disguise mandatory. For the moment even his harness was safe inside the trunk of the BMW Bolan had "borrowed" in Zurich.

There were probably three thousand people in a town whose usual population was about two hundred. There was free and spirited drinking, and the oompah bands played everywhere. Rifle shots rang out from surrounding fields, from the marksmanship competitions for schoolboys; the value of a good eye and steady hand was as important here as skill at mathematics.

Bolan's eyes took in everything, memorizing his surroundings, marking the killground. He'd especially been watching the Chinook. The ceremonial guard surrounding it sported the traditional red-and-white uniform and tall bearskin hat. The uniform jacket would cover the combat harness just fine. If he could get close enough to the chopper, he could take it. And one of those uniforms would sure help him get close. Nightfall wouldn't hurt, either.

He stopped to lean against a small statue of a printing press, apparently a homage to the famous local counterfeiter. He looked up the hill at the castle and pretended to drink his beer. It was a rough route any way but by air, and by air was going to be a million-to-one shot.

Dennison, who looked quite natural with his long hair and leather outfit, angled up to Bolan's position, standing with his back to the castle. He pretended to drink his beer.

"Any luck?" Bolan asked.

"There's a guy who'll rent me a balloon at dusk," Dennison said, "but he wants it back before dark. No one's willing to let them go up after dark."

"Dusk it is," the Executioner said.

The man grinned at him. "You know, it just occurred to me that I can't lose with this proposition. If you kill the Vulture and get away, there's a chance I'll profit. If you kill the Vulture and die, I'll definitely profit. If the Vulture kills you, oh well. I'll profit and move far away."

"You just help me up that hill," Bolan said. "That's the only thing you need to be thinking about." He showed the inside of the pouch he wore over his shoulder. It contained their climbing gear, plus several empty bottles.

"I grabbed three or four good-sized bottles from the streets," he said. "We'll find a few more along the way."

"Bottles?"

"Yeah. We'll take them out to the car later and siphon the gas out of the BMW to fill them."

"You want me to drop Molotov cocktails?" Dennison asked.

"Only enough to make them think there's an attack coming from the other direction," Bolan replied. "Enough to grab their attention. After that, you're free to go."

"If I have any gas left in the BMW."

"Don't mess with me," Bolan said. "Just keep up your end of the bargain. You know how to pilot a balloon, don't you?"

"The guy said he'd show me."

"Great." He pushed Dennison out of the way to

watch the chopper slowly descend from the lofty peaks just as a convoy of several large trucks rumbled down the mountain trail into the city.

"What's happening?" Bolan asked.

"The trucks are delivering barrels of wine for the festival from the baron's cellars, made in his own vineyards. That's probably him flying down right now to officially dedicate the festival."

"Why didn't you tell me this before?" Bolan said. "I could have set up down here and gotten away in the crowds."

"I'd forgotten," Dennison said. "Hell, I've just been here once. You can't expect me to remember everything."

Bolan briefly considered trying to grab a rifle and take the man cowboy style, on the fly, but something held him up. So far the Vulture had lived a charmed life. But he was careful, too, a planner. Knowing the Executioner was in the village would be enough to make him alter his normal routine.

"Let's see how close we can get," Bolan said.

They packed in tightly around the square, getting within thirty feet of the landing pad, and Bolan noticed Mulroy in charge of protecting the bird when it landed.

"There's your blond friend from the Little Madam," Dennison said. "I'd hoped we wouldn't see him again."

"Look at his hand," Bolan directed. "It looks like he's missing a finger."

Dennison had small opera glasses to his face. "It's not missing," he explained. "It's hanging from a string around his neck."

"And that's how the Vulture treats his friends," Bolan said. "That's what he got for letting us slip through at Marta's house."

Four open-backed trucks rumbled into the square, and a thunderous cheer went up from the assembled. As the chopper descended to the city, men rolled barrels to the edge of the truck backs and tapped them, and the wine flowed unchecked.

The helicopter reached the square but didn't land. It hovered, blowing full skirts and tablecloths and trash in billows around the square.

"My friends," came the Vulture's booming voice through a loudspeaker system on the chopper itself. "Welcome to our festival!"

Bolan couldn't see the man in the bay. The voice sounded recorded.

"Unfortunately, due to some poor health today," the voice continued, "I am unable to join you in person for the opening of the festival. To do the honors for me this year, I introduce you to someone far easier to look at. I give you a goddess of the American cinema, and my very dear friend, Kimberly Adams."

A woman in a lime green chiffon evening gown with three-quarter gloves appeared in the bay, waving as the crowd cheered. Hell, they'd been drinking since early this morning; they'd cheer anything.

"The baron sends his regrets," she said. Her voice was loud, and feedback forced everyone to put their hands over their ears. "But I want you to know I'm taking very good care of him!"

Loud laughter and cheers stoked a black anger in Bolan. He wondered if the woman knew exactly who it was she was selling herself out to.

"And now it is my great honor and pleasure to officially open this year's von Maur Wine Festival with a gift to you from the baron from his vineyards—von Maur burgundy, the finest in the world! Enjoy, people!"

The crowd charged the trucks then, and the chopper angled off. "He's not coming down the mountain today," Dennison said.

"No. He's waiting for me to come to him. Let's wander around a bit and enjoy the festival. We've got hours until dark. Study the town. Maybe it will present something to us."

"I've got something for you to see," Dennison stated. "If we're not too late. Come with me."

They walked through town, past a field where a number of circles of sand had been piled for Swiss wrestling, a popular local sport. Six matches were going all at the same time, spectators betting and cheering on their favorites.

Next to the wrestling field was another field, this

one also surrounded by spectators who were cheering and cajoling. But Bolan couldn't see anything happening in the clearing itself. Two cows, little cows at that, were quietly eating grass and swatting flies with their tails.

They joined the circle watching the two little cows. The men were pointing and betting. "I give," Bolan said. "What's going on?"

"Cow fights," Dennison said.

"Cow fights," Bolan repeated, as if saying the words would put it in perspective for him.

"Yeah. Those cows are small, but they're Eringers, a very aggressive breed. These are the toughest from two different herds. It could be a good match. This man next to me just bet a million francs on the one with the dark spots."

"How do cows fight, Rennie?"

"Oh, I don't know. They just kind of...butt up against each other, you know?"

"Not really. When does it start? Do they ring a bell or something?"

"No. The cows just have to get around to it whenever they feel like it."

"And how do we know when the fight is over?"

"When one of the cows runs away."

Bolan smiled and lifted his stein to the man on his right. This was the craziest place he'd ever seen.

THE GREAT HALL TEEMED with life, and the Vulture was basking in his role of lord of the manor. His eye had hurt steadily for several hours, yet no trace of Belasko had been found. He stood with Count and Countess Wolfstein near the tables, where a feast of the foods of three countries was spread for all to share. The great hall held up to four hundred, and there were at least that many here now, their talk and laughter creating a constant echoing rumble in the mammoth cathedral ceiling.

A sixteen-piece jazz band played on a raised platform. Jazz was another of the Vulture's loves, another art form created out of synchronistic change and pain. He found its permutations endlessly fascinating.

"You are such a rogue, Baron," the count said, sipping a gin and tonic. "You are reported to have one of the world's great Impressionist collections, yet you do not have it out for everyone to see."

"My dear Count," the Vulture said, "in order to achieve a great private collection in this day and age, one must necessarily heed the word 'private,' for there aren't a great many works of the mid-nineteenth century up for sale through altogether...legal channels. One must go where the art is."

"I understand the nature of collecting," Wolfstein agreed. "My wife is obsessed with Delacroix. We have had to resort to the basest of means to satisfy her."

The Vulture turned and smiled at the woman, a stern, midfifties, matronly type. "Why Countess," he said, "you have a bold streak. Delacroix. Decisive. Swift. The beating heart of Impressionism was born in his style."

"His work is so active," she returned, flushing slightly. "And his portraits of the Hapsburgs..."

"I own several Delacroixs," the Vulture boasted.

"No," the countess said. "Which?"

"Several of those Hapsburg portraits you talked about," he explained. "But I have one I believe would tempt you more."

"Is your artwork for sale?" the count asked.

"Everything is for sale, Gregore," he returned. "It's all just a question of prices."

"Which painting?" the countess asked, and the Vulture enjoyed watching the avid fire come into her blue eyes. It made her much more attractive. No wonder the count catered to her obsession.

"I'm not going to tell. You'll just have to see it."

"Now?"

"Why not, but we must tell no one else, eh?" He looked at the count. "I hope you've brought your checkbook, Gregore. This may prove to be a very expensive day for you. Follow me upstairs." He turned to Kimberly at his side and smiled. "My dear? Will you join us?"

He took her arm and led her up the stairs. He liked this one a lot. She'd been an animal the night before. He was always an animal.

"I don't understand what's going on," she said. "Why can't we say anything about your paintings?"

"I'm a very bad boy," he returned, leaning down to kiss her on the cheek. "As you said, 'dangerous.' Many of my paintings were acquired over the black market."

"Stolen paintings?"

"I prefer to think of them as homeless."

They reached the mezzanine, the open balcony running around the great hall on three sides, with doors leading to bedrooms and studies.

He walked them along the balcony, stopping to unlock a door with a key from his pocket. They walked into the gallery, a long, richly decorated room fifty feet long. It was jammed with paintings, from waist level all the way up to the top of the ten-foot-high wall.

"Oh, my," Jessica Wolfstein said. "This is amazing."

And truly it was, several of the world's most famous paintings fighting for space within one room.

The countess charged around the room, squealing like a schoolgirl, while her husband backed slowly into the center of the room, turning a slow circle.

"I'm amazed," the count breathed.

"You should see what I have in storage," the Vulture commented, walking to the countess. "Jessica, my dear. Here is what you want to see."

He led her down the wall, stopping near the corner

and pointing to the picture at eye level. The woman's mouth fell open.

"The Death of Sardanapalus," she whispered, a hand going to her throat. "But I thought—"

"There's a perfect facsimile at the Louvre," the Vulture said, watching the woman's growing excitement. It was a painting of the potentate Sardanapalus preparing to immolate himself, his servants bringing his favorite wives, horses and dogs in to cut their throats before him. It was considered scandalous at the time.

The countess turned to her husband. "Gregore," she said. "I must have it."

"What's going on outside?" Kimberly asked, staring out from one of the tall, narrow windows.

The Vulture joined her and watched the men unpacking crates marked with danger signs from the huge trucks below.

"I've decided to give my guests and the townspeople an extra treat tonight," he said. "When it gets dark, I'm going to put on the greatest fireworks display Switzerland has ever seen!"

He expected the big man to come with the darkness. When the fighting began, the fireworks would cover the noise and the explosions.

"Now, we *are* friends," Wolfstein said. "You wouldn't overcharge a friend, would you?"

The Vulture smiled. "This is business, Gregore.

Market value is what a picture's worth to the individual. Let's see what it's worth to Jessica."

Schwander appeared in the doorway, a cell phone in his hand. "Baron, someone from Bank Leu wants to speak with you."

"Tell him it's Wine Festival. I'll deal with it—"

"He says it is extremely urgent."

"Excuse me." The Vulture moved to take the phone out onto the mezzanine.

"This is von Maur," he said.

"Baron," came a frightened voice—his accountant. "This is Grauwiler. Something is seriously wrong with the books."

"What are you talking about?" the Vulture said angrily. "Don't you know I'm in the middle of—?"

"Your money's gone," Grauwiler said.

"What do you mean, gone?"

"I was transferring funds," Grauwiler said, "wanting to buy American dollars from the numbered account while they were low. There was no money to transfer. Have you put it into another account?"

"Of course not. That's your job."

"We show a transfer going into another numbered account yesterday."

"How is that possible?"

"We were hoping down here that you could enlighten us."

"Someone stole my money! Get it back!"

"It's not that simple," Grauwiler answered, his

voice shaking. "First of all, we can't just go into another numbered account and take the money away without reason."

"It's *my* money! That's your reason!"

"Baron...please. This is difficult enough as it is. There will have to be a formal investigation, charges brought, a hearing in court before—"

"You know I can't do that!" the Vulture snapped, then lowered his voice to a desperate whisper. "I can't deal with the law...I won't. There must be another way. Get the money back. Tell whoever you need to tell that there will be a generous reward for my money's safe return, no questions asked."

"You still don't understand. From the numbered account, the money was transferred again, into a dozen banks and brokerage houses in a dozen different parts of the world. We can't just take that money away."

"Why not?"

"No one will give it to us. It was put there by the owner of the numbered account. Without the court proceedings—"

The Vulture bellowed, "The name, Grauwiler. What name is attached to this number?"

"Baron," the man whispered. "You don't know the trouble—"

"You want trouble, you bald-headed idiot, I'll give you all you can handle. Give me that name or I'll cut your tongue out and make you eat it."

The man's voice quavered fearfully as he said, "My contact at the bank would only say it was an American customer. You must realize—"

The Vulture threw the phone down the mezzanine. Belasko had managed to do it. And it had to be Dennison, the computer whiz. That's who'd grabbed the money. This was no longer a diverting game, but a true life-and-death struggle. The Vulture hadn't survived to this point by being stupid. He knew that all that surrounded him—everything he had, every friend he knew, every woman who loved him—was bought and paid for. Without money he was just another cheap gun for hire, like Mulroy. Since he had no heart, he had to buy the hearts of others. It was the closest to really being alive he ever got.

He couldn't give that up. He would die without it.

He pulled the knife out of his tuxedo jacket and cut himself on the hand, across the palm. Blood welled up quickly to sheet down his hand and drop on the floor. Pain flared along his nerves. He used it to stoke his internal fires and prepare for battle.

CHAPTER SEVENTEEN

Bolan now had his means of admittance into the castle. He'd relieved one of the men in the Swiss guard uniform of his outfit and left its owner tied up in the bushes.

He buttoned into the red trousers, a trifle large, stuffing the shirttail into the pants. Then he tried on the red-and-white wool jacket; its larger size would leave room for the combat harness.

He quickly moved through the grass a thousand yards from the edge of the city, carrying the bearskin cap under his arm and tugging at the fake beard.

He jerked hard, and the beard ripped off, stinging his face. He put on the black frame glasses he'd taken from the guard, and the world blurred immediately. He slid the glasses down his nose and looked over the rims.

He angled back in toward the city lights, reaching the distant parking lots where they'd left the car this morning. They were close enough to town to hear the music, especially the tubas, and the laughter of the crowds—all potential enemies now. He stared up the castle looming forbiddingly above.

They were parked amid a thousand cars, and Dennison was busy siphoning gas from other cars.

Bolan slipped into the harness with its protective body armor and put the coat back on. It worked well. He pulled on the tall cap, hooking the strap under his chin, then adjusting the clunky glasses.

"Next step," he said. "I walk up and get on the aircraft and take it to the castle while you drop Molotov cocktails on the western slope from your balloon."

Dennison shrugged. He looked into the sky. "Getting dark."

"Yeah," the Executioner said. "It's time. Good luck to you."

"You're the one who needs the luck. You realize I think you're mad to take this on?"

"Luck's fickle, and maybe *his* luck is ready to desert him. You think *me* mad, but he is rabid. So let's forget the talk, and just do it."

"Sure," the man said. "Why not? This is totally weird."

"No…last night at the bank was totally weird. This I understand. It's very direct."

They moved closer to the city, picking up a dirt road leading in. They sank into themselves, each preparing in his own way. Bolan considered the possibility of defeat. As difficult as it was going to be getting in, he had no way out planned. It was the ultimate cowboy job in the final analysis. He was the most confident man in the world, but this was different. It was personal. There was no risk unacceptable, no odds too high. No hasty exits like in Paraguay. He would either succeed in killing the Vulture or he would die in the attempt. One thing he knew, if he went down, it would be because the Vulture's whole damned army had taken him down. That's what it would take.

The dirt turned to cobblestones, and the city rose around them. The sky was cherry pink as they rejoined the street crowds and moved along the main drag toward the square, to the sounds of the singing crowd.

"Strange," Dennison said. "There's a girl in the crowd moving just ahead of us who looks like Marta."

"Leave it alone."

"Did she tell you where she was going that day?"

"Just leaving town for a few days of vacation time. Look, here's the balloon. Let's do this part now."

The balloon was tethered in the middle of a blocked-off street. Gray houses rose on either side of it, the balloon almost touching their facades. It was emblazoned with a smiling sun face.

"See you on the other side," Bolan said, giving Dennison a starting shove.

Dennison nodded and began to maneuver himself out of the flow of the crowd.

And then it happened: everything changed in the blink of an eye. A woman just a few feet in front of him stopped walking and turned. It was Marta.

Bolan tried to get next to her, but it was not to be. Her head cocked to the side as she caught sight of Dennison, doing a double take when she saw the fake beard, then laughing and shaking her head when she knew it was truly him.

She broke immediately from the crowd. "Rennie!" she called. "Rennie Dennison!"

Dennison froze, his shoulders hunching up. She ran to him, and Bolan slid out of the crowd to watch from the shadows of the house beside the balloon.

He turned to her, smiling slightly. "Uh, hi, Marta."

"What are you doing here? And in that beard?"

The man turned and put the sack full of Molotov cocktails and climbing gear inside the balloon's basket. He turned back around, his eyes scanning wildly through the crowd. "Wine festival," he said. "Had to come back after last year."

"And the beard?"

"It grows…really fast."

Bolan saw the cordon of men moving relentlessly through the crowd toward the balloon. Mulroy was in their midst, talking on a cell phone, probably setting his men up to draw the noose tight.

Civilians were everywhere. As usual, the Vulture

had picked an impossible place for a firefight. Bolan sank back in the shadows, watching several men pass him on their way to spring the trap.

MULROY MOVED through the crowd like a vampire stalking a victim, his eyes scanning every human being he came in contact with.

He'd been moving through the darkness of the side streets, and now his quarry had been identified for him. What a piece of luck, he thought with rising excitement.

It was him, the man who'd started all of this. Sprecher's friend, the man with the computers and the crypto.

He slid closer, pulling the cell phone from his belt and pushing the button that put him in touch with his people on the streets. "We've got the younger one," he said softly, "at the corner of Kleinstrasse and Marktplatz. Long hair, phony beard. Get here now. We'll take him on my signal."

As he crept through the shadows, he scanned the surrounding crowds, looking for Belasko. If one was here, so was the other.

He watched his men positioning themselves. "Move in slowly," he ordered, switching the phone to his bandaged hand and pulling the nickel-plated .45 out of the garrison belt.

He strode toward the man, still straining to watch the crowd. Dennison was talking to the woman when he walked up, cocked the gun and stuck it against the man's temple.

"Hey, Rennie. I've been looking all over for you," Mulroy said.

His men rushed up then, over a dozen. They grabbed Dennison and seized the woman when Mulroy nodded toward her, too.

"Quick…down here," he said, moving into the darkened street. A phalanx of men totally surrounded Dennison and the woman, dragging them down the street. The woman tried to scream, but one of Mulroy's men slapped her and muffled her mouth with a big hand.

Mulroy picked a house in the middle of the block and kicked open the door. Everyone filed into the darkened house, spreading out. The owners were at the festival, like everyone else.

"Where is he?" he rasped in Dennison's face, then knocked him to the floor when he didn't answer quickly enough. "Where's the big man?"

The woman was crying. Mulroy twisted his good hand in her hair and pulled her to her knees beside Dennison. Paybacks were great.

"He's…in the city," Dennison said, not looking up, blood bubbling from his lips. "We'd just split up."

"What's your plan of attack?"

"Listen, we weren't—"

Mulroy shut him up with a jackboot to the gut. Dennison doubled up into the fetal position and began throwing up. "Let the woman go," he said through clenched teeth from the floor. "She has nothing to do with this."

"Nothing to do with it?" Mulroy looked at the group of men jammed around him.

"Get out of here," he said. "Go watch the balloon. Just leave a half dozen in here."

His men filed slowly out. "Where were we?" Mulroy asked, jerking on the woman's long brown hair, nice hair, like his mama's.

She cried out just like his mama, too.

"Oh, yeah," he said. "You were saying how she didn't have anything to do with this."

"Let her go," Dennison said, half rising, his arms wrapped around his stomach.

Mulroy kicked him again, this time in the face. "This is almost too easy," he said as Dennison fell heavily to the floor. "Now look at me."

Mulroy pulled the woman up against his legs and shoved the .45 against her ear. "Here's what she has to do with it. If you don't tell me the game plan as soon as I'm finished talking, I'm gonna blow her brains all over you, and you'll *still* end up telling me before we're through."

"No!" the woman moaned, in the grip of terrible fear.

"Will you let her go if I tell you?"

"Sure. I'm easy."

"I was supposed to take a balloon and create a

diversion while he commandeered the chopper and went for the castle."

Mulroy laughed. "That son of a bitch has fifty-pound balls, don't he?"

"Now let her go," Dennison said.

"Soon as I'm through with her." Mulroy smiled, awkwardly pulling the cell phone off his belt with his wounded hand.

"Looks like you're falling apart," Dennison said, nodding toward the finger on the string. "Is that the punishment for screwing up at Marta's house?"

Mulroy kicked him in the face again, knocking him back hard to the floor.

"What about my house?" Marta said, wincing.

"It's gone, honey," Mulroy said. "Blown to hell."

She looked at Dennison. "You blew up my house?"

The man shook his head, spitting out a tooth. He pointed to Mulroy. "No, *he* blew up your house."

Mulroy connected with the chopper station. "Is the bird in the nest?" he asked.

"We're waiting for it to come down from the castle."

"Okay." He punched up the baron's number in his study, and he answered immediately.

"This had better be good news."

"I don't have the big man," Mulroy said, "but I've got the other one, the hippie. You want me to kill him now?"

"No, no, no," the Vulture returned, excitement in his voice. "Please. Whatever you do, don't hurt Mr. Dennison. I must speak with him immediately. This is excellent work, Willy. Excellent. I am very proud of you. Bring Dennison to me. Bring him now."

"He said the big guy's gonna try and take the chopper," he said.

"Where is it now?"

"At the castle, waiting to ferry people back to the town."

"Drive up," the Vulture instructed.

"Don't you want to stop the chopper from comin' down the mountain?"

"No, Willy. We will prepare the chopper on this end for a reception worthy of our adversary."

"But not Dennison?"

"Dennison is my best friend at this moment. Bring my friend safely to me. Drive. Is that clear?"

"I guess so. But I don't underst—"

"You're not supposed to. Hurry, Willy. Hurry Dennison to the castle. He and I need to have a conversation about computers."

"There's a woman with him."

"How nice. Bring her along, too." The Vulture hung up.

Mulroy looked at the men remaining in the room. "Bring the car around," he said, "but keep an open-line contact to me the entire time. There's a man hiding out there who could kick all of your asses with his eyes closed. So watch it.''

They hurried out. Mulroy noticed through the open doorway that the fireworks display had begun up on the mountain. Brilliant streamers of flashing, glittering colors gilded the clouds above and reflected on the snow below. But the real fireworks would start later—that much he knew.

BOLAN WATCHED from the rooftop across the street as Dennison and Marta were dragged from the house and shoved into the big white Mercedes as fireworks exploded brilliantly overhead.

A number of factors were immediately obvious. First, there was nothing he could do for Dennison at this moment. Any rescue attempt would surely end in disaster for both Dennison and Marta, and it would be foolish to risk losing his main target. Secondly, judging from Dennison's condition, he'd obviously told Mulroy the plan. If the chopper wasn't held up at the castle, it would come down loaded for bear. Thirdly, he couldn't figure out why Mulroy hadn't killed Dennison immediately, unless there was already feedback from last night's theft.

If that was the case, Dennison might not be in any imminent danger—not until after he was forced to capitulate and return the stolen money. He could see absolutely no other reason for the man to be still alive.

The Vulture wouldn't hesitate to have him killed immediately if he had no use for him.

The car disappeared along the road up the mountain. Bolan slid along the high-peaked roof to shinny down the drainpipe four stories to the ground.

He moved cautiously into the dark street. All the noise, light and action were a block farther north, where throngs of people danced and laughed, pointing up at the fireworks with collective oohs and aahs. He walked slowly back toward the action, briefly considering riding the balloon as an alternative.

He could have the sky immediately, but with no control. He'd be at the whim of the wind and would risk being blown off target, or worse, hovering for hours while they shot him down.

Taking the Chinook was still the best shot. He looked up at the castle, so small yet imposing in the distance, and smiled when the chopper crested the top of the wall and angled down toward the town square.

He picked up his pace and walked into the square. The uniform was serving as a better disguise than he'd originally expected. The Vulture controlled an army of strangers. No one would shoot the uniform until he had thoroughly checked out the man wearing it, lest the same thing happen to him.

When he walked into the square, the chopper was nearly halfway from the castle. He began looking for a target. He zeroed in on a huge, bearded tough-

looking man dressed in short leather pants, but nobody would ever dare tell this guy he looked silly.

He was standing, talking with a group of men who
were all drinking. The men were leaving, and the big
guy waved to them as they moved off in a happy
mood. Then he turned to the woman at his side,
snarled something at her and shoved, sending her
sprawling. It must have been jealousy because now
she was crying and trying to button her revealing
blouse. The big man narrowed his eyes and looked
around just as Bolan approached him with a friendly
look. The chopper just hit the pad fifty feet behind
him.

"Excuse me," Bolan said in English. "There's
something I must do."

The man smiled, gesturing broadly with his hands
to indicate he hadn't understood.

Bolan saw that the chopper was down, idling on
the pad, no one getting in or out. He had to make his
move now, Bolan decided.

Without another word, he came around with a hard,
stiff right to the man's gut. He was muscled, but doubled over anyway, and Bolan grabbed the back of his
head and held it as he slammed a knee to the man's
nose.

The man went down, blood spurting from his nose.
"I have him!" Bolan yelled in English, which seemed
to be the official language of the Vulture's multicul-

tural army. "I have the big man! He's down! Hurry! Hurry!"

The crowd swept back as men rushed from their hiding places to converge on the scene and scrambled from inside the Chinook.

The big man growled from the ground, then got immediately to his feet, anger burning in his eyes. He was talking away, but Bolan didn't understand a word.

Just as the mob of mercs reached them, Bolan stomped hard on the big man's foot. The man screamed loudly, swinging a beefy right hand that connected solidly on Bolan's jaw, driving him back into the pack.

The hired guns jumped the man, and Bolan stumbled back through their midst, then staggered, hand to his aching jaw, toward the helicopter.

Two men armed with M-16s guarded the open bay of the Chinook. "They got him down there," Bolan said.

"Looks like he got you," one of the men said.

"Go ahead if you want to get in on it. I've had enough. I'll watch the bird for a minute."

They were off in a flash. Bolan pulled off the glasses and hat and immediately jumped into the bay. He jerked out the .44 and the Beretta, much to the surprise of the three heavily armed men in snow camouflage who sat on the metal bench seat welded to the frame.

Fire spit from both barrels, and they all went down, unable to even fire their weapons. But the sound would bring back the others and timing was critical. Bolan turned and kicked out at the small cockpit door, prepared to force the pilot into the air, but the pilot had other ideas.

The pilot was trying to pull a pistol out of his belt, but it got hung up on the control panel, snapping free only to discharge beside his head. He turned and looked blankly at Bolan for several seconds before sighing loudly and sinking back in his seat, his brains running down the side of his face.

Bolan pulled the pilot out of his seat and took the controls, lifting off before any of the mercs could return to the chopper. The rotor wash drove everyone back as the chopper swung in a wide arc. Bolan watched through the bubble windshield as the square came into view. Bullets pounded the side of the chopper, and Bolan pulled up hard just as his bubble front was ready to smash into a parked bus. The bird rose quickly, and the city was suddenly small beneath him.

CHAPTER EIGHTEEN

Rennie Dennison sat beside Marta. Both of them were handcuffed behind their backs. She leaned her head against his shoulder and sobbed quietly, fearful of Mulroy's rage. But the rage hadn't been there, not since the phone call.

Dennison smiled. The money. The money was keeping him alive right now.

"What did you do?" Marta asked him. "Why did they blow up my house?"

"It's complicated," Dennison replied, his mind working the possibilities. Bolan had taught him one thing: life belonged to those who took the possibilities without hesitation. To the bold. It had worked so far.

"It ain't complicated," Mulroy said from the front seat, turning to face them. He shrugged at Marta Kleppe. "We were after the guy your boyfriend hangs around with, so he goes along with the deal. He's a government snitch, your boyfriend. You just happened to own the house."

"He's not my boyfriend," Marta said.

"Whatever."

"You certainly misunderstand the importance of my role in all this, Mr. Mulroy," Dennison said, trying some bait.

"No way," Mulroy said. "You got lucky with Sprecher and snitched, hopin' it'd help you escape Zurich."

"What's wrong with Zurich?" Marta asked.

"Nothing," Dennison said. "I love Zurich." He turned back to Mulroy. "I'm sure that the baron told you on the phone to treat us properly, correct?"

Mulroy's slack face spoke volumes.

"Do you want to know why, Mulroy?"

The man made a fist to punch him, then looked down at his bandaged hand. He stared at it for a minute, then looked back at Dennison. "Why?" he asked.

"Because I stole all his money."

Mulroy's eyes went wide in the multicolored lights of the fireworks. "All of it?"

"All except for pocket change," Dennison said. "Fifty million American dollars."

"Fifty...million?" Marta repeated.

Dennison nodded. "I hope the baron hasn't written any checks to pay for the festivities tonight."

Mulroy just stared at him.

"Think about this," Dennison urged. "We'll go up to the castle and I'll negotiate with the baron, probably cut a deal with him pretty quickly. I'll get all his money back for him and get a hefty percentage for my time. In fact he may even want to use me in future on a consulting basis so something like this doesn't happen again. You, however, screwed up one thing and have to wear your finger tied on a string."

"Son of a bitch," Mulroy said.

"Let us go, Mulroy," Dennison said. "I'd just as soon cut my deal with you and the gentlemen in this car as with Long John Silver up on the top of the hill. What would you say to about ten million in American dollars?"

"Twenty," Mulroy said.

"Fifteen, no more."

"Seventeen-five."

"Seventeen and a quarter," Dennison declared emphatically.

"Deal," Mulroy said as the other men in the car spoke among themselves.

Mulroy's phone rang. He put up a hand for quiet and answered. "Yeah? Yeah…how the—?" He slapped the driver. "Stop the damned car."

They jerked to a halt a hundred feet from the first checkpoint. Mulroy kicked open his door to stare into the night sky, while Dennison leaned over to look out the back window.

"What is it?" Marta asked.

"It's that damned Belasko," Dennison said. "All we needed."

The Chinook was angling away from the village, moving inexorably in their direction. Belasko.

"He's coming this way," Mulroy said into his phone from the pitted blacktop. "Notify the checkpoint. Everybody open fire. We'll bring him down."

Mulroy leaned back into the car. "Everybody out! Take your guns. A million francs to the merc who brings down that chopper!"

"Let us go now," Dennison said to him. The merc's face was hard as the large car emptied, the door on Dennison's side left standing open. "Just uncuff us and we're gone."

"Yeah...that's what I'm afraid of," the man answered. He pointed skyward. "Until this is finished, all deals are off."

Mulroy was out of the car then, directing his men off the roadway and into the snowbanks to get the best angle on the incoming chopper.

Dennison turned to Marta. "You have small hands. Work them, try and slide out of the cuffs."

"They're tight. They hurt."

"Just keep trying." he answered, sliding toward the door. "Come on. Let's get in the front."

He slid out as the chopper came in overhead. Mulroy and his men opened up on it, the lower battlements joining in a moment later, rattling the night.

Dennison turned to open up the driver's-side door to let Marta slide in first. He then slid awkwardly behind the wheel, which jammed into his stomach because of the position of his hands. He couldn't close the door.

"What are you doing?" she asked.

"Taking advantage of an opportunity," he returned, leaning in her direction to push the gearshift into neutral with his body.

"But what about your deal?"

"You can't make deals with animals. Are you working on your cuffs?" he asked as he raised a knee, bringing it back to his chest.

"Yes," she said. "They're coming. It's not easy."

"Hey!" someone called from the field. Mulroy was running back toward the car with several of the men.

"Fine," Dennison said, and tripped the handbrake lever with his foot. The car immediately rolled backward.

"What the hell are you doing?" she screamed.

"Get out of the cuffs!" he yelled back, bringing up his other knee, steering with them as they rolled backward.

One of the mercs jumped on the hood. The driver's door flapped, then tore the other way, snapping, flying off the hinges and wiping Mulroy off the road.

"You're crazy! You're crazy!" Marta yelled at him as she pulled her hands against the metal cuffs, twisting her arms.

"We're still alive!" he returned, working his knees furiously to get them around a small curve. They were picking up speed, the incline steeper at this point. "Hang on!"

Her hands suddenly came free from behind her, the

wrists red and raw, a little bloody. They were going fast now, a hairpin curve coming on them, a forest of thick trees jammed around it. His knees couldn't do it.

"Grab the wheel!" he screamed, taking his knees off and straightening his legs, jamming his feet down hard on the brake pedal.

The car skidded, then slid and turned as Marta fought the wheel while he pumped the brakes.

And they were suddenly facing forward going into the turn. Marta's hands were blurring on the wheel as she worked the turn, the Mercedes sliding into it but pulling out, moving forward, the speed dying as he kept working the brakes.

He stopped the car and climbed immediately out of the open space where a door had once been. "We'll change places," he said. "You okay to drive?"

"After what we've been through," she replied, climbing out and helping him slide back in, "I could get away with anything."

She climbed behind the wheel and jammed it into gear, burning rubber as they took off. He could see her face wide-eyed and intense.

"Where?" she said.

"My car...in the lot outside of von Maur. We've got bolt cutters."

"Then what?"

"Your call," he said.

"Did you really steal fifty million dollars?"

"It's waiting for me in Geneva. John Smith, glad to know you. I'd shake hands, but..."

"Rennie," she said. "I've never seen this side of you. You were always so sullen and morose. I loved you, but I didn't think I could live with that."

"I...couldn't tell you I was a spy," he said, rolling with it. "I still love you."

She looked at him as she buzzed into town. Everyone on the streets was watching the skies, the flight path of the chopper set against the exploding rockets of the fireworks.

She half smiled at him. Her eyes were alive, dancing in the fireworks. "Maybe I was hasty when I broke off with you," she said.

"This wouldn't have anything to do with the fifty million dollars, would it?" he asked. "Turn left here."

She turned into the road leading to the parking lot. "I'm Swiss," she said proudly. "I'm many things, but I am also practical. I will love you for the rest of our lives and help you spend your fifty million properly."

"That's the best deal I've heard all day," he said. "Right in this next line of cars."

"I can't believe we got away with it," she said.

"It's my new philosophy," he declared. "Live... big. I like that. Live big. There's the BMW."

She stopped and they got out of the car. Marta fished his keys out of his pocket to open the trunk. She got out the long-handled bolt cutters that Bolan insisted on bringing and snipped the chain binding his cuffs.

"Oh, yeah," he said, moving his cramping arms. "That's better."

She handed him the keys. "Let's just go right to Geneva," she said. "When the banks open in the morning, we can withdraw the cash, make the preparations and get out of the country on an evening flight."

She got into the passenger side while Dennison moved to the driver's door and climbed in. He stuck the key in the ignition but didn't turn it.

"Come on," she said. "Let's go."

He sat there for a long moment, then looked at her. "I'd love to but I can't," he said.

"What?"

"I made a deal with Belasko. He takes up the chopper and I take up the balloon and drop Molotov cocktails on the western slope."

"So?"

"So, he's fulfilling his end of the bargain. I'm going to fulfill mine."

"This doesn't sound like you at all."

"The new Rennie, remember?"

He opened the car door. "Take the car. Find a place to hide for tonight. I'll call you at work tomorrow if I make it. We'll go from there."

He scrambled out and started to trot toward town. He'd almost reached it when she drove up beside him.

"I'm going with you," she said, stopping the car and opening the door.

He climbed in the passenger side. "It's dangerous," he warned.

"It's a fifty-million-dollar gamble. Live big, remember? Besides, you'll need somebody to light your Molotov cocktails. It works better that way."

He stared at her. "Maybe we're more alike than we realized."

They drove up the back street to the balloon, passing the place where he'd been beaten by Mulroy. His ribs were still throbbing, his face simply numb.

They moved to the balloon unmolested. Everyone else was a half block up the street, watching the spectacle as cannons were brought to bear to try to down the Chinook.

They climbed into the basket, his bag full of homemade bombs right where he'd left it. Each taking a side, they unsnapped the tethers. The balloon rose, the houses moving by on either side.

There was a large tether rope meant to hold them back; the owner wasn't willing to rent his balloon without a two-hundred-foot guarantee. Dennison used the pocket knife Bolan had made him carry to cut through it as they rose.

In a moment the city was beneath them and they were floating into the blazing night sky. Silently. Majestically.

BOLAN FOUGHT THE CONTROLS, the dead man bouncing in the seat beside him. He'd taken a hit somewhere vital, and smoke was pouring from the back rotor. The engine was coughing, wanting to stall out.

He needed altitude, but it was all he could do to keep from plummeting to earth. He juiced the dual throttles and wobbled higher, the machine shivering the entire time. The altimeter read two hundred feet and climbing. The cockpit was shot to hell; .50-caliber shells had torn right through fabric and sheet metal.

A ground-to-air rocket exploded fifty yards from the cockpit. It was coming from the line of bunkers below. Then another exploded just overhead, shaking the bird. And all around, other rockets of happiness exploded, showering the colorful stars and wheels of celebration over the village of von Maur.

He continued the slow, shivering rise, reaching three hundred feet. He kept pushing it, with the machine straining loudly beneath him as it continued to rise.

He heard the crack of a cannon and looked down to see an M-1 tank bleeding smoke from the 105 mm gun. The cannon fired again as more rockets leaped at him. The sky exploded like chain lightning all around him, and he was at four hundred feet above the up-sloping ground.

There was a double hit to the tail section. A gust of fire blew through the aircraft, and it was only the cockpit door that kept him from burning to death. And when he saw the back rotor go flying off the machine, gliding to earth, spinning and fluttering, he knew that the bird was going down and that he was a dead man.

He sat in a burning fireball, suspended hundreds of feet in the air. He charged through the pilot's door and looked into the brightly flaring night, amazed at what he saw.

A hundred feet below him was the balloon with the sun face on it, drifting languidly with the wind. He heard a rumble in the tail as the cockpit door crashed inward followed by a ball of fire. Bolan jumped from the open doorway, spreading himself out full as he fell into the night.

Whooshing air screamed past his face, and he heard a *whump* from above. The fuel tanks had exploded on the Chinook, pieces of the chopper zinging past him on an explosive rush to ground.

A second later he slapped into the top of the balloon, sinking deeply into the bag of hot air then popping back out as the balloon ejected him.

He grabbed at the restraining ropes as his body tried to slide off the curved surface. The burning hulk of the helicopter was plunging toward earth, passing the balloon and missing it narrowly as it fell.

Sore and bleeding, he scurried down the balloon's ropes and dropped into the gondola to find Dennison and Marta Kleppe staring at him with wide eyes.

The still-flaming chopper hit the ground, spreading flaming wreckage everywhere.

Below he could see men running out of the fortified bunkers, the first defensive line, to try to shoot the balloon down.

"Crank the fire up!" the Executioner yelled. "Let's try and get out of range! Marta...help me with the bombs."

They dug into the leather pouch. Bolan grabbed a liter wine bottle full of gas, with a torn-up shirt sticking out of its mouth. They were an unmissable target, and bullets screamed through the basket or punctured the balloon itself as Dennison turned the burner up full. The whole balloon glowed brightly, its sun smiling happily down on the troops below.

"Light me!" Bolan called.

Marta fired a Zippo lighter to set the rag aflame, and the Executioner chucked it toward the closest bunker and the men outside it.

When it hit the bunker's concrete top, liquid fire exploded outward. White-suited mercs lit up like torches, running through the snow screaming.

The tank fired its cannon again.

"Down!" Bolan yelled.

The three of them hit the deck as the shell exploded near the basket, rocking them wildly, its concussion blowing the balloon higher. Bolan dug another bottle out of the pouch.

"Lights!" he yelled.

Marta, grimly determined, torched the liquid bomb.

He threw it at the tank below and hit the turret. Fire sprayed onto the gunner on the cannon, and the man toppled back into the machine, flame shooting out the top.

"Yes!" Marta said, and Bolan had another bottle in his hand.

They were still rising slowly as the .50-caliber machine guns opened up on them from another bunker, and another tank clanked across open ground to have a go at them with the big gun.

The shot hit the balloon, blowing a huge hole in it. It deflated, falling slowly as part of the bag still desperately tried to hold air.

Bolan grabbed more bottles out of the pouch, and Marta lit them even as they fell back to earth. The Executioner hurled them in all directions to try to keep back the charging troops.

They were coming down near the tank he'd hit. Two burning men climbed out of it to fall onto the ground. Bolan ripped the Desert Eagle out of his webbing for a mercy shot at one of the screaming men; the other merc was already still on the ground.

"Hang on!" he yelled as the balloon sputtered out the last of its air, and plummeted earthward from fifty feet.

They came down hard. The snow cushioned the fall somewhat, but the impact still sent them flying out of the gondola to land near the tank.

Bolan was up immediately, grabbing the satchel and firing at approaching troops as Dennison ran to help Marta.

"Get her into the tank!" Bolan yelled. "It's our only shot!"

The woman was dazed but able to get to her feet and aid in her own escape. Bolan jumped onto the treads, then the turret, making the cupola as Marta was climbing in. The stench of burning flesh was nearly overpowering; all of them were gagging but not turning down their only port in the storm.

Bolan swung the cupola toward the advancing troops, opening up with the antiaircraft machine gun, tearing a blood-drenched swath through their ranks from thirty feet away, driving them back.

"What's it like inside?" he called down to Dennison as he swung the gun in the other direction to hold back the troops who were making their way through the burning wreckage of the chopper and the still-flaming bunker.

"Awful," Marta cried out.

"How about this?" Dennison yelled, and put the tank in motion, clanking them through the snow.

Bolan let himself slide in, closing the hatch and locking it down tight. It was awful, with the cloying smell of burned flesh. One of the operators, probably the one he'd hit with the cocktail, lay dead on the floor, twiglike.

Bolan slid into the driver's seat and revolved the

turret, watching the countryside through the view plate, stopping when he saw the other tank rumbling toward them.

"Load the cannon!" he yelled. "The shells will be stored in that case behind you."

Dennison got into the case, hefting out a 105 mm shell and moving to slide it into the already opened breech of the cannon. Bolan pulled the lever that locked and armed it, then moved to the computer board. "Dennison," he said. "Juice this thing up and lock on to that oncoming tank."

"I've never—"

"It's a computer."

The man dived for the board, his fingers running over a small keyboard. "Yes," he said. "Yes. No sweat."

Bolan looked down at his screen, saw the cross hairs line up the tank. He fired without hesitation, just as the other tank fired at him.

The blast rocked them, smoke bleeding from the control boards. The Executioner jumped up to look through the periscope at the other tank. Its turret was blown off, and thick smoke poured from the hole. It was dead.

"Take over!" Bolan said to Dennison. "Move us toward the siege line. Marta, reload the cannon."

Bolan moved away from the periscope and turned to the ammo cabinet. "This thing should do thirty," he called as he slid open the cabinet, finding three extra canisters full of ammo for the half-inch gun. "Open her up!"

Dennison kicked it and the tank jerked forward, picking up speed as Marta reloaded the big gun and levered it into firing position.

"My mother will never believe this," she muttered as she looked through the periscope.

Bolan was climbing the ladder, hefting the heavy canister under his arm to place it.

He popped open the hatch and stuck his head outside, grabbing a breath of fresh air. Troops were falling back behind them as the tank picked up speed.

He turned the other way. The siege line was still a mile ahead. Maybe time enough.

The spent-cartridge canister pulled easily out of its nest beneath the machine gun. He threw it out and slid the full one into the space just vacated, pulling the feed through the top slot to lock into the antiaircraft gun.

He slammed the breech closed just as a Jeep with a mounted machine gun in the back roared through a spray of snow toward them. He swung the machine gun in their direction and fired a three-second burst at the windshield. He wanted to kill the men, not the car.

Glass exploded in a shower of red, the car rocked and the back gunner was thrown out as the driver tumbled through his door. The car traveled on by itself, pointing downward and coming to rest in a snowbank.

Bolan jumped from the tank and charged toward the jeep. He hopped in and raced back to pass the tank, driving in front so they could see where he was, waving, then taking up his rear position again.

They were rapidly approaching the siege line, designed to slow any advancing force. Defenders could be deployed to their position through the gates of the main road only. He'd learned that by watching drills the day he'd climbed the Little Madam with Dennison.

The siege line gradually became something other than a pencil line across the horizon. They reached it quickly, stopping as Bolan pulled up beside them. Both Marta and Dennison poked their heads out of the turret to stare in disbelief at a sea of wood and wire six feet high, stretching a football field's width and completely encircling the entire mountain.

"What'll we do?" Dennison asked.

"Back up a touch," Bolan called back, looking up at them from the jeep. "Turn on that searchlight you got on the turret and take a look at those poles. Then start blasting with the big gun and see what happens. Do it now. They'll be here pretty quick."

Their heads disappeared, and several seconds later the searchlight came on, bright, shining on the siege line. The light was also marking their position. He heard distant gunfire and answered with a quick burst from the machine gun, just to make sure it worked.

The cannon fired, blasting splinters out of the big trees. Five seconds later it fired again. Five seconds later again.

Bolan could see dozens of men running toward them several hundred feet distant, illuminated under the light show still pumping furiously overhead.

He quickly turned to the siege line to see twenty to thirty feet of defense blasted or torn away, a crater gouged from the line.

Dennison didn't need to be told the drill at this point. Starting up the tank, he drove right into the notch and fired again, clearing more away, creating a narrow channel for the tank to pass through.

Bolan jumped behind the wheel and followed the tank into the corridor, watching the advancing troops getting closer as the cannon blasted again. He was only wishing he'd counted the shells. He hoped they had enough to get through.

He drove right up on their tail, forty feet into the line. Wire snapped and curled into itself, and huge, splintered logs were blown apart and shoved aside.

The cannon fired again, and he slammed on the brakes and jumped into the back to man the machine gun. White-suited mercs charged into the breach three abreast. Bolan let them get ten feet into the chamber before cutting loose with the .50-caliber weapon. It bucked solidly in his hands, his teeth clenched, vibrating.

The strains of death rolled out of the staccato drumming of the machine. The men were totally trapped in the confined space, and he mowed them down, four rows of three writhing to the ground, piling up like cordwood, the others ducking out of the tunnel to take cover.

After another blast from the tank, the Executioner climbed back behind the wheel to follow it another thirty feet into the line. They were nearly a third of the way through. He caught up; their progress had slowed to a crawl.

He stopped the Jeep and jumped on the hood, then onto the back of the tank as it blasted again. He grabbed two of the ten-gallon extra fuel tanks tied to the side of the tank and walked around to the front. Setting one down, he tossed the other as far in front of them as he could, then did the same with the second can.

He moved back. The cannon fired again, shaking the tank, igniting the gas and spewing it outward in a large path.

Behind him the white-suited troops were rushing the Jeep. Bolan jumped down from the tank and ripped the Beretta from the harness, firing as he ran.

He jumped to the hood of the Jeep and leaped to the machine gun in back. Grabbing the handles, he hit the thumb triggers.

The machine gun erupted, spraying the corridors. Men fell, shot and sliced to pieces by the razor wire. One of them jumped up with him, and Bolan swung the barrel around to knock him off the Jeep and into the razor wire, then swung back to open up on the troops again. The belt vibrated, spent shells flying through a curtain of acrid smoke.

The mercs turned and ran, leaving another pile of bodies behind. Bolan grabbed the Beretta and finished the man still writhing on the razor wire.

He jumped behind the wheel and caught up with the tank again. A major portion of the surrounding defensive line was burning out of control.

The tank stopped again, and Bolan vaulted onto the wide back, then up to the turret.

"We've only got three shells left!" Dennison called loudly up to him as Bolan opened up with the anti-aircraft gun, hosing down the men behind them.

The fire was surrounding him completely, and its fiery heat was chasing his assailants totally out of the corridor. Bolan dropped into the interior to escape the heat, but it was far worse down below. They were in an oven. Both Dennison and Marta were red-faced and dripping sweat.

"Let's take our shot," Bolan said. "We're going to cook if we don't. Blast the three shells, get a running start and hit the barricade with all you've got."

Dennison nodded, then looked at Marta. "Ready?" he asked.

The woman nodded, hefting up another shell, arm muscles tensed.

Dennison fired the three shells, blasting the wooden barricade in front of them.

"Back it up!" Bolan yelled. "Get a good jump on it!"

Dennison complied without hesitation. The tank moved blindly backward, banging quickly into the Jeep, shoving it, then bumping over bodies, flattening them.

Bolan looked through the front viewport to see nothing but fire before them. "Enough," he said. "Let's do it."

Dennison started forward, and Bolan grabbed the ladder while Marta climbed into the nearly empty ammunition cabinet.

They picked up speed. Faster. Faster.

Then they hit the siege line at full speed. A terrible bellow roared as irresistible force met immovable object. The impact threw Dennison off the controls to spin into the stairs. The machine was still moving and Bolan rushed to take his place. The machine was struggling to free itself from a fiery tomb, but slower. Ever slower.

"Come on!" Bolan yelled. "Come on!"

Through the view plate he saw fire, endless, churning orange. Fire, nothing but—

Suddenly the mountain was in front of them.

They'd broken free. Bolan hit the brakes, then

struggled up the ladder to open the hatch for oxygen. It streamed in, sweet, cold air rushing in.

Bolan climbed into the night, amazed to find a growing ring of fire threatening to consume the entire siege line. The castle walls were glittering up a steep slope a thousand yards ahead, with nothing but space between them and the wall.

And then he saw them, emerging from the snow itself. Dozens of men stormed the tank, on it in seconds, swarming like army ants.

CHAPTER NINETEEN

Bolan tried to pull down the hatch, but mercs were grabbing it.

He struggled up farther, trying to free his arms from the hatchway. A merc jumped on the cupola to kick him in the face, and Bolan fell back down the hatchway to flaring pain in his jaw.

He came down hard, right beside Dennison, instinctively reaching for the Beretta. Like a boxer taking a beating, he moved through sheer training and experience, firing straight up. The man who'd kicked him tumbled back into the arms of his fellows.

Bolan rose, still dizzy, and climbed the ladder, firing the entire time to keep them from bringing guns to bear on the hatchway, which would be the kiss of death.

He'd lost count of spent shells in his haziness, and hoped as he crested the hatch that he had something left. He came out, twisted behind him, firing at a man who'd thrown his body over the hatch itself. The shot gutted him, and the man jerked and rolled back onto his men.

The hatch lay open. Bolan grabbed it even as gunfire spit at him and seared across his shoulder. He turned and fired indiscriminately at the scrambling men. The gun emptied, spent, as he slammed the hatchway on someone's hand, pulling hard, four fingers dropping into the hatchway with him as he clamped it shut and let himself fall to the floor of the interior.

He held on to consciousness, twisting to look at his shoulder. It was a clean flesh wound that had done a decent gouging job. It was bleeding but wasn't serious.

"Dennison!" he called. "Shake it off. We need a driver!"

Dennison was on his knees weaving, shaking his head. "Did we make it through?" he asked.

"Yeah," Bolan said. "Get us to the wall quick!"

The man staggered to the controls. Bolan slid painfully out of the wool coat and checked his wound. With some pressure, the bleeding would be staunched.

"I need a bandage," he said as the machine reluctantly started up and clanked forward.

Marta Kleppe moved quickly to him, grabbing a long scarf out of her coat, which was covering the burned corpse they'd shoved to the side as much as possible. She moved to Bolan, and though she looked shocked and wild, her eyes showed simple jungle survival.

"What about the men on the tank?" she asked as she wrapped the wadded scarf over the wound and tied a knot.

"If they want to ride, let them. We'll hit the castle defenses in a minute. Riding this tank will not be the place to be."

"What happens when we reach the castle?" she asked.

"We get through the walls."

"How?"

Dennison turned and stared at them, raising his eyebrows. "We climb them, just like we climbed the Little Madam."

Marta looked surprised. "But that's out in the open, exposed—"

"That's why you're going to keep them off us," Bolan said.

"How?"

"The antiaircraft gun on top," he said. "And you'll have to reload it, too."

Dennison and Bolan took turns at the controls while preparing their climbing gear, then Bolan made Marta carry a heavy canister of the ammo up the ladder to see if she could do it. They even cracked the hatch so the Executioner could show her how to pull the breech and load the belt. That's when he saw the parapets.

The spire, rising well above the rest of the wall and bulging out from it cylindrically, was spitting .50-caliber death in their direction. The shape of the parapet, however, kept it partially hidden from half the battlements, the closest half. It would be their best route up, especially since the gunners in the turret itself wouldn't be able to tilt their weapons far enough down to hit them.

But much, ultimately, depended on Marta's ability to quickly reload the antiaircraft gun.

They closed the hatch and prepared for combat. Marta found side arms for herself and Dennison in personal lockers. They were closing on the castle quickly, with bazooka hits now pounding down from the high walls, hitting near the tank, shaking the ground around them.

"Pull up on the side of the closest tower," Bolan directed. "Try and get in the center, blocked from the two side walls."

"Got it!"

He turned to Marta, taking her by the shoulders. "They're going to come at you from the castle gates and from the walls above, and they're going to be fired up. Keep them back. Always work first on the men on the battlements. They've got the best angle on you."

She nodded. "Will you and Rennie each take a canister up with you when you go? Leave it on the turret. That way I won't have to come back down for it."

"Good," he said.

"I'm getting there," Dennison said, turning them hard left at the top of a long upgrade.

Bolan threw lengths of rope over his good shoulder.

"Let me be lead," Dennison said. "I'm faster up, and you're a better shot."

"No argument."

They shuddered to a stop. Dennison also grabbed rope from the satchel. "Look for cracks in the wall," he said, "spaces between stone blocks. Jam your crampons there. They'll hold. If there're enough cracks, maybe we can forego the rope and pitons and just scurry up."

"Go," Bolan said, then turned to Marta. "Good luck. You're a hell of a woman. When we take the tower, lock yourself in here and just drive, get as far away from the castle as possible."

She nodded. Dennison was already up the ladder, opening the hatch, driven back by gunfire from the battlements two hundred feet above.

Bolan took his place, jumping into the cupola and grabbing the antiaircraft gun. He pounded the notched battlements, driving men back. Then he swung the other way as Dennison, canister under his arm, moved past to set down his burden and jump to the wall, crampons holding fast.

The Executioner ducked into the tank, grabbed another canister and put it up beside Dennison's as he took control of the antiaircraft gun again, firing single shots at the notches.

Above, the fireworks continued, with twenty to thirty going off one after another, indicating the big finish.

He aimed at the other wall. Dennison's climb was a lot slower than it should have been. He fired ten times and started to worry about ammo right away. The two side walls he could see were well over a hundred feet long, each topped with a turret similar to his.

"Hit the searchlight!" he called down to Marta. The light came on, and he could see maybe fifty men creeping out of the gate in the wall. They jumped with the light, bringing their weapons to bear, but the Executioner was already up in the cupola and working the machine gun.

Bolan emptied the entire canister into the advancing column, driving the survivors back into the gates. He tore out the empty canister and reached for another, slamming it into the nest and feeding the belt into the exposed breech, then snapping it closed.

A rope dangled down to him. Dennison was secure forty feet above, continuing upward as distant shots gouged the wall near him.

"Pick your shots!" Bolan yelled down to Marta as he clamped the rope to his utility belt and pulled himself up, walking quickly up the wall.

On the gun below, Marta tried to lay down covering fire.

He felt death ricocheting off the walls beside him and knew this was too slow. They'd have to go for it. The hell with any thought of safety.

Unclamping the rope, he jammed a crampon into the wall and started climbing, grabbing for handholds on protruding rocks and crevasses. "Forget the ropes, Dennison," he called up to the man. "Go! Just go!"

The man dropped the ropes from his shoulder. Bolan did the same and scurried as quickly as possible for someone climbing a sheer cliff wall.

Bolan looked down from a hundred feet to see Marta preoccupied with the gate, not noticing a squad of mercs charging from the direction of the blazing siege line. He pulled the Beretta and realized he'd emptied it while trying to close the hatch earlier.

Holstering, he awkwardly got hold of the .44 as he clung precariously to the escarpment. Holding it against the tower wall with his head, he primed it with his free hand, then grabbed it.

The assailants were just reaching the tank when he looked down again. He fired once, then again, and two men fell to roll off the tank. The sound alerted Marta, who swung the big gun around and blew away the other ten men from nearly point-blank range.

Bolan stuck the .44 in his garrison belt and started climbing again, straining for cracks and protrusions in the wall. Dennison was far above him now, past the top of the wall and moving just on the tower itself.

The Executioner picked up the pace, his hands, arms, and legs straining, his resolve shoving the pain away. He let the wall take him instinctively, moving steadily as the machine gun stopped below while Marta reloaded.

Firing came from everywhere—the walls, the ground, bullets pinging just beside them.

Dennison started to move faster. Bolan followed suit and he'd crested the wall and was continuing up as Marta began firing again, driving back those on top of the wall who'd been positioning themselves to kill the climbers.

Dennison was barely a foot beneath the slot windows, where men poked their heads over the big barrels of the machine guns to peer down. Bolan joined Dennison and, holding on with one hand, pulled the .44 with the other. Dennison nodded and drew his side arm, a 9 mm Ruger, priming it the way Bolan had done. They could hear confusion within the tower as men called down on cell phones for information. It had to happen now.

Bolan saw a nice crack about eight inches up and over from his left foot. It would put him right in a bow slot. Unfortunately a barrel would be jammed into his chest. He pointed and nodded to Dennison, and they both took a step at the same instant. Bolan came up to the bow slot and blasted a surprised gunner right between the eyes. The man fell back, blood pumping out of his head even as Bolan was turning and firing randomly into the small, circular room.

Ten men jumped and danced under a relentless hail of shells with nowhere to run. Blood spurted everywhere as both Bolan and Dennison emptied their clips into the room, its darkness flashing lightning.

One more step and they were inside. Bolan grabbed a .50-caliber machine gun with a fresh belt attached. They stood atop bodies. There was no other room. Marta had stopped firing below—Bolan hoped because she was escaping.

"Now what?" Dennison asked, breathing heavily through teeth clenched hard, his face set hard. He was a warrior after all.

"They know we're here," Bolan said as he jerked the belts out of the other machine guns and threw them over his partner's shoulder, then handed him the canister containing the belt already loaded into the gun. "Movement is our only friend." He nodded to the ammo belts. "Feed me. Let's go!"

They walked across bodies to the door. Bolan kicked it open, knocking a white-garbed killer off the stairs to plummet down the parapet.

The stairs down were lined with men, but Bolan came out firing, assailants crumpling and falling down the tower. Both men moved forward, always forward, down the stairs, firing at anything that moved below them. Above them nothing lived.

They wound around the tower, reaching the doorway, nearly taking off the head of a man coming in as the weapon ran dry.

Bolan peeked out the door as he jerked open the breech. Dennison fed him from one of the heavy belts on his shoulder. Snapping the breech closed, Bolan immediately jerked back the bolt to activate live ammo. They stood beside a pile of moaning, dying bodies ten feet high, the men who'd fallen from the stairs.

"Here we go," Bolan whispered, and stepped out of the open stone doorway and onto the battlements.

Lines of men on the walls turned their guns on the intruders, but Bolan emptied the belt in a long, sweeping spray. Knocking them off the walls before they could respond, Bolan then jumped back into the tower to reload.

"Once we stop moving, they'll nail us. Movement is the key, trust me," Bolan said.

"Ideas?"

"Yeah. The courtyard's fifty feet down. It's filled with cars, filled with cover. There are stairs to our left. Here, hold this." He handed the bulky weapon to Dennison, who jumped, burned, under the hot barrel. Bolan pulled the Desert Eagle and the 93-R from his webbing and dropped in the clips, reloading.

He took back the big gun as Dennison reloaded with another clip from his holster. "We empty this on them," the Executioner said, "then run for the stairs down."

"We'll never make it all the way down."

"I know," Bolan answered. "Get halfway and jump into the space beside the stairs, then run for cover in the cars. Okay?"

"Sounds just crazy enough," Dennison said. "Let's do it."

They charged out again, their assailants better positioned this time behind bodies and buttresses. It was unravelling quickly.

Bolan fired from the hip, sweeping the walls in a back-and-forth arc, driving them all back to cover, giving the two men several seconds of reaction and aiming time.

When the gun ran dry, Bolan threw it and charged onto the stone stairs down to the courtyard. They got close to halfway before return fire rang out. Both men jumped from twenty feet, falling into the shadows created by the stairs.

"Go!" Bolan yelled, jumping immediately to his feet and running the twenty feet toward the crowd of limos parked haphazardly around the chopper pad. All they had on their side was reaction time.

He pumped hard, and Dennison caught up to him just as the impacts of automatic fire tore up the ground around their feet. Both men dived into the sea of cars and crawled quickly on hands and knees as bullets thudded into metal and windows shattered, showering them with glass.

Then the firing stopped, and there was deadly calm, frightening calm.

"I don't like this," Bolan said. "Keep moving toward the hall. Watch for—"

"You sons of bitches!" came Mulroy's screaming voice from the helipad.

"Keep moving," Bolan whispered.

"I'm going to tell you straight up, Belasko!" Mulroy yelled as the fireworks above abruptly stopped, the sky now dark. "I've got fifty men left. Fifty! And they're all here, all looking for you."

Bolan glanced back to the walls. The battlements had been abandoned.

"They're going to close you in, tighter and tighter, until you got nowhere else to go. Then we're going to take you. If not alive, hell with it."

Bolan looked at Dennison. "Did you offer him a deal on the money?"

The man shrugged. "It almost worked. I could've been halfway to Geneva by now."

"But you're here."

"So I am."

"We've got your woman, too, Rennie!" Mulroy called back. "We've got lots of plans for that bitch. The man who kills you gets her first!"

Dennison stiffened, but Bolan put a hand on his

arm. "He's just making that up, trying to get you to give your position away."

"What if he's not?"

"Marta's got a side arm," Bolan said. "She'd never be taken alive by these animals."

Dennison relaxed, frowning. "Okay."

"If you come out with your hands up," Mulroy said, taunting, "we'll take you alive to the baron. I'm sure you can still make your deal, Rennie!"

Bolan could hear them approaching in the silence—the swish of material, the soft padding of feet. The sounds came from everywhere, and not that far away.

"Okay!" Mulroy shouted. "Time's up. Guys, sweep slowly in, be thorough. These men are dangerous. Shoot to kill and then keep shooting. Do not let them slip through your dragnet or I will kill *you!* Go!"

They were moving faster, bobbing up and down, occasional interior car lights coming on as insides of vehicles were checked. The noose drew tighter, choking.

"What do we do?" Dennison whispered urgently.

Bolan looked him hard in the eyes. "Take off your shirt," he ordered.

CHAPTER TWENTY

Dennison stared at the Executioner. "My shirt?"

"Yeah," Bolan said, tearing off the remnants of his own shirt. "We're going to make a couple of big Molotov cocktails."

Dennison hurried out of the shirt, pulling the suspenders of the short pants back up over his shoulders.

They crept to the next row of cars, finding two whose gas tanks faced one another. They quickly pried off the caps with their pocket knives, then dipped the shirts down into the tanks.

"They're getting closer," Dennison whispered.

"You got a light?" Bolan asked.

The man shook his head. "Marta took my Zippo."

Bolan had nothing in the uniform pants or the harness. He slipped into the limo and killed the overhead light, then pushed in the lighter.

"Would you hurry!" Rennie rasped urgently. "They're on us!"

The lighter popped, and Bolan jerked it out. "We're going to have to shoot some of them," he said, tying the shirts together and laying the coil lighter against the gas-soaked material. "Then make your way up two cars and get in the back seat of the Caddie. I've already checked—it's open."

"When do—?"

The shirts burst into flame just as they were spotted from both directions from several cars away. Both men ripped their weapons out and fired at the dark figures coming for them. The shooting would attract the rest of the mercs, but Bolan kept firing into their ranks. With his back glued to the Executioner's, Dennison fired the other way and moving toward the Cadillac.

"It's going to go!" Dennison yelled as they reached the limo and tore open the door, diving inside onto facing seats.

The two gas tanks went up simultaneously. The blast slammed closed the limo's still-open back door and rocked the car. Windows shattered, and a tongue of orange fire shot through the windshield space, setting the front seats afire as burning fuel spewed over the whole area.

"Let's get out of here!" the Executioner yelled.

He opened the door on the other side and fell out into fire. Dennison followed, nearly landing on top of him.

They were up, weapons in hand, charging toward the great hall. Fire was everywhere, burning men twisting and screaming all around them, the living jumping up and firing, but the Executioner dropped them on the fly, blowing away shadows.

And before him, his goal, the great hall and a date with the Vulture. He charged toward death. Dennison at his side.

THE VULTURE, like everyone else in the great hall, turned toward the front of the building when the explosion went off in the parking lot.

"My friends!" he called from the food tables just as he was about to ask Kimberly Adams to become a more permanent house guest. "No need to be alarmed. I'm afraid we've had an accident with the fireworks. Enjoy yourselves, I'll attend to it."

A sea of guests, toasting and laughing, opened a wide channel for him to pass to the door, Kimberly hurrying up beside him. But as he reached the middle of the hall, the front doors burst open and Willy Mulroy stumbled in, his clothes and face burned. He was stooped over with pain.

"B-baron!" he called, stumbling in to gasps from the crowd, falling to the floor five feet from the Vulture. He rose to his knees. "That g-guy...that big son of a bitch. He's...he's in."

His rage bypassing his brain, the Vulture jerked his Ruger from his belt and shot Mulroy in the chest several times. "You're stupid!" he screamed, shooting him again. "Why did I take you in! Idiot!" He shot him again as two men charged through the door.

Jerking the gun up, he shot at movement immediately, dropping the long-haired man with two hits. But the big guy dived left and rolled.

The Vulture fired twice at Belasko before he got cover behind a pillar. Expecting movement on the other side, the Vulture fired five more times into his own guests. People screamed, Gregore Wolfstein went down—but no Belasko.

The crowd swept backward, leaving two dead behind. At least the Vulture had a clear field of fire now and a shield. Kimberly Adams stood, stupefied, beside him, her mouth and eyes open wide as she stared around in horror. That's why the big man hadn't taken him down. He didn't have a clear shot.

"Hey, Belasko!" he called. "Look what I've got."

He grabbed Kimberly Adams, pulling her hard against him as she gasped. "No. No...please," she whispered.

"Belasko!" he screamed, and pointed the revolver toward the ceiling, pulling the trigger.

It was spent, empty. He hadn't even noticed. The gun dropped from his hand.

Bolan walked out from behind the pillar, the Desert Eagle in his hand. The Vulture dropped the gun and reached into his pocket in a blur. Within two seconds the little blade was lying against the woman's throat where he could slash both the carotid and the jugular in one swift movement.

"Put the gun down or she's dead," he barked.

MACK BOLAN STOOD ten feet from the man he'd come halfway around the world to kill, a young, fragile woman in a chiffon party dress the only thing separating them. He recognized his own knife at her throat, wondering how many others had been killed with it.

"I have something to return to you, no?" the Vulture said, smiling down at the knife. "Put down the gun, and I won't have to get it all messed up with someone else's blood before giving it to you."

The Executioner smiled. He had no doubts about the man's weakness. He wasn't a real human being. He just imitated. "Why should I give a holy damn about her?" Bolan asked. "I got here by being just like you. Think about how much her life is worth to you, and you'll know how I feel."

Bolan raised the weapon to eye level and kept moving forward. The Vulture's eyes narrowed as he tried to imagine the possibilities of someone being as soulless as he was.

Bolan smiled, closer still. He wanted to get close enough that the terrorist would think he still had options. "I'll shoot her out of our way if you want."

The surviving mercs charged in, taking to the stairs and positioning themselves around the mezzanine, rifles pointed downward.

With that the man made the move Bolan had expected. He shoved the woman hard toward him, following with the knife pointed at the Executioner's throat.

Ready for it, Bolan never lost his sighting on the man's fist. He fired over the woman's shoulder from a foot away, and bright blood flowed over the knuckles of the Vulture's left hand. The knife clattered to the floor as the woman slammed hard into him, sending him reeling backward as the Vulture doubled over, going to the floor, cradling his bleeding stump, several fingers lying on the ground.

Bolan shoved the woman away.

"Kill him!" the terrorist shouted to his men. "A half billion francs to the man who kills him. Shoot him now!"

Rifles were raised all over the room, and a shot rang out from the floor beside Bolan. Mulroy, dying, had shot a huge, ugly man with thick lips, throwing him back against the wall.

"Don't fire!" Mulroy called weakly, trying intently to rise to his knees without success. "He can't give you any money. He doesn't have any! These guys stole it all! It's gone!"

The riflemen hesitated. "There's too many dead people piled around here for this to go away," the Executioner said. "It's a mess and it's over. If you get out now, you might be able to outrun the trouble you're in."

That was it. The Vulture's army disintegrated on the spot, its members charging down the stairs and out of the house in disarray. Bolan looked down at Mulroy; the man was dead, his eyes staring blankly at the ceiling.

The Vulture had risen, cradling his hand, his face pale. "My friends," he said, "please don't let this man destroy me. I've been cruelly attacked, maimed. Kimberly, dear." He moved, staggering, toward her. "You understand. You—"

She swung her hand out at him, long-nailed fingers digging into his flesh, four long, bloody trenches left in their wake. Kimberly Adams turned and stalked away without a word.

"My friends..." he began again.

"Your friend," Bolan said, "is a vicious killer who goes by the name of the Vulture."

There were gasps through the great hall.

"He's not a proud mercenary! He's not a benefactor to Switzerland. He's a pathetic monster who kills innocent people for money! Is that your friend?"

"No," the terrorist protested. "Look what I've done for you. The feast...the music..."

He walked to a group of tuxedoed men, his good hand outstretched. "Roberto," he said. "Henri. Remember Cannes last year? Remember the fun?"

One of the men punched him, knocking him back, while the others moved in to beat him.

"Leave him," Bolan said as he heard the sounds of distant sirens.

The men backed off. The Vulture was still on his

feet, bent over, staring in hatred at the Executioner. Suddenly he bolted forward, his right hand streaking toward his waistband.

Bolan flashed out with the blade, running true and straight, and it plunged into the man's remaining eye, sinking it deeply into the brain.

He went down, screaming and writhing, his legs kicking wildly on the ground, thrashing the death agonies. It didn't last long enough.

"You keep the knife," Bolan said, then turned and hurried to Dennison.

Uniformed police were rushing through the doorway along with medical personnel with stretchers.

The warrior knelt beside Dennison. The man was breathing heavily, labored. His eyes fluttered open. "Did we get him?"

"Of course we got him," Bolan said.

The Executioner picked him up, ignoring his own pain, and carried him toward the doorway as crying and horrified people crept guiltily from the great hall.

He came face to face with Stiler, the detective from Zurich. No wonder help had gotten there so quickly. "Conscience bother you?" he asked the man, who stiffened, staring.

Bolan took Dennison to a gurney just being wheeled into the huge room from outside, and a doctor bent over him immediately, taking vital signs and ordering up morphine.

"Belasko," Dennison said, taking hold of his arm. "I helped you all the way, top to bottom."

"You did good."

"The money," Dennison said. "What are you going to do about the money?"

"You're a thief, Rennie."

"You said if I helped you, you—"

"I'd think about it," Bolan said. "Who knows. Maybe I'll think about it just a little longer since it looks like you'll be laid up for a while. I've got lots of time to think about it. Take it easy, kid."

"Belasko," he said, "this isn't fair. It's not right."

"See you sometime." Bolan smiled, walking off.

"Don't you touch my money!" Dennison yelled.

Bolan turned to wink at him, then left, moving into the profusion of flashing lights and uniformed cops who filled the courtyard. A large group of men was putting out the fires still burning there.

He smiled, spotting Marta Kleppe walking slowly, gingerly through the courtyard toward the great hall. He was glad she'd made it. When she saw Bolan, she ran to him, hugging him.

"I'm so glad you came through," she sobbed. "I was so worried, I...Rennie, where's Rennie? Is he...he...?"

Bolan shrugged. "He got shot up a little bit," he said, pointing over his shoulder toward the hall, "but he's too ornery to be hurt bad."

Her face lit up like the balloon's sun face, and she

touched his arm with a glad cry before running to the hall. The look he saw in her eyes had nothing to do with money.

Good. Better than good. It's what made Bolan go on.

He moved into the sea of cars and cops, picked a Jaguar and climbed in. The keys were inside, so he started it up to a rumbling roar and drove out through the gates.

He was free of Paraguay finally.

CHAPTER TWENTY-ONE

Geneva, Switzerland
July 25, 10:00 a.m.

The cabdriver pulled up before the small bank buried deeply within the confines of Geneva's old city. The former fortress town, surrounded by enemies, was now the capital of peaceful negotiations. An international city.

Bolan climbed out of the cab and asked the driver to wait, then walked into the five-hundred-year-old structure with the three teller windows and the walk-in safe-deposit-box rooms. This was not Bank Leu, but he had the feeling that it did business just as sharply.

He bypassed the windows and moved to a secretary's desk that sat before an important-looking office.

"My name is John Smith," he said.

The woman's eyes widened slightly, and she said, in heavily accented English, "You will wait a moment, please."

She rose and disappeared into the office, returning within a moment with a tall, older man. His hair was white and he was thin, bent over. But he had piercing blue eyes that tore right into Bolan's.

"So you are Mr. Smith," he said, offering Bolan a chair, not willing to take him back into the office. "I am Mr. Durer, president of this establishment. Do you mind if I look at your papers?"

Bolan sat, producing the fake identity papers he'd invented in Sprecher's forgery room. The man went through the papers, smiling at the photo page. "Nice picture," he said, handing back the passport. "You understand the need for confirmation?"

"Certainly," Bolan said. "Is my transaction ready?"

The man looked at his secretary's desktop. She was nowhere to be seen. "You must understand, Mr. Smith," he said, "that your request is highly unusual. We've never done anything quite like—"

"Sir," Bolan said. "It was my understanding that Swiss banking is capable of accomplishing anything. If you cannot honor my request, perhaps I should take the rest of my money and put it somewhere—"

"Don't be hasty." The man smiled, reaching into the secretary's drawer and withdrawing a long white envelope. "We have done as you've asked. We just fear for its format."

"I'll be careful, Mr. Durer," Bolan said, standing, taking the envelope and shaking the man's hand. "It has been a pleasure doing business with you. You'll hear from me again."

He turned and left them, figuring that Marta Kleppe and Rennie Dennison could get by on a little less than fifty million. The cab was still waiting. He climbed in happily and closed the door behind him. "Airport," he said.

ANNIE TRIPP WALKED reluctantly into the lobby of the First National Bank of Patterson, New Jersey. She moved slowly, looking around for the man who'd called her on the phone and told her he had something from Gene.

Everything was so confusing. There was the horror, then the funeral just yesterday. She couldn't seem to focus her mind; the empty place in her heart was as large as the sky. She hadn't even begun to believe he was really gone. So soon. So very soon.

Then the phone call, her family begging her not to go alone, as the man had suggested, a man who wouldn't leave his name.

But what did it matter? She was a new widow with a stack of bills and a government life-insurance policy that barely covered burial expenses. What could it hurt to meet the mystery man, probably someone trying to scam her out of her insurance money?

"Mrs. Tripp?" came a gentle voice.

Annie turned in surprise to see such gentleness

coming from such a large man. "Do I know you?" she asked.

"I knew your husband, ma'am," the big man said. "I was...with him when he died."

"You were?" she said, taking him by the arms. "Did he...did he say anything? Did he suffer?"

"He went quickly," Bolan said, "but he had a lot to say about how much he loved you and how he'd put a little something aside for you two to take a cruise after his retirement."

She smiled with the thought. "Gene was always talking about us taking the big trip," she said, "but we never had any money. He didn't suffer?"

"No, ma'am," the big man said. "He gave me something for you and told me to make sure you got it."

"What?"

Bolan held up the safe-deposit-box key and the information. "This is for you," he said. "If you want, I'll walk you back to the box."

"All...all right," Annie said, confused again.

When they went through the sign-in process, Annie knew as she saw the signature card that Gene had forged her name on it. He was always doing that.

They moved back with the bank official, both of them using their keys, the box in Annie's hands. The big man watched until the teller was gone before speaking again.

"I just want you to know that what you find in

there is yours to keep. It belongs to no one else. And it's legitimate."

She nodded, setting the box on the table in the center of the long, narrow room. She worked the key slowly, not knowing what to expect now. She opened the lid to find several thousand dollars in cash and smiled. He'd probably spent the past twenty years saving that money.

Then she noticed the envelope, taking it out to open it. She looked at it for a long moment before actually realizing what it was—a cashier's check for ten million dollars.

"I don't understand," she said, turning to the big man.

But he was gone, vanished. Only the cashier's check remained in her hand.

The Destroyer takes on a plague of
invisible insects—as the exterminator

Destroyer

#107 Feast or Famine

Created by
WARREN MURPHY
and RICHARD SAPIR

Is the insect kingdom mobilizing to reclaim the planet...or
is something entirely different behind it all? Unless the
Destroyer can combat this disaster, a whole nation may
start dropping like flies.

Look for it in April wherever Gold Eagle books are sold.

Don't miss out on the action in these titles!